DEAD FRENZY

VICTORIA HOUSTON

Adams Media
An Imprint of Simon & Schuster, Inc.
57 Littlefield Street
Avon, Massachusetts 02322

For information about special discounts for bulk purchases, please contact Simon & Schuster Special Sales at 1-866-506-1949 or business@simonandschuster.com.

The Simon & Schuster Speakers Bureau can bring authors to your live event. For more information or to book an event contact the Simon & Schuster Speakers Bureau at 1-866-248-3049 or visit our website at www.simonspeakers.com.

Cover design by Frank Rivera.
Cover image © iStockphoto.com/elenavolkova.

Manufactured in the United States of America

ISBN 978-1-4405-8223-3

DEAD FRENZY

VICTORIA HOUSTON

one

"A lake is the landscape's most beautiful and expressive feature. It is earth's eye; looking into which the beholder measures the depth of his own nature."

—Henry David Thoreau

The morning was so still not even the wind whispered as Osborne sipped from his first cup of coffee. But as he sat, the woods awoke. A woodpecker rattled on a dead aspen and overhead a squirrel chucked.

He tipped back in his chair, closing his eyes and lifting his face to the sun. Below, just off his dock, a canoe paddle dipped. Henry Darden out for his morning cruise. Mollie, his wife, would be in her paddleboat heading straight across the lake. You could set your clock by those two codgers—on Loon Lake at the dot of seven any day it was decent.

A fish jumped. Even with his eyes closed, Osborne sensed the circles radiating out across the black surface. From the sound of the splash, he guessed a smallmouth. Loon Lake was rich with bass these days. He resisted the urge to trot down with his fly rod and tease a few, too darn cozy right where he was. And his rig was too light for bass anyway. He inhaled. Such peace, such solitude. Such a fine life. Even tonight would be good: He had a date to fly-fish with the woman of his dreams.

Osborne sighed happily. Then he grimaced. Things would not stay this calm for long. The news in the morning paper, folded on his lap, was good and bad. That national bass-fishing tournament set to open in ten days would pump a lot of bucks into the Loon Lake economy. With two warm winters sabotaging their snowmobile tourism, the little town needed the action. But geez Louise, the *Milwaukee Journal Sentinel* was estimating 15,000 visitors. Fifty professionals paired with fifty amateurs—and the rest *gawkers*?

Fifteen thousand was triple what the president of the chamber of commerce had told the city council when they voted to allow the tournament. This was bass country and the tournament had been angling for several years to have access to the three hundred–plus lakes in the region. Lakefront owners like Osborne had balked at first. The fishing tournament featured afternoon boat racing, which tended to draw too many cowboys. In the long run, no one could resist the money.

But that wasn't the worst of it. Twenty miles away, on the very same late July weekend, Tomahawk was hosting their annual Harley-Davidson Rally—another 30,000 razzbonyas. What a contrast: one crowd decked out with bass poppers and miles of monofilament while the other flashed chrome and leather. Problem was, both drank way too much beer. On the roads and on the water, the northwoods would be a zoo. Lew would have her hands full.

Yep, Osborne thought as he opened his eyes and sipped from his mug. She just might need some help. He smiled. Every day he was amazed. Who would have ever expected this sixty-three-year-old retired dentist to be courting a police chief?

Not Henry and Mollie, that's for sure. He could imagine the expressions on the faces of those two every time Lewellyn Ferris's squad car passed their kitchen window, two doors down from his, on its way to Osborne's. He wouldn't put it past Mollie to sneak by in the wee hours to see if Lew was spending the night. They had nothing on him yet, but boy, hope springs eternal.

As if in answer to his thoughts, tires crunched in the driveway. Lew. He heard the door slam and waited for her whistle. It was a habit they had fallen into while grouse hunting last fall—makes it easy to know exactly where someone is in the woods so you shoot a bird and not a buddy. These summer mornings she often used it to see if he was already out on his deck.

But today—no whistle. Instead, footsteps through the house and the porch screen door banged. Heavy feet hit the wooden stairs behind him.

"Ray? Grab a mug." Eyes closed again, Osborne kept his face to the sun as he waved his hand toward the coffeepot on the table beside him. He was surprised. The fishing guide was usually on the lake by now, with or without a client. Had he caught his limit already? Or more than that? Ray bent the law whenever he needed to.

When there was no answer, Osborne turned around.

He was surprised to see his daughter standing there, eyes red, arms crossed tightly across her body as if she was holding herself together. She wore jeans and an old purple T-shirt. Her pale blond hair was pulled back in a single braid. Her face looked pale, washed out.

"Erin, honey!" Osborne dropped his feet from the deck railing and stood up, a terrible feeling in the pit of his stomach. "What's wrong—are the kids okay?"

"Kids are fine, Dad."

"Are *you* okay?"

At the sound of his three simple words, his daughter collapsed onto the steps, covered her face with her hands, and sobbed.

Osborne watched in astonishment. He had just seen her two days ago and she was as lighthearted as ever. What on earth? He stood there, unsure what to do as the younger of his two daughters cried her heart out. Finally, wiping at her nose with the back of one hand as if she were three instead of thirty, Erin looked up, her eyes desperate.

"Tell me this—are we dealing with a life-and-death situation?"

"The dream is back, Dad . . . and there's a reason. Can we take a walk?"

"Of course. Let me unplug the coffee."

He knew the dream. It had taken two years of expensive psychological counseling and weekly trips to Wausau to push it out of her head. Why the hell was it back now?

Erin walked past him down off the deck toward the driveway. He followed her up the driveway to the road. Osborne's home sat on a peninsula between two lakes in the Loon Lake chain of five lakes, each identified by a number. He expected her to turn left or right to follow the road, but she crossed instead. The overgrown path ahead of her would take them into an old hemlock forest and over to Second Lake.

"Erin . . . wait." He wanted her to stop. She hadn't been in there for seventeen years.

He hadn't either. In fact, he had no intention of ever going in there again. "Erin, please stop. Where are you going?"

She marched ahead as if she hadn't heard him. Osborne hurried to catch up. Maybe it would be okay. After all, things had changed. A cottage now graced the path that led into the old forest. He wondered if they weren't trespassing and hoped no one was home.

But as he followed Erin into the woods, he could see one thing had not changed. The old hemlocks stood guard still, as menacing and secretive as ever. He had played there as a boy and even then would stay for only a short while. The forest floor beneath the trees was dark and shadowed and silent. He felt like he always had: that he was being watched. Erin must have sensed it, too, because she slowed and dropped back as if to be closer to him.

The old hemlock loomed ahead. The fallen one, the skeleton.

He caught up with her just as she stopped. She was looking down. His gaze followed hers into the cave that nature had carved under the branches of the ancient tree. And as if it were yesterday, he remembered every detail of that awful sight.

He had arrived home early from the office that late summer day seventeen years ago. He was planning to change, meet Dick at the landing, and get in a good evening of muskie fishing. But when he drove into the driveway of his new home, it was filled with cars. Mary Lee's bridge group was running late. He'd hurried into the kitchen only to find Brenda Anderle, a pretty redhead who had just moved in down the road, on her knees trying to comfort Erin.

"She's upset about something, Dr. Osborne." Brenda had looked up with concern in her eyes.

"Paul—I *told* Erin I'll help her out in a few minutes. I have one more hand to play," Mary Lee called out from the living room, exasperation in her voice.

Meanwhile, Erin was looking up at him, eyes wide and terrified. She was wearing her Brownie uniform as was another little girl, standing by the back door, whom Osborne didn't recognize. "Oh, Daddy," Erin said, "we found a dead thing in the woods. I think it's a person and it's . . . it's too scary, Dad—"

"A deer carcass, Erin. Don't worry about it." Osborne interrupted, feeling as impatient as his wife. These kids had imaginations out of control and he was already running late.

"No, Dad—it's not!" The child was trembling. Osborne had never seen her so upset. The other little girl had begun to cry.

"Okay, okay. Let's hurry then and take a look."

He followed the girls across the road and down the path past the orchard and into the hemlocks. The stately timbers stood high against the sky, shutting out the light. As they ran, the girls told him how they had found this thing. Searching for mosses for their forestry badge, they had been feeling their way through the tangled roots of the old trees.

"I'm the one who found it, Dad," said Erin, calming now that someone believed her.

"Okay, hon." Osborne was so sure they had stumbled onto a dead deer that once they pointed to the cave beneath the tree, he hurried over and thrust his face forward so fast that he almost hit it with his nose. He backed off fast. Very fast.

Two arms reached up at him. Human, oozing and green, thrusting their way through a large burlap sack torn by animals. Later, he thought the smell should have warned him but the wind, at that moment, was from the east and masked the odor.

"OhmyGod," he had managed just before vomiting.

Later that evening they learned that the corpse was what was left of a teenage girl, a local girl baby-sitting for a family of tourists from Illinois. She had been missing from the family's cabin for two days but they thought she had run off with a boy. It was also learned that a desperate Loon Lake man, a patient of Osborne's, had been seen with the girl and, later, seen leaving the woods. Before he could be arrested, he shot himself. The murder was considered solved.

"But why deal with this now?" he asked Erin. "That was a long, long time ago."

"I was so frightened, Dad. But I got past it, didn't I? And I can stand here today and it won't hurt me, will it?"

"Of course not, sweetheart. You know, you're not making much sense to your old man."

"They found the man who killed her, didn't they?"

"I believe so," said Osborne. He hesitated. Should he say it? Since he didn't understand why they were here in the first place, would he make it worse if he told her he never had believed Jack Schultz was guilty? Osborne decided to keep his mouth shut.

"Let's go down and see if that old bench is still by the water."

Again, he followed her. The bench was there, weathered, the red paint long gone, but sturdy enough for the two of them to sit.

"Well, Dad," Erin managed a grin as she sat down, "I survived that—so . . . I guess I can survive this." Tears squeezed from her eyes. She wiped them away.

"Erin." Osborne put his hand on her knee. "I don't understand what this is all about. Survive what?"

She sat back, sniffled, crossed her arms again, and took a deep breath. "Mark left me two days ago. I don't know where he is. I thought he would be back yesterday, but he's gone. Oh, Dad, I am so frightened."

"What! Mark's gone? Well, how do you know he left? Maybe something happened. He fell out of his boat—"

"He left me a letter, Dad."

"Oh."

Stunned, Osborne pulled her close. She breathed in deeply as if to settle herself but all the extra air did was flush out more tears. He rocked her as she wept. Erin, happy, ebullient Erin with the perfect family. How could this happen?

"Take it easy, now. It can't be as bad as it seems. Mark's a good man. Let's take some time and figure this out."

Deep down Osborne had a hunch. Much as he loved her, he knew her to be too much like her late mother in one way: too full of her own life, always overprogrammed. Even he found it hard to make her stop and listen.

"And there is certainly no reason to be afraid."

"But I am. I am so afraid. I know that's why I'm having that nightmare, Dad."

He gripped her shoulder and felt defeated. For two years after finding the girl's body, little Erin would wake up screaming, haunted by a dream of bloody arms in a wooden box reaching out to grab her. How many nights had he held that terrified little body? If this was Mark's way of getting attention, he was having one hell of an effect.

They sat in silence, arms around each other. Osborne listened to the hollow roar of the wind overhead. He watched the whitecaps rolling at them, ferocious and foaming. This peninsula always amazed him—you cross a twelve-foot road and walk half a mile into a different world. First Lake would be still and Second Lake wild. Like life, calm one moment, out of control the next.

Yes, he thought, Erin has a serious problem at hand. But she brought up another one that concerned him just as much. A problem long forgotten but as potent today as it was seventeen years ago. If he believed that Jack Schultz did not kill that girl—and he had good reason to—then who did? And where was the killer today?

two

*"The last point of all the inward gifts that doth belong
to an angler is memory. . . ."*

—*The Art of Angling,* 1577

Thrusting his hands into the pockets of his khakis, Osborne stood in his driveway watching Erin's van as she backed out. He waited until she was out of sight, then dropped his head in thought for a long, long minute before turning back toward his house and yard.

Mike, always the happy black Lab, was busy picking up and tossing a bright green tennis ball, all the while eyeing his owner eagerly.

"Not today, guy," said Osborne. "I just don't feel like it, sorry."

Looking past the dog and down the hill as he opened the gate to the yard, he could see that First Lake, his lake, was as serene as it had been an hour earlier. He wished he could say the same about his life.

Patting Mike's head absentmindedly, he mulled over what to do next. He'd lost the urge to join the boys for morning coffee at McDonald's—this would be the first morning he'd missed in six months. He glanced at his watch. It was too late anyway.

Osborne was the first to admit he did not handle conflict well. Maybe that was why he'd let Mary Lee run his life for so long: the easy way out.

But this situation with Erin, this was different. Different even from a year ago when Mallory, his elder, had announced her decision to divorce. That husband he had been happy to see go. Never did like the guy.

But Erin and Mark? They seemed so right for each other, they complemented one another. Sure, she's the front man, thought Osborne in defense of his daughter's outspoken ways. She has the ideas, the charm, and the outgoing personality. But while she might appear to run the show, it was Mark—quiet, solid, calm Mark—who kept it all together, the one who built her dreams.

Osborne did a quick run-through of his son-in-law's virtues: a successful young lawyer, so good with his hands he could fix just about anything, a decent fisherman, granted he was better at hunting deer than birds—Erin was the grouse hunter. And a good father. A very good father.

Negatives? Osborne pondered that. Too quiet. Yep, the kind of guy who might let a problem build too long before saying anything. And bullheaded when he was convinced he was right. "Bullet head," Ray called him. Of course, Osborne shrugged, what the hell did he know—he didn't live with the guy.

So okay, you have a quarrel with your wife, but why on earth would you leave your children? He could understand Mark stomping out for a few hours—but to be missing for a night and a day? He should have asked Erin what was in that letter Mark had left behind.

Osborne rounded the corner of the house and started up the stairs to his deck. Someone had been there. A golden lattice-topped pie sat on the small table that held the coffeepot. He walked over and brushed his fingertips along the sides of the glass pie dish. It was so fresh-baked, it was still warm to the touch. He bent over and inhaled deeply. Ray, you son-of-a-gun, you know I love peach pie. His heart lifted ever so slightly. Little did the rascal know that this was the perfect moment for a peach pie. At least something was right in the world.

"Hey, Ray—I'm out here," he said in a loud voice, certain his neighbor must be inside looking for him or just leaving through the yard on the opposite side of the house. No answer. Something rustled in the yard behind him. Osborne glanced back over his left shoulder toward the garage and the screened-in corner porch that he used for cleaning fish and storing some of his less expensive equipment. He thought he saw movement.

"Ray? Is that you over there?"

Silence. Not a leaf or a pine needle moved. The dog was busy chasing a squirrel at the far end toward the lake. Osborne looked past the fish hut through the stand of red pine that separated his property from old man Balser's. The longer he looked, the more he was sure he had seen something, but it didn't make sense. Ray lived on the other side of his place. And old man Balser was no baker of pies, that's for sure. He spent his days going to yard sales, filling his tumbledown garage with junk. Osborne made a mental note to ask the old geezer again if he was interested in selling. He would love to have a buffer of land between him and the glut of year-round homes popping up around Loon Lake.

With a shrug, Osborne turned away. He checked to see if the pie was cool enough to pick up. Slipping his left hand under the glass plate, he reached with his right to shove open the sliding screen door. This time he was sure he saw a flash of movement to his right. The dog saw it, too. Mike was up and nosing around the fence on the far side of the fish hut. He gave a low growl and crouched back. Someone or something was definitely there.

"Hel-l-o-o, who's there?" Holding the pie in both hands, Osborne walked over to the deck railing. No answer. He waited, Mike waited—then the dog snuffled off after something more interesting. Whoever, whatever, had moved on. Balser's barricade of balsams along the road made it impossible to see anyone walking off to the east.

Kids! Osborne gave up and walked back to his doorway. Normally he would have checked out any trespassers—he kept enough fishing gear on the little porch that he didn't need youngsters nosing around. But not today. He had too much on his mind.

The house was cool inside, the kitchen meticulous. He made it a point to keep it that way in case Lew dropped by. Setting the pie down in the middle of the kitchen table, he leaned back against the counter with his arms crossed. He wished he could think of some piece of advice, some . . . thing that would put Erin's life back together. As if shoveling through a junk drawer, he reached back into the memories of his therapy sessions in rehab.

Were there clues in the map of his own misguided emotional history that might help this daughter he cherished?

He was concentrating so hard, he didn't even hear the soft padding of moccasins across the deck and onto the front porch. Mike, used to those particular footsteps, didn't bark.

"Doc?" said Ray, looking toward the bedrooms as he stepped into the living room.

"Out here, Ray," said Osborne. He moved around the counter so he could see into the living room. "Thanks for the pie."

"What pie? I haven't been baking pies—I've been digging graves since the crack of dawn. Don't know what got into everybody, biting the Big One on a gorgeous day like today."

. . .

Ray's lope across the living room reminded Osborne of
nothing so much as a young buck caught in the headlights: four limbs exploding in different directions simultaneously. At age thirty-four, Ray still found six feet five
inches of height a lot to handle. The rest of him was better
organized.

This morning he was so freshly showered that moisture
still glinted on the random gray hairs curling through his
russet-red beard, a beard that had only recently been
trimmed to a more civilized length of four inches from his
lower lip. No such concession had been made for the
crazed mass of curls on his head. Those he shoved behind
his ears and hoped for the best. Ray had too much hair,
true, but at least he kept it clean.

Maybe more than clean. Osborne had good reason to
suspect that Ray spent nearly as much time in the mirror
as a teenage girl. And why not? Any guy would if he had
what Ray had: a lean body, a deep tan, an engaging grin,
remarkably good teeth, and the kind of eyes (according to
his daughter Mallory) that women love to fall into. Actually, Osborne liked his eyes, too. They were honest.

The only thing Ray lacked was steady income. But
being in his early thirties, that could change. At least,
that's what the women always thought. People who knew
him well knew better. All it took to make Ray happy was
a few bucks in the wallet, no limit on his catch, and a
place to sleep close to the water. He bragged to his clients
that success was matching lure, weather, and the correct-
weight monofilament to make for an excellent stringer of
fish—be it walleye, bluegill, bass, or muskie. As he always said when he hooked a big one: "Life don't get
much better 'n this."

"You didn't leave this peach pie on my deck a few minutes ago?" said Osborne.

"Nope, but I sure can help you out if it's more than you can handle."

"Well, that's strange," said Osborne. "I wonder. . . ."

"The lovely Lew perhaps?"

"I doubt that—but we're fishing tonight so I'll ask her. What's up?"

"Not much—need to borrow some flour. I'm all out and I got a mess of bluegills to fry up."

"Help yourself."

"Thank you, sir."

Ray walked into the kitchen and over to the cupboard where the staples were kept. An excellent cook, he was always short of something. Chances were good he knew Osborne's kitchen better than his own. He glanced over at his friend as he reached up.

"Doc, you seem preoccupied . . . is anything wrong?" he said as he pulled a tall silver canister down from the cupboard.

Ray had an uncanny ability to read the weather—in the sky, on the water, and in a man's face. While it might make him one of the premier fishing and hunting guides in the entire northwoods region, it was a talent not always appreciated. And right now Osborne did not feel like talking about Erin, not even to the man he considered one of his closest friends.

"Nah, I was just thinking about that girl whose body they found across the road years ago, back in the stand of hemlocks. The one they pinned on Jack Schultz—remember that? Or were you too young?"

"Oh, I remember that all right," said Ray. "A bunch of us kids rode out from town on our bikes to watch the cops pick it up. I remember that like it was yesterday, those bones. The hands with the flesh falling off, y'know—and they were reaching up. . . ."

Ray mimicked what he'd seen with a sudden thrust of

his own arms. "I don't think I've ever seen anything so desperate in my life."

"C'mon, you were a kid, you don't remember all that."

"Doc . . ." Ray leveled his eyes at Osborne. "The stuff I remember most clearly is the stuff I saw as a kid. And I will never forget that night. A lot of excitement at home, too, because no one knew who the killer was, remember? Those days my folks never locked their doors and that night they were frantic—couldn't find the key—and they sure as hell weren't going to bed until every door and window was locked up tight. One of the Ginzl girls, wasn't it? I remember you were living here in those days, Doc."

"Yep, we had just built this place."

"So why are you thinking about that today?" said Ray as he scooped a cup of flour into a plastic bag.

"I never thought Jack Schultz was the killer. He was a patient of mine, we'd fished together once or twice . . . and I've just never thought he had it in him. . . ." Osborne paused, then decided. "You know, I'm going to ask Lew if I can take a look at the file on that."

Ray turned and looked at Osborne, measuring cup in hand. "You didn't answer my question, Doc. Why . . . are you . . . thinking . . . about that . . . *today?*"

Ray had an annoying habit of stretching out his vocabulary when making what he considered a very important point or asking what he considered a very important question—making it impossible to ignore him.

Suddenly, inexplicably, the inside of Osborne's eyelids felt hot and wet. He bent his head to run a hand through his hair and hide his face.

Ray reached for the pie. His voice softened. "Hey, you old jabone, you. Time for a good breakfast and a slice of homemade peach pie. C'mon," he urged with a shrug of his left shoulder. "Whatever it is, Doc, you are not going to solve it standing here."

three

"Some men fish all their lives without knowing it is not really the fish they are after."

—Henry David Thoreau

The walleye fillets were long gone, the butter mopped up with whole wheat toast, and the pie almost half-eaten when Ray pushed his chair back from the table, extended his long legs, crossed his arms, and gazed out the window at the lake.

"So Mark changed jobs a year ago, huh?"

It was a rhetorical question. Osborne knew he was well aware that Erin's husband was no longer the district attorney for Loon Lake, the man who went a little easy on him when he was caught inhaling on the Willow Flowage.

"Wonder how he likes private practice. He joined Chuck Kasmarek's firm, didn't he?"

Osborne nodded with a grimace. He hadn't said anything to Erin and Mark when that decision was made. They were so pleased with the huge increase in salary—and with three young children, they needed the money.

"Now there's a razzbonya." Ray continued to look out the window as if the answer to Erin's dilemma might roll in on the next whitecap. "Guided him and a bunch of his law school buddies out fishing muskie a couple years back. They hooked a big one all right. One of their own right in the schnozz."

"Emergency room?"

"Nah, he didn't deserve it. I whipped it out with my fish pliers."

"Ouch."

"He'd had so many brewskis, he didn't even know what was happening. That's a hard-living crowd in that firm, Doc. I know for a fact Chuck's at the casino almost every night."

"Oh boy."

"You didn't know that?"

"Mark never talks about his work."

Ray was quiet again for a while. While his friend ruminated, Osborne stood up, picked up both their plates, and walked them over to the sink. The house trailer might appear small from the outside but indoors it was open and airy and kept as tidy as Ray's boat, which was always in perfect order. Osborne felt welcome any time. He had his own chair at the old oak table with its blue-and-white-checked placemats, and his own coffee cup, white background sprinkled with trout flies. Ray had bartered for it with the owner of the fly-fishing shop up in Boulder Junction: one coffee mug for directions to a tiny private lake bursting with brook trout.

Ray's yellow Labs, Ruff and Ready, were sleeping soundly on the overstuffed couch in the living room. The aroma of fresh-caught fish sauteed in butter still hung lightly in the air, and a lake breeze fluttered the white cotton curtains framing the open window above the kitchen sink. Osborne turned on the faucet to rinse the plates, then set them on the drainboard and dried his hands. Yep, it was a happy, homey place all right. You just had to get past the rusty exterior with its humongous neon green muskie leaping at you.

Two springs earlier Ray had used his downtime between the ice going out and opening day of fishing to paint the "fish of 10,000 casts" smack dab across the front of his trailer, positioning the monster so visitors had to enter through gaping jaws. Then, just before the arrival of a new guiding client, Ray would position himself behind his kitchen curtains and wait—ready to judge his new client by the expression on their face as they got out of their car.

"Tells me everything I need to know about a person, Doc, everything."

"I don't know about that, Ray—that's before they've met *you.*"

In Osborne's opinion, the true test was when and if a new client agreed to entrust their life and the lives of their loved ones over deep and unfamiliar waters to the man who stepped out of that trailer wearing a stuffed trout on his head. And he wasn't the only one who felt that way.

Ray's approach to a day's guiding was a frequent source of commentary among Osborne and the rest of the guys in the big booth at McDonald's. Meeting every morning from seven to eight-thirty or so, the six regulars, all of them experienced fishermen, relished a critique of the man who lived a life they envied. Most had fished with him; almost all had sent friends Ray's way for guiding. While they admired his talent for locating trophy fish, they were well aware of his faults, not the least of which could be poor judgment in personal relations.

To a man, they had nodded in agreement with Osborne when he said, "That client makes up his mind when Ray comes down those two stairs with that damn hat on— *that's* the moment that tries the soul."

"You betcha," said five guys simultaneously.

But whatever the exact moment of truth, the reality was that if you were new to fishing with Ray, the outcome of your day was determined in the seconds that passed between the time you got out of your car and shook Ray's hand. No smile and a thin lip line broadcast that you were worried over getting your money's worth out of an individual who appeared to need electric shock treatment.

Ray knew instantly what was on your mind and he would plan accordingly: If you looked tense—that thin lip line—you got textbook technique, not too many jokes, egg salad on wheat for lunch, and a decent stringer of bass and walleye. If you were a real pill, you got suckers. And he didn't want to see you again either.

"On the other hand," he said to Osborne one night as they sat on Ray's dock enjoying a peach and lavender sunset, "if the party at hand registers less chagrin—well hell, I'll give him a day he'll never forget."

He would, too, which was why, after all the discussion, the boys at McDonald's would still book any visiting relatives they knew and loved for a full day of fishing with Ray. It was a day guaranteed to deliver two-word pointers that could change your luck (if not your life), a steady supply of "Ray jokes" (slightly off-color even if females were along), sautéed-in-butter catch of the day (lightly seasoned with fresh ground pepper), directions to at least one "secret" fishing spot (including advice on how to deal with the game warden if arrested)—and a whole lot more fish than the thin-lipped client ever imagined could be caught. The only fish Ray could not deliver on command was muskie but he'd sure as hell help you try—even set you up with a long-term plan you could do on your own.

Ray was not stupid—he knew a happy fisherman when he saw one. He knew who tipped better and who was a heck of a lot more likely to come back even if the weather was lousy. That was how he handled his live clients.

Summers, Ray split his time between guiding fisher-

men and digging graves for Loon Lake's Catholic cemetery. Winters he spent ice fishing, shoveling snow, carving
wooden muskie lures, and defrosting the ground for the
internment of less lively Loon Lake residents. The coffee
crowd agreed on one thing: Ray was a marketing genius;
he could make a buck off anyone—living or dead.

"I'm not sure Kasmarek's the sharpest knife in the drawer,
Doc."

"I wouldn't argue that, Ray," said Osborne. "But he
sure as hell makes money."

"Easy money. Bought and sold by the mining interests
moving in from Canada."

"You can't fault free enterprise, Ray. He's not the only
one—but I wouldn't be surprised if he doesn't have more
than that going on."

Again Ray gazed out at the water. His tone was softer
and thoughtful when he finally spoke. "Kasmarek is dangerous, Doc. He's not very nice and he's not very happy."
He looked away from the window to Osborne. "He'd be
tough to work for . . . maybe old Mark is having a career
crisis of some kind. He wouldn't be the first to bring work
problems home, y'know. He *is* a bullet head, Doc. We've
agreed on that before—maybe he and Chuck locked
horns."

"I'd like to think it's that rather than something between him and Erin."

"Tell you what. . . ."

Ray pushed his chair back from the table, stood, and
reached for the trout hat sitting on top of the refrigerator.
Summertimes, he anchored the treasured fish to a baseball
cap, the head and tail extending to the right and left over
his ears. That way he could wear the hat backward and
still get the same effect. He stepped down into his living
room and looked into the mirror hanging over the sofa
where the dogs were sleeping. Setting the hat carefully on

his head, he tucked a couple rogue curls up under the sweatband, then tipped the stuffed trout slightly forward and to the right.

Osborne waited patiently, watching Ray complete an act he performed many times a day and always with the same slow precision he used when casting for trophy fish. Frustrating as it was for friends and relatives, Ray did not rush through life. There was virtue in that, Osborne knew, but it did not make being around the guy any easier. At least watching him, you could see progress. A telephone conversation was something else: Punctuated with long pauses, the wait could be torture. At last, Ray was ready.

"I've gotta go by the bank this afternoon, Doc," he said, ambling past Osborne to open the screen door. "Kasmarek's law office is right around the corner from the drive-in and one of the gals who works there is a real sweetheart. She wants a pup next time I breed Ready. I'll stop by and chat her up a little, see what I can find out. You home later?"

Osborne followed him out the door. "Lew and I are fishing the Wolf—heading out around five if she doesn't get held up." Even Osborne heard the lack of enthusiasm in his voice. Ray gave him a sharp look.

"Now, Doc," he coaxed, throwing his arm over Osborne's shoulder as they stepped into the sunny clearing he used for a driveway, "lighten up. You can't live Erin's life for her."

"I know that. . . ."

"No, you don't. I can tell from the look on your face you don't. Doc . . . step back and look at the sit . . . u . . . a . . . tion." He stretched out the word as he looked hard at his friend. "What's . . . the worst . . . that can happen?"

Their eyes met. They had shared too many sessions in the room behind the door with the coffeepot on the window. Osborne knew right where Ray was going and he knew it was exactly what had been bothering him since Erin's visit that morning.

"I wouldn't worry about *that*," said Ray. "It was Erin who got you into rehab, she's the one who led the intervention. She's taken the lead with Mallory. That's one family tradition your daughter is not going to follow. Believe me, she's not. So . . . given that, what's the worst?"

"Suicide?"

"Be serious."

"Okay." Osborne let his shoulders slump under the weight of his worry. "If they break up, she'll be so unhappy and my grandchildren . . ." He couldn't finish.

"True—but geez, we all have times like this, Doc. You and I both know you can't beat life, right? So . . ." Ray resumed the drill. "Is that the worst?"

"I'll bet you anything Erin will have to go to work full-time."

"Now that *would* be terrible," said Ray, arching his eyebrows. "A full-time job? That would kill *me*, I tell ya!" And he meant it.

They both burst out laughing. Osborne felt a little better. Ray was right, he had to step back and let Erin find her way. Nothing he could do or say could change a thing.

"You don't have the whole story yet either," said Ray. "Two days from now everything may be just fine. If you ask me, knowing your daughter and Mark—I'm sure it will be."

"You're right, Ray," said Osborne with a grudging smile. "Y'know, I can always count on you to be really right—or really wrong. Today, for a change, you're right."

Minutes later, walking up his neighbor's rutted drive toward his own place, Osborne's step was much lighter than it had been on the way over. Just talking to Ray had eased his mind. Taking care not to drop what remained of the peach pie, he checked his watch. Only nine and a half hours until he would see Lew. That was not a bad thought.

Not a bad thought at all. She might know something about Kasmarek, too. In fact, the more he thought about it, the more he thought Ray might be on to something.

By the time he got to his back door, he had decided to surprise Lew with a picnic dinner. If the mosquitoes weren't bad, they could take a break from their fishing and eat on the riverbank. Mallory had just sent him an easy recipe for making a roast lemon chicken and an equally simple orzo salad to match—"Just boil the stuff and add herbs, Dad."

He had to admit he was enjoying Mallory's interest in his relationship with Lew. She might have her hands full with her divorce, her therapy, her AA meetings, and being back in school, but his elder daughter wasn't letting any of that or her Chicago location get in the way of helping her old man upgrade his dating techniques. And she seemed to really like Lew. Instead of asking questions, she sent recipes, which he appreciated. Not the recipes so much as her willingness to keep a lid on the questions. Questions he couldn't answer if she did ask.

He decided to try his hand at the orzo dish, too, and for dessert, they could finish off the pie. Osborne found himself whistling as he checked his shelves for ingredients. Cooking would be an excellent way to take his mind off Erin and bodies rotting in burlap potato sacks.

Half an hour later, list in hand, he headed off to Loon Lake for groceries. The day was exquisite—sunny and breezy and tempered with light gusts from the west. He decided to shop as quickly as possible, put the chicken in the oven, and see if he couldn't get a little time on the lake in his canoe. Days like today were at a premium in the northwoods.

Actually, Mary Lee's unexpected death two years earlier had taught him that days like today were at a premium *period.*

He scanned the roadside, on the alert for a mother bear and two cubs he had seen earlier in the week. Mother bears were hard on old Subaru wagons like his, plus the cubs needed a mom.

four

"Fish and visitors smell in three days."

—Benjamin Franklin

Summertime is crazy time in the northwoods. Even in little Loon Lake with its population of 3,112, midday traffic on a nice day can reach gridlock proportions. Tourists cram sidewalks, intersections, and parking lots as they rush to stock up for cruises on the decks of their pontoon boats, which would soon perpetrate the same gridlock in the narrow channels between lakes. But Osborne had to admit the tourists weren't the only ones at fault.

Loon Lake is distinctive for being the last town of any size on the way north to Lake Superior. It is also the county seat and—not least—it boasts a Wal-Mart. Add to that two good-sized grocery stores and Main Street is ripe for crowd control. From mid-June to late August, thousands converge for supplies, to see their lawyer, or to visit family and friends.

When it comes to the latter, a small but potent group arrives to visit relatives incarcerated in the brand-new jail adjacent to the courthouse. Though Lew would never say as much, Osborne could tell just from watching and listening during the midmorning cup of coffee they often shared in her office that she was quite proud of the building she had helped plan and design. It certainly raised her profile among the law enforcement professionals in the region—though the effect was not always positive.

More than once she joked about a less welcome effect the new building was having on her career, calling it "the jealousy factor." She could always see it coming, too—unpleasant assignments that sheriffs from nearby towns, large and small, would try to fob off on her department with the excuse that Loon Lake had the better facility.

"I hear what you're saying, but it's your problem, guy," was her polite but firm response. "Nope . . . nope . . . your problem. Sorry, wish I could help you."

Osborne would do his best not to grin as he listened. She was as deft at dodging her colleagues as she was at dropping a trout fly under an overhang of brush in a narrow creek. And she was adamant. He felt sorry for her competitors as he had yet to see her hedge on her priorities. And those were three: Get the job done for Loon Lake and Loon Lake only, get it done right—and get on with the fly-fishing. He liked to think that one of these days, if he was lucky, he might be added to that list.

Osborne loved to shop for groceries. Not the shopping so much as the other shoppers, which was why he favored the Loon Lake Market. Yes, the newer, bigger North Country Grocer had a wider selection but at the Loon Lake Market he could count on running into friends or former patients—people he could trust to have the latest in local news. Also, the Market's bulletin board was still the best in town for anyone with something to sell.

This morning he was lucky to get one of the two remaining grocery carts. Hoping that was an omen, he headed to the produce section for packages of fresh basil and tarragon. Also, aware that it was later than he had planned, he wasn't disappointed to see that the faces of his fellow shoppers were unfamiliar. The strangers crowding the aisles also appeared more affluent than the average Loon Lake resident, an opinion Osborne could safely base on thirty-five years of practicing dentistry in a town where his year-round patients were easily distinguished from summer "one-shots"—in manner, manners, and appearance.

Halfway down the noodles, rice, and pasta aisle, searching for orzo, he found his way blocked by a woman with a young child. He waited patiently as the mother, whom he'd never seen before and who appeared to be in her early forties, let herself be tortured by a little girl in a hot pink two-piece swimming suit. Osborne guessed the child to be five or six years old—old enough to know better.

"Celia, ouch! Please don't do that," the woman said as the kid ran their grocery cart up the back of her ankles. It was obvious the mother was a tourist. A Loon Lake parent would have said nothing and whacked the kid. Forget discussion.

Osborne watched a sly smile cross the little girl's face as she backed up, waited for her mother to look away, then ran at her again. This time she drew blood.

While the mother bent over to reason with the little monster, Osborne edged his cart around them, resisting the urge to prescribe homicide. That was one virtue of being retired from his dental practice: He no longer had to deal with spoiled brats—and the summer patients had been the worst.

Wandering up and down the aisles, list in hand, Osborne was pleased to find every item he needed, including a fresh, creamy-skinned, never frozen, six-pound capon. Then, in an aisle devoted to local farmers, he came upon an unexpected treat: a pint of fresh-picked raspberries for his cereal the next morning. That reminded him he was almost out of milk.

He hurried toward the dairy section, which was located at the far end of an aisle of frozen juices. Going a little too fast as he rounded the corner, he nearly crashed into what appeared to be a large loon reaching for a quart of half-and-half. It wasn't, of course; loons don't drink half-and-half. Able to stop before inflicting injury, Osborne could not help staring at the vision blocking his access to low-fat milk.

The loon-like image was imprinted on a stolid, very tall individual; as wide as it was tall and wearing clothes that offered no clue, the figure challenged Osborne to decide on its sex. Unable to see the face, which was turned away, he finally decided it was female. She wore faded Levi's and a black leather vest zipped tight over an ample bosom. A leather fanny pack hung off her left hip.

But what was so striking were her arms—tattooed from the wrist up to her shoulders, where they disappeared into her vest. Looking for all the world like the plumage of a mature loon, the arms were covered with dots, stripes, and cross-hatching executed in black and a brilliant white. Osborne was mesmerized. The woman reached for a gallon of orange juice. Then, to his surprise, she just stood there, continuing to block his way. It wasn't until he looked over at her face that he realized he was himself being observed.

"Dr. Osborne?" The voice was deep, raspy, and familiar. But it was a voice he hadn't heard in years. And without that voice, he would never have recognized the girl who had once worked for him. She'd been slender then and quite pretty. But slender had given way to burly, and the cheekbones that had once defined a heart-shaped face were bulbous under skin hammered by sun and wind and feathered with smoker's lines.

But the ice blue eyes were bright and amused. Friendly, even. Much friendlier than the day he had fired her. Even though it had to be twenty years or more since they had last spoken, the sound of her voice and the amusement in her eyes prompted exactly the same reaction he had had that day so long ago: fear. A deep and abiding fear of a young woman half his age. A fear that time had proven to be ridiculous.

"Catherine!" Recognition tinged with guilt. How unfair had he been so long ago?

"Dr. Osborne, you don't recognize me?"

"I do now. Are you visiting?"

"Hell no, I live up near Manitowish Waters."

"No kidding. Why did I think you were in Hawaii?"

"That was years ago—fifteen, seventeen maybe. Before moving back here, I lived in San Francisco for seven years and I've been here now for almost three."

"Oh," said Osborne, unsure what to say next. He reached for a quart of milk.

"How's Mary Lee—and your daughters?"

"The girls are fine. Erin lives in town with her family. She married Mark Amundson and they have three children. Mallory is single, living in Lake Forest, and Mary Lee . . . Mary Lee passed away two years ago."

"Oh," Catherine stepped back. "I'm sorry to hear that. Was it—?"

"No, no," said Osborne. "Very sudden. She came down with a viral bronchitis of some kind that went into a killer pneumonia in the middle of the night. By the time I got her to the hospital, it was too late."

"Whoa, one of those things, huh?"

Catherine didn't look all that unhappy at the news. Maybe she could see from his face that he was long past grief. Maybe she had been one of Mary Lee's targets, too. It was only since Mary Lee's death that Osborne had begun to get some measure of how vicious she had been to so many people.

As if she knew what he was thinking, Catherine said,

"Your wife didn't like me much, Doc. I think she thought I was trying to put the make on you."

"*What?*" Osborne could feel his face flush. He was thankful there were no other shoppers nearby.

"And I was!" said Catherine, flashing a smile that lightened the hardness in her face. "But you didn't have a clue."

Osborne was so speechless and embarrassed he didn't know what to do or say. He just wanted out of there.

Catherine didn't know how right she was and he would never forget that summer. Mary Lee had accused him of being more than the target of Catherine's affections. She had been convinced he was involved with her. The only justification she had was Catherine's lush beauty and her reputation. And Catherine was something in those days. By the time she left Loon Lake, she had scored way too many married men. But the unforgivable sin, in Mary Lee's eyes, was that Catherine left with her head held high—she married the scion of a wealthy summer family. Yes, she was pregnant but she *was* married.

"Oh, come on," said Catherine, her eyes twinkling at his unease. He remembered that about her now: She loved to make people uncomfortable. "You were the best-looking man in town. You still are, Doc. What are you . . . fifty-five?"

Her flattery pleased and alarmed him.

"I'm at least your father's age," he said, responding in his most professional, authoritative tone. He wasn't, of course, but he was desperate to change the subject. "So, Catherine, now that you're back—are you retired?" He didn't dare ask if she was married. God forbid he find out she was single.

"Oh, God no," she said, concern crossing her face as if it were her turn to decide exactly what to say. "I build docks."

"Docks? What kind of docks?"

"Custom docks—you know, with pilings."

"They sound expensive." Osborne inched his cart away, anxious to end the conversation.

"They are—but that area up around Manitowish Waters, Winchester, Boulder Junction. People are building ten-thousand-square-foot log homes. They can afford my docks. You should come up and see 'em someday."

"I should."

"We've got a big sign on the road—just drop by if you're ever in the neighborhood."

Whew, thought Osborne, she said "we." Thank goodness.

"I'll do that," he said. "Nice seeing you, Catherine."

Ten minutes later, as he carried his groceries to his car, he heard the voice again. Just his luck—Catherine's van was parked three spots down from his own car.

"Doc! I want you to meet my husband," she called, waving as he walked toward her. She had opened the back doors to a silver-gray van and was loading groceries inside. As he neared, she walked to the front of the van and yanked opened the driver's side door. "Jimmy, get out, I want you to meet someone."

A leg clad in grimy jeans reached for the ground as a chunky figure backed out from behind the steering wheel with all the grace of a garbage truck. Jimmy was one of those men who wear their pants so low that you see things you never want to know about. Osborne kept his eyes averted, concentrating on the lurid pattern stenciled onto the back of the black leather vest facing him.

Both feet on the ground at last, the man turned to face Osborne. Unlike Catherine's, his vest was open, exposing an impressive acreage of hairy chest and belly. The landscape could hardly be ignored given that it featured black and white tattoos identical to those running up both Catherine's arms. And his own, though Jimmy's arms were thicker and wider, allowing for more variation on the theme. Hard to miss these two.

Osborne extended his hand. "Glad to meet you, Jim. Paul Osborne."

"He's the dentist I used to work for—I've told you about him," said Catherine, poking her husband with her elbow. Osborne cringed. Discussed by this pair? That wasn't a happy thought.

"Oh, yeah, I know who you are." Jimmy reached down to slip both thumbs under his waistband. Once his pants were safely anchored over his hips and under his belly, he offered a four-fingered, half-handshake, the kind that Ray liked to call a "sucker grip."

The lower half of Jimmy's face was hidden behind a short, ragged light brown beard that matched his hair, which was long and pulled back in a ponytail. His eyes were red-rimmed and half-focused somewhere over Osborne's head as they shook hands. Osborne had spent enough time around Ray to know when someone was stoned. This jabone was on another planet.

"Those are quite the tattoos, you two," said Osborne to Catherine. She grinned and pointed to a decal on the side window of the metallic silver van: TAKE PRIDE IN YOUR HIDE. Other, ruder decals decorated the window as well. Osborne made an instant decision to avoid Manitowish Waters for the rest of his life.

"We got these done in Italy last year," said Catherine, holding her arms out and twisting them from side to side to display the full effect. Cost five thousand bucks."

"I can believe it," said Osborne. "The dock business is thriving, I take it."

"The what?" said Jimmy. He looked back and forth between his wife and Osborne. "The duck what?"

"The *dock business*," said Catherine loudly, as if the man were hard of hearing. "I told Doctor Osborne we build custom docks."

"Oh," Jimmy grunted as he backed his way into the van, shoveling his butt onto the driver's seat. Catherine walked Osborne to the back of the van, where she slammed the doors shut.

"Really nice running into you, Doc. Hey, are you still practicing? I just broke a crown."

"Oh no, I'm retired. Very nice seeing you, Catherine."

Back in the safety of his own car, Osborne sat quietly for a moment. He watched the van back out and drive off. Catherine was something else, always had been. Building docks? With that animal? Something smelled less than fresh: the thought of those two in a legitimate business.

So Catherine Steadman was back in town. . . . Osborne backed out of his parking spot carefully. No, wait . . . Steadman was her name from her first marriage. He knew she had been divorced at least once. Wonder what number husband Jimmy was? He should have asked her name— oh well, with luck he wouldn't run into her again.

Catherine Steadman, maiden name *Plyer.* She had been dangerous once—but to people other than himself. Mary Lee's accusations had been way off the mark. Catherine was a problem, all right, but in a way his wife would never support. He'd never let her in on it either.

He was halfway home and deep into memories of the young Catherine before he remembered that he had wanted to stop by Erin's house to see if she'd had any news from Mark. He decided to give her a call as soon as he had the chicken in the oven.

five

"The charm of fishing is that it is the pursuit of something that is elusive, but attainable, a perpetual series of occasions for hope."

—John Buchan, former Governor General of Canada

Lew was early by twenty minutes but Osborne was ready. He knew what drove that woman. Alert to the thermometer mounted on his deck, he was well aware that the late afternoon temperature had dropped about ten degrees—an excellent harbinger for trout during a month that tended to be too hot. No, sirree, if he could predict anything about Lew Ferris, it was that when conditions were right, her internal clock matched that of the hatch.

"I feel helicopters," she said, confirming his hunch with a big grin through the open window of her truck as she shifted the well-worn Mazda into idle. She waited as Osborne hurried to the back of the truck to load the gear he had already set out in the driveway.

"Sixty-three degrees, Lew, could be a good day," he said loud enough so she could hear. He was a little taken aback by how happy he felt suddenly, but Lew had a way of doing that to him. "Now when you say 'helicopters,' you mean spinners, right?"

He hoped that was what she meant. The vocabulary of the fly-fishermen who knew their insect hatches was a universe that he was struggling to master: spinners, sinkers, helicopters, woolly buggers. . . . geez. At least he wasn't still a rank beginner thinking only dry flies and wet flies. And if he died still short of being able to identify the damn things, at least he would die happy—he had had a great teacher.

Lifting the cardboard box packed with his picnic surprise, he wedged it tight between his fishing duffel and the inside wall of the truck so it wouldn't slide around. When Lew drove off-road, the little vehicle could lurch so violently that he wanted to be sure nothing would tip or spill.

"Need some help?" she asked over his right shoulder. He hadn't heard her come around the truck. She looked at the box, then up at him. Her eyes were quick and dark, eager. "Hey . . . what have we here?"

"Nothing . . . just a little something for later," said Osborne, throwing his waders over the box to hide it and trying his best for a casual, noncommittal tone.

Lew looked as good as ever, her face glowing dusky and tan against her light khaki fishing shirt. She always wore the same shirt fishing and he loved her in it. Loved the hint of her breasts against the pockets, loved how she tucked her shirt down into her pants so her waist emphasized the firm curve of her hips.

Once, when she was in uniform and he was waiting for her, he had found the shirt thrown onto the front seat of her truck. Holding it to his face, he inhaled deeply. For a woman who wore no makeup that he could discern, it surprised him to find she smelled of fresh-baked bread and lily of the valley—she wore perfume. Later, the first time they embraced, as he rested his face against hers, he had smelled it again—a light, lovely fragrance.

Tonight the shirt was tucked neatly into a pair of comfortable-looking faded Levi's, which fit snugly but not too tight. Lew was not a small woman. About five-eight, she had wide shoulders and hips to match. But she was toned and strong. She made women like his late wife seem soft, too soft. In sharp contrast to Mary Lee, Lew had a hard, muscled body and was easily able to shoulder half a canoe, whether wood, aluminum, or fiberglass.

Osborne could feel her peering over his shoulder. He had folded closed the top of the box, partly to keep the contents cool and partly for the surprise effect. He lingered, enjoying the feel of her standing so close. Curious, she didn't back off. But Osborne refused to give away his little secret until the time was right. Leaning back as he pulled down the hatch, he grinned down at her. His lips could have grazed her forehead under the baseball cap that she clamped down over her dark hair, but he resisted the urge. He knew better than to push his luck.

And he was very pleased with how everything had turned out so far. The chicken legs moved easily in their sockets (Mallory's test for doneness); the tiny orzo pellets had boiled themselves up into a reality that he still couldn't quite believe. And at the last minute he had decided to tuck in a blue-checked tablecloth with matching napkins (a set Mallory had given him for Father's Day) so he had quite a spread with which to impress her later.

The only unfinished business was that Erin had not answered his phone calls. Even though he knew he could try again later, the lack of contact nagged at him. He resolved to set that worry aside until he could do something about it.

"Well, I have my own surprise tonight," said Lew, walking around to the side of the truck near the driver's seat. "See those?" She pointed to the interior of the truck.

Osborne had been concentrating so hard on getting his box of food situated that he hadn't even noticed two large inner tubes crammed into the back.

"Float tubes, Doc. We're going up to a secret place of mine and give these a try."

"Are both those yours?" What had looked like tubes at first glance, Osborne now realized, were more like large inflated chairs covered with zippers.

"Ralph let me borrow one for you—he usually rents 'em out but I told him I had a new fly-fishing pal who just might turn into a customer."

"Did you name names?"

"Of course not," said Lew as she bounced up into her seat and tipped a sidelong glance his way. It was no secret between them that Lew deliberately did not tell the pretentious owner of the local fly-fishing shop just how much time she spent fishing with Osborne.

In Osborne's opinion, Ralph was obsequious when it came to Lewellyn Ferris, downright *obsequious*. Ray had confirmed Osborne's worst suspicions, too. The jerk might be married, but Ray had learned from some of the fishing guides working the lakes north of Loon Lake that he had shown up at more than a few fish fries in Boulder Junction with a woman who wasn't his wife—hard evidence Ralph fooled around.

Nope, Osborne didn't trust him for a second around Lew. Instinct triumphed over logic when it came to assessing the competition. He figured Lew found it to her advantage to keep Ralph guessing, guessing and falling over himself to supply her with the latest weather, water, and hatch updates, not to mention new equipment to test.

Osborne climbed up onto the hard vinyl seat on the passenger side. Pulling off his fishing hat, he set it on the seat between them. The fishing truck might be twelve years old and lightly rusted on the exterior, but Lew kept old Nellie so pristine that the inside looked brand-new.

As she turned the key in the ignition, Lew said, "With
the temperature like this—and no humidity—we may get
lucky tonight, Doc. Plus, we've got an early start," she
added, checking her watch. "It's only five o'clock and no
overcast—we could get more than four hours of light
even."

Osborne watched Lew as she backed out of his driveway. Black ringlets of naturally curly hair, which she
often cursed, escaped from under the forest green cap,
clustering over her ears and across the back of her neck.
The extended brim framed her face, emphasizing the firm
lines of her jaw and cheekbones.

Once upon a time, before he understood the basics of
making a living, he had considered sculpture as a career.
While his father cured him of that idea quickly, he had
never lost his eye for volume, space, and defining line. It
was one reason he had come to love dentistry. And silly as
it was, nothing matched the pleasure he got from letting
his eyes linger over the curves and hollows of Lew's face.

That, plus she always looked younger than he remembered. Better yet, she always looked happy to see him.

How many years had he arrived home after long hours
spent bending over to work in small, often diseased,
spaces—only to see irritation flicker across his late wife's
face. It wasn't Mary Lee's fault; her mother had prepared
her: Men were good for paying the bills, the rest you put
up with. He had laughed, during their courtship, when she
told him how her mother blocked out one hour every Sunday afternoon for Mary Lee's father. Ten years into their
marriage, he found he had inherited that hour—and he
was lucky if it was once a week. But Osborne had to
admit he'd been warned: He and Mary Lee had dated for
a year before their wedding.

The wedding. He would never forget that night. Mary
Lee had allowed twenty minutes for his husbandly rights.
Granted they had been together once before then so it

wasn't exactly a ceremonial event. But he never expected what followed. She leaped from the bed, turned on all the lights, and spent the next hour and a half opening cards and counting money. Actually, now that he thought about it, she spent the next thirty-eight years counting money!

But those days were past and tonight it felt good just sitting next to Lew. He liked to kid her that she loved to fish so much just the *sight* of a fly rod made her sparkle. Her response was an unladylike snort. Sparkling or snorting, Lew's good humor was contagious to the point that tonight she made even Erin's situation seem a little less serious.

"Boy oh boy, did I run into an old nightmare today," said Osborne as Lew turned onto Highway 45 heading north. He wasn't quite ready to break the spell of the late afternoon with talk about Erin.

"Oh yeah?"

"Remember Catherine Plyer?" said Osborne. "She's older than you, I think—had two younger brothers, both troublemakers, and her father was a general practitioner in Rhinelander."

"I knew Patty Boy. He was a year behind me in high school. There was a kid had problems—"

"Everyone had problems with that guy," said Osborne, interrupting her. "He was trouble right from the start. Yep, he was the younger of the boys. Dickie's the other one. I think he moved to Florida. Anyway, I hired Catherine to work in my office one summer. She was seventeen and I needed a receptionist for two months while the woman who had been working for me took a maternity leave.

"Everything was just fine at first. Catherine was a tall, attractive, articulate young woman. She was very good on the phone, friendly with patients, could type, help with the billing. And it was only a summer job—what could possibly go wrong, right?"

Lew looked straight ahead. "Plenty, if I remember right. I know the old man drank himself to death, died in a gutter down in Madison. The mother left years before, when those kids were still small, I think. What I remember most was those brothers and their father—they were tall, good-looking men. You would never expect such . . . well, that was one crazy family."

"Oh, you have no idea—" Osborne turned toward her eagerly, but just as he looked over at Lew, his eye was caught, as they passed, by rapid movement in the window of a black Mazda Miata pulled off the road heading in the opposite direction. Lew saw it, too: a woman's hands fluttering like a grouse in flight.

"What the hell—?" She slammed on the brakes.

Before Osborne could manage an answer, Nellie was in a power slide sideways up Highway 45.

six

"The congeniality and tact and patience demanded by matrimony are great, but you need still more of each on a fishing trip."

——Frederic F. Van de Water, author

"Dammit!" Lew smacked the steering wheel with the heel of her right hand as the truck eschewed along the shoulder back toward the parked car. "I knew I should have a radio installed in this truck. Damn! Damn!"

Arms up against the dashboard, Osborne braced himself and said nothing. He had mixed feelings about that. The most selfish was knowing full well that having a radio in the truck would sabotage the few hours of uninterrupted fishing that Lew was able to squeeze into her busy days.

As head of the department, she was already on call twenty-four hours a day every day. All she ever tried to take off was an hour or two—well, okay, three if you added in travel. And she always left someone in charge. Plus, this was Loon Lake, for God's sake—how much could go wrong in that short a time? No-o-o, thought Osborne to himself, no radio if he could help it. On the other hand, if not having a radio meant they were about to lose the person in that car . . .

Before Nellie had skidded to a stop behind the Miata, Osborne was out the door in a dead run.

He didn't even have to think. When it came to CPR, he was on automatic pilot—able to see pages of the training manual in his mind. Throwing open the door of the little car, he wrenched on the seatbelt, then pulled the young woman down onto the pavement.

No longer convulsing, she was unconscious. Not breathing? He straddled the limp form, gripped the jaw hard with his left hand, and thrust his finger down, searching for the tongue. Then lifting and pressing, he was forcing air into her lungs even as Lew ran up.

"Cell phone on the seat!" he rushed the words as he lifted his head to inhale.

"Let's hope to hell it works." Lew leaned into the car to grab the phone. She punched in numbers and waited.

Tourists were always stunned to discover their cell phones didn't work in the northwoods where few cell towers existed and even those were good only within five miles of the nearest town, sometimes not even that. And a town could be forty, fifty miles away. Until Sprint PCS executives felt a driving need to be in touch with the home office while *they* were fishing, cell phones would remain next to useless in the northwoods. For Lew, the radio in her police cruiser was still the best option.

"Doc, it's ringing," said Lew, relief in her voice. "Hey, Chief Ferris here—I need an emergency vehicle on Highway 45 about five hundred yards north of Ginty Road. Tell 'em to come across County C! Right now, the victim is . . . victim's convulsing.

"Yes, we're doing CPR but the victim is not conscious. Okay, I'll hold. . . ."

Osborne kept working. Phone to her ear, Lew waved off a car that had pulled over.

"EMT's on their way? Good—then patch me through to my switchboard. No, I have no idea what the problem is. We saw her convulsing or choking—I don't know. Please, I need my switchboard—"

Lew looked down with exasperation. "Doc, sometimes I wonder. . . ."

Just as she spoke, the girl moaned. Osborne slowed his movements. The girl gagged and coughed. Off in the distance he could hear Lew giving directions to whoever was on duty at the police switchboard, but his focus was the limp form beneath him. The girl was still a strange blue-white, her eyes rolled up behind the lids—but she was breathing.

Raising himself up onto his knees, he listened . . . she kept breathing. He moved off to the side, never taking his eyes off the girl's face. The eyes remained half-open, unseeing.

"Looking better, I hope?" Lew leaned in for a better view.

"Slightly." Osborne laid the back of his right hand against the girl's forehead, "I'm guessing but I think she's got a high body temp, Lew. It's not that hot out. . . ."

"Her hair is wet with sweat," said Lew. "I thought she was choking—"

"Looked like convulsions to me," said Osborne. He felt around the girl's neck, just under the edge of her collar, then glanced down to her wrist. "No ID necklace or bracelet to indicate she's got epilepsy or diabetes."

"Fever, maybe?"

Osborne shrugged. He could hear the wail of the approaching ambulance. They would know the answer to that.

The girl was slight, blond, and dressed in a short-sleeved lime green T-shirt over a pair of slacks the same color. No bra, which had made Osborne's efforts easier. The left foot still wore a matching lime green sandal; the other had fallen off when he pulled her from the car. Lew stooped to remove the other sandal, then set both neatly on the front seat of the girl's car. As she did so, she picked up a tan leather fanny pack that was lying there.

Opening the fanny pack, Lew pulled out a small French coin purse. Tucked into that was a driver's license. "Ellen Andrews . . . age nineteen . . . Wausau street address." Lew turned the license over to examine it. "If it said she was twenty-one, I would say it's a fake ID—but this looks like the real thing."

Just then three EMTs, two women and a man, jumped from the ambulance and ran toward them. "Good, Chris is on tonight. I know him," said Lew of the stocky, fair-haired man leading the way. Osborne guessed him to be in his mid-twenties.

"Jessie?" said Osborne as the women neared. He was surprised to see that one of the two was a former patient. "What are you doing here? I thought you worked in advertising."

Even as he asked the questions, Osborne stepped back and out of their way. Jessie could answer his questions later. Lew, meanwhile, had run off toward two more cars that had pulled over. With an emphatic swing of her arm, she motioned for them to keep going.

Osborne stood back and watched the EMTs, relieved to turn over the responsibility. Jessie certainly seemed to know what she was doing. Oldest of the four Lundberg kids, she was tall, slightly overweight, and quite a pretty brunette with soft, round features and shy brown eyes. He knew from the years of annual school checkups that she had a voice that matched her eyes: soft and pleasant.

Jessie was one of Loon Lake's stars. Now in her early

thirties, she had logged ten years as a television news producer in Australia and on the East Coast, only recently returning to her hometown to open a small ad agency producing television commercials.

All of Loon Lake had speculated on the reasons for her return. Erin was convinced she was recovering from a broken heart. Mallory, who had been a year ahead of Jessie in school, thought otherwise. Jessie was so softspoken and gentle, it was Mallory's guess that she lost out to the hard chargers in her field. Whatever the reason, her little agency had already snagged the account of the local hospital and seemed to be doing nicely. At least, that's what Osborne had heard from her father over coffee at McDonald's.

Jessie must have seen the look of astonishment on Osborne's face because she stood up and stepped back to stand beside him while her two colleagues continued hooking up an IV and preparing to roll the young woman onto a stretcher.

"Tell me when you need help, guys," she said, then turned to Osborne, "Surprised to see me, Dr. Osborne?" she said. "I've been training as an EMT this past year, taking classes at Nicolet College over in Rhinelander. I got certified a couple months ago, now I'm training for the next level."

"Wow," said Osborne. "After a long day in the office?"

"Well . . . I don't have a personal life," she grinned a little sheepishly. "And I've been thinking about making a career change—maybe going back to school in medicine, so I thought this would be a good test."

"You don't want to give dentistry a shot?" he kidded.

She gave him a quick smile and shook her head. "How come *you're* out here tonight?"

"Chief Ferris and I were on our way to do a little fishing when we saw something was wrong—"

"Oh?" Jessie glanced over at Lew, then back at Osborne. A funny look in her eye triggered a feeling of mild embarrassment, which Osborne did his best to shake off. But Jessie's amusement faded fast. "Whatever—that girl is lucky you two came by. Excuse me—"

At a wave from Chris, Jessie stepped forward to carry the IV and supplies as the other two lifted the stretcher. As another siren wailed in the distance, Lew and Osborne followed the EMTs as they carried the stretcher to the ambulance.

"Chris, is she in good enough shape for you to wait until my deputy gets here? He's about thirty seconds away," said Lew.

"Sure," said Chris, "she's stable. We can wait a few minutes, Chief." He appeared to be in charge of the operation.

"Chris?" Jessie called out from inside the ambulance as they eased the stretcher into place. "Do you know Dr. Osborne? He's a dentist in Loon Lake, friend of my dad's."

"Retired," added Osborne, shaking Chris's hand.

Jessie backed out of the ambulance and looked at her male colleague. "This looks like another overdose to me, Chris. What do you think?"

"What do you mean *another*?" said Lew with an edge in her voice.

Stripping off his disposable rubber gloves, Chris paused before answering. "I'm just a paramedic, Chief, but I think you should know that we got a call on another young kid, a boy, about two hours ago. Similar symptoms—high body temp, seriously dehydrated. He wasn't convulsing but he'd passed out. My guess is Ecstasy.

"Picked that one up down near Elcho. Bunch of kids held a rave back in on some farmland over off Highway 55 this weekend. I heard they had ten thousand people show up."

"Ten *thousand*?" Osborne gasped. "Where do they come from?"

"Everywhere," said Jessie. "Wausau, Madison, Milwaukee. And they party all day and all night. It's crazy."

"I can't believe I didn't hear about this." Lew looked at Chris as she spoke.

"When we brought the boy in, someone at St. Mary's called the Rhinelander cops," he said. "First they heard anything, I know. Shouldn't they have called you, too? Those kids are going in all directions."

"Hell, yes, they should have called me," said Lew. "But what really makes me mad is I'll bet those jerks down in Wausau knew all about this and never said a word to any of us up here. Elcho and that area off Highway 55 may be out of my jurisdiction but this location sure as hell isn't."

Chris looked uncomfortable. "I have no idea what the story is—but I'll sure have someone at the hospital get in touch with you."

Just then one of the Loon Lake police cruisers pulled up behind Lew's truck. A slight man, late middle-aged and balding, hurried over. The expression on his face was always the same: a mix of worry and hesitation as if he was about to be asked to do some real work.

Poor Roger. Osborne was quite familiar with the deputy's distress. Several years earlier, the man had made a bad decision. Thinking he had discovered an easy way out, he had traded the pressures of running a small insurance agency for a position as a police officer, a deputy. Roger's plan had been to coast into an early retirement with a nice pension.

He had assumed his most serious duty would be the emptying of parking meters. But life took an unfair turn. The northwoods became a "lifestyle destination" for young professionals from Milwaukee and Chicago. Almost overnight, the population base outside the township limits exploded as monied newcomers bought up lake property. Tourism had always added twenty thousand people to the summer population—now that number was soaring exponentially as well. Loon Lake had become a magnet for real estate investment and all the attendant misbehavior.

Then Lewellyn Ferris was promoted to chief of police. With the full support of the mayor and city council, she took an aggressive stand when it came to errant fishermen, hunters, snowmobilers, and idiots running their personal watercraft too close to shore. No more meter maid for Roger; he had to perform. And he wasn't happy. Nor was Lew for that matter; she was counting the days until his retirement. Meanwhile, she had to make the best of it.

"Roger," said Lew as the deputy edged his way toward her, shoulders hunched as if he expected to duck a flying object, "I want you to follow this ambulance and stay with the victim. I want confirmation from the emergency physician on duty that this is a drug overdose. *Under no condition* do you let this young woman leave the hospital until I am able to question her when she regains consciousness. Understand?"

Roger's face brightened. Sitting outside a hospital room? Reading magazines? He could do that.

Lew turned to Osborne. "Doc, I better pass on fishing tonight. With Roger at the hospital, I need to head back. Someone has to be available if we have any other problems tonight and Todd Reimer is at a training session in Green Bay." Todd was her other Loon Lake police officer.

Phooey, thought Osborne. What a frustrating day this was turning out to be.

"Chief Ferris?" Chris called out from where he had just

climbed into the driver's seat in the ambulance. Jessie had climbed in beside him and both their windows were down. "I don't know that it's really necessary to have an officer at the hospital," said Chris. "I understand your concern but no one has to accompany us. This girl will be kept overnight for observation, regardless.

"When there is any question of drug use by a person under twenty-one—and there certainly is in this case— our policy at the hospital is no release until family members arrive to sign her out. You go fishing, Chief; she'll be in supervised care through tomorrow morning, I promise."

"I'm on duty until midnight," said Jessie. "I'll keep a close eye on her, too. This is probably the most activity we'll see until the drunks head home after closing time."

"You might have more of these kids," said Lew.

"We don't think so," said Chris. "Rhinelander sent two cops over to clear the area. This girl must have left just before they got there. We would know by now if there was any trouble between here and there, I'm sure."

"Well . . ." Lew hesitated. "Roger, just to be sure, why don't you drive down that way. Doc and I have to buy licenses at the Michigan border and I'll call in to see if everything is okay."

"Lew . . . you need a break," said Osborne. "Roger can handle anything that comes up. As far as this young woman goes, even if she were to leave the hospital, you have her home address. She's not a hardened criminal— she's a kid who partied too hard." He knew that sounded a little light, given drugs were involved, but he had seen and heard enough when he went through rehab at Hazelden to know that the girl wasn't going to be moving too fast too soon.

Lew looked up at him and sighed. "I'm less concerned about that than who's supplying these kids. That's the real problem here."

"True," said Osborne, "but is that something you need to handle tonight?"

To his credit, for once Roger stepped up to the plate. "Look, Chief, I'll get her car towed, I'll call the family. I'll call around and see what the story is on this rave thing, okay? I've got everything under control—you go fishing."

"Nothing's under control, Doc, not a thing," said Lew as they climbed back into the fishing truck. She turned the key in the ignition and waited for oncoming traffic to clear.

"That's not true," said Osborne. "You run a disciplined operation."

"Yeah, but we're so small." Lew shifted then, forgetting she had already turned the key once, she gave it another turn. Nellie responded with an angry grinding.

"Ouch! Sorry, Doc, I'm just so stressed right now. I've got that fishing tournament coming up with the damn motorcycle rally the same weekend. Then today I get a call I have to be at a five-county emergency task force meeting in Park Falls at the crack of dawn tomorrow. Who knows what the hell *that's* all about. Jeez Louise!"

"All the more reason to take a break while you can," said Osborne.

"You're right." She pulled onto the highway and swung the truck around to head north again. "By the way, thanks, Doc." She reached over to pat his hand.

"For what—insisting you go fishing? Count on me for that anytime, kiddo."

"I mean for the CPR. I had no idea you could do that."

Osborne shrugged off the compliment. "You can't practice dentistry these days without knowing CPR, Lew. Half your patients are scared to death just being in the chair, the other half forget to tell you they're allergic to anesthetic. You better know CPR or you'll never see a paid bill."

Lew laughed. He loved the sound of it. That, plus the truck windows were down and the flow of warm air felt good against his face. It occurred to him suddenly that he was very happy she didn't have a radio in the car—no one could stop them now.

"Oh, one good thing happened today," said Lew, turning right down a gravel road. "I got your buddy, Ray, a job."

Osborne sat back in the seat and stared at her. "You're kidding, of course."

Lew loved to make the point that Ray was *Osborne's* friend. Yes, she acknowledged Ray's talents as an expert tracker through the forests and slash and dark waters of the northwoods. "Outstanding, Doc, I agree."

But she never let Osborne forget that the guy who had an eye rumored to be as keen as an eagle's also had an inch-thick file in her office, one that lent new meaning to that word *outstanding*.

"Misdemeanors today, felonies tomorrow," she loved to trill when they discussed his neighbor. Osborne had to concede she was right. Ray's file had been hefty before he was out of his teens, and his efforts at agriculture throughout his twenties only added to the department's paperwork.

Still, on occasion, Lew would draft him as a deputy. While his reputation as a pothead and his penchant for poaching gave the good mayor and certain city council members bad dreams, it also gave Ray access. Access to walking, talking human nightmares. And Loon Lake had a few too many of those.

"Ray? You aren't hiring him on during the tournament next week?" Osborne's heart sank; he'd been hoping she would ask *him* to help out.

"Heavens no. Rhinelander is lending me two deputies.

You know I can't deputize Ray unless I've got a serial killer on the loose. Nope, guess again."

"A new guiding client—a *rich* guiding client."

"Uh-uh." Lew shook her head and gave him a sly grin. "Guess again."

"O-o-kay . . . some dead out-of-towner needs a grave. An *obese* out-of-towner who needs a grave wide enough and deep enough to pay Ray's overhead through Christmas?"

"No-o-o!" Lew chortled. "*Bodyguard.* I got him a job as a bodyguard for this woman. You may know her. She's the star of one of the fishing shows on cable. Her name is Peyton or Hayden, something like that."

"Ah," said Osborne. "I heard that ESPN Two is coming in. But I don't watch enough TV to know who you're talking about."

"I set it up so he'll be paid a fair amount, too. They asked me what we pay our deputies—and I doubled it. We don't pay our people enough, so the hell with that approach."

"I'm surprised Ray didn't say anything when I saw him today."

"The Steadman people didn't call until late this afternoon."

"The *Steadman people*?" Osborne repeated blankly. His first thought was of Catherine with the beat-up face and her garbage truck of a husband. Those idiots with the loons tattooed all over their bodies are on television?

"Yeah, you know Parker Steadman—the billionaire who owns all the sporting goods stores, the one that started this bass tournament. He's coming to Loon Lake later this week and bringing his wife and her television crew. Apparently they're making a documentary of his life—the wife is, which is why she's coming. She's the one who needs a bodyguard.

"Hey!" Lew looked over at Osborne. "Were you his

dentist? Maybe they'll interview you. I'm sure they'll
want to talk to people who knew him when he was growing up. . . ."

"Well, that's not me. Parker Steadman is ten, maybe
fifteen years younger than I am. And he didn't really
grow up here, Lew. His family is from Chicago. They
owned a lot of potato land up here and had a huge summer place out on Lake Consequence. Even though he
spent his summers up here, Parker Steadman's really a
city boy."

And a major razzbonya, Osborne might have added.
Up until ten years ago, when he began to make his name
in sporting goods, he was better known to Loon Lake locals following his exploits in the *Wall Street Journal* as
Parker the Predator—he had skirted the SEC more than
once with a habit of raiding companies. But he was
shrewd: Buy cheap, restructure, let the stock run up, and
sell. A little too often the stock would crash shortly
thereafter.

"Why on earth does his *wife* need a bodyguard?
Parker's the one investors might have the urge to kill."

"The person who called me said she's been the target of
death threats——"

"From someone in Loon Lake? Does anyone here even
know her?"

"Not *from* Loon Lake, Doc. The threats are being
phoned in from somewhere outside the state—they didn't
give me details. They said they're afraid whoever it is will
follow her here.

"They seem quite worried. The woman on the phone
kept insisting that I assign an officer *full-time*—twenty-
four hours, in fact. I told her that was absolutely impossible. It is, you know. We don't have the budget for that.

"So I gave them Ray's phone number and told them
that he's done very good work for me as a deputy on special projects. I said, hey, you want someone who knows

their way around, who can keep a sharp eye out—he's the best. Don't you agree?"

"Lew," said Osborne, only half listening to what she was saying, "do you remember what I was saying before we stopped to help that girl? I was telling you that I bumped into Catherine Plyer today. She's a Steadman—she was Parker's *first* wife."

seven

"Regardless of what you may think of our penal system, the fact is that every man in jail is one less potential fisherman to clutter up your favorite pool or pond."

—Ed Zern, *Field & Stream*

It had been over twenty years since he had last seen Catherine Plyer Steadman but he had not forgotten a moment of those final hours. Nor would he ever.

Osborne had just turned forty. In fact, Mary Lee still had some leftover birthday cake sitting on the counter that June morning that Tim Knudson stepped out in front of him, blocking his way to the door that led to the stairs to his office over the Merchants State Bank building.

"Doctor Osborne? Do you have a minute?"

At first, given the intense look in Tim's eyes, Osborne assumed he was in pain from an abscessed tooth. Tim's uncle and Osborne frequently fished muskie together in those days, and Tim had been a patient of his for several years.

Osborne checked his watch. "I have a patient in ten minutes, Tim. I'm sure we can work you in later this morning."

"No, no, that's not the problem. Dr. Osborne. . . ." Tim, who was the operations manager for the telephone company, whose offices were right around the corner, looked hard at Osborne before saying, "Are you all right?"

Osborne chuckled, taken aback. His first thought was that his buddies were pulling a prank of some kind. "Am *I* all right? No, I'm not all right, Tim—I'm forty."

But the man wasn't kidding. "Dr. Osborne, someone is making obscene phone calls from your office. The police will be in touch with you shortly, but I talked to my uncle and he suggested that I talk to you first. We, ah, neither of us can believe that you're the type that—"

For a brief moment, Osborne was speechless. "My office? Are you sure . . . *my* office?"

"Someone has made half a dozen calls to three different women in the last week. Not only have we traced the calls to your office phone but the women—they're all patients of yours, Dr. Osborne."

Osborne didn't know what to say.

Tim continued, "The calls were all made at seven forty-five in the morning and it's a man's voice. . . ." Tim waited. The sad, worried look on his face told Osborne everything. "I thought . . . well, the police are willing to keep this confidential if we can work something out."

Osborne resisted an overwhelming feeling of rage. Anger would not help. He took a deep breath, dropped his head, and thought hard for a long minute.

"Tim, I don't get to the office until eight or five after, my first patient is at eight-fifteen. I have a ten-minute walk from my home, which I do every morning, and I have several neighbors or friends that I greet on the way—so you can check on my whereabouts at the time the calls are made.

"My receptionist isn't here much before me—*and* it's a young woman. I'm assuming you've tapped the women's lines? Did you tape the calls?"

"Just the last one. She got called two days in a row so we were able to set up and wait. We were lucky—the calls aren't made every day. Doctor, who besides you has access to your office and your office phone?"

"No one—no, wait . . . I gave Catherine a key so she can open and close. I wonder if someone might have gotten a hold of her key. Come on up and we'll talk to her. Oh yes—and there's the woman who cleans for me."

"It's a *man's* voice." Osborne could see the uncertainty in Tim's face. He wasn't sure yet that Osborne was not the perpetrator. Osborne could understand that. One of his best friends in college had turned out to be a peeping tom, had terrified neighborhoods for months before he was found out. Who was to say a dentist couldn't be off-kilter.

"Any call this morning?" asked Osborne.

"No, we waited until just before I walked over here—nothing today."

"Tim, let me go upstairs and think about this. Maybe I'm forgetting something—"

"I'd like to go up with you and look around if I may."

Osborne balked at that. What would his patients think?

"I know, I know." Tim raised a hand. "I'll just say we've got a line out of whack. But I would like to check this out. I'm afraid it's either me or someone from the police department—"

"Fine," said Osborne, giving up.

They were nearing the top of the dark, narrow stairway that opened into a hall at the end of which were Osborne's offices, when the door at the bottom of the stairs opened. The light, lovely eyes of seventeen-year-old Catherine Plyer looked up at them.

"Sorry I'm late, Dr. Osborne," she said, bounding cheerfully up the stairs. Osborne decided not to say anything yet; he didn't want to frighten her.

While Tim walked through the examining rooms and the hallway that made up Osborne's dental office, Osborne hung up his sport coat, pulled on his light blue gown, then stepped into the bathroom to scrub.

He looked at himself in the mirror. He looked like he always did: wavy jet-black hair, black-brown eyes, and a deep tan from the sun reflecting off the waters he fished at least four to five times a week. He might be forty but he prided himself on looking much younger thanks to the high forehead and strong cheekbones that he owed to his Meteis grandmother. He knew he was a tall, good-looking man. What he didn't know was if he was losing his marbles. How could someone be making obscene phone calls from his sacred space without his knowing?

Just then it dawned on him. "Tim!"

He stepped into the hall and motioned to Tim to follow him into the back room. Once there, he closed the door and indicated with his hand that they should keep their voices low. The room where they were standing was a combination study–supply room. Quite small, all it held was an easy chair that faced two windows four feet away, a coat rack to the right of the chair where Osborne hung his sport coat, winter coat, and an extra dental gown. The rest of the space was given over to shelving on which he kept a selection of dental supplies.

"I forgot about this," said Osborne, pointing to a door at the back of the room. He opened it and flipped a light switch. This was a storeroom. Very tidy with more supplies neatly stacked on shelving in front and to the right of them as they peered in. To the left was another door.

"I keep this locked," said Osborne. "It opens into the McKenzie law firm's front office. When I moved in here, their offices and mine had been used by a title company. They were split to make room for us."

"So someone from the law firm could enter through here?" said Tim.

"If they had a key."

"Doc, do you have a key?"

"Yes, right here." Osborne reached into his pocket for the ring with his three office keys. "Downstairs front door, my office door, this door." Osborne noticed Tim's use of the more familiar "Doc." He felt a glimmer of relief.

"Does that young woman at the front desk have copies of all three?"

"No, not the key for this door. No reason for her to."

"Okay—let's go next door," said Tim.

Fifteen minutes later, after a brief talk with a shocked Harry McKenzie, Tim and Osborne left his office. Harry, who was just back from a two-week fishing trip to Canada, had an alibi so his involvement was out of the question. But he was quite shaken at the thought that one of his two partners—or their paralegal—might be up to no good. Osborne felt sorry for him but he was enormously relieved to see the suspicion shifted.

Still, someone was invading his office and, worse, terrorizing his patients.

Between the three of them, they decided on a plan. Now it was Harry's wish to avoid any more police involvement than was absolutely necessary. Assuming the perpetrator was someone in his firm, he would hope to negotiate a warning rather than an arrest. After a quick call from Tim to the police officer handling the complaints, they had an approval to proceed.

At six-thirty the next morning, Tim and Osborne arrived at Harry's office. He was waiting. No one else had arrived yet. A quick glance down the hall showed that Osborne's office was dark, too.

Entering the storeroom through the door in Harry's reception area, Tim and Osborne opened the door that led to Osborne's study. The office was dark and silent. They decided to hide in the bathroom. Osborne checked his watch: six-fifty.

At seven thirty-five, they heard a key turn in a lock. It was the front door to Osborne's office. The door opened, closed. Footsteps. Tim and Osborne looked at each other. What if Catherine was early? Would she need to use the bathroom? They would scare her to death. The two men waited anxiously but the footsteps stopped at the front desk.

Tim cracked the bathroom door slightly. Papers rustled, the wheels on the receptionist's chair squeaked. Silence. Then the sound of a rotary phone dialing.

A man's voice, low, insulting, obscene. Tim edged toward the bathroom door. They knew whoever it was could make that call and leave before Catherine arrived. Neither Tim nor Osborne intended for that to happen.

Just as they were ready to throw open the door, the man's voice changed its low, intimate, insidious mutter. It took on a shrill, angry tone as it shouted, "Lady, this isn't your husband! This is an obscene phone call." And the phone was slammed down hard.

Tim bolted for the hallway, followed by Osborne.

The caller stood over the desk, hand still resting on the phone. Tall, angry, and dressed in a short white nurse's uniform. It was Catherine. Or as Osborne would always remember it——the *other* Catherine.

Tim stepped back as Osborne moved forward. "Catherine . . . you——?"

She turned and stared. Her eyes were dark, burning. Then she started to walk toward him, her head high and thrust forward like the rabid raccoon that had stalked him in his yard that spring. Fear galvanized Osborne. He backed away.

"Out, get out," he managed hoarsely. "Get the hell out of my office."

Catherine laughed. A harsh, deep laugh. Without taking her eyes off Osborne, she reached down for her purse and swung it over her shoulder. Then, in a swift move, she grabbed the phone and threw it at them. Osborne ducked. By the time he looked up, she was gone.

Catherine Plyer was the daughter of a prominent professional man. No one wanted to make an issue of the situation, certainly not the police. As far as Osborne, Tim, and Harry McKenzie ever knew, she wasn't even warned. But the phone calls stopped.

"Hmm," was all Lew said when he'd finished. "Hmm." She drove in silence for about a minute. "You must have run into her after that—what happened then?"

"I didn't, actually. The few occasions that I might have seen her, like at the grocery store, I managed to avoid her. The family wasn't Catholic so it's not like I would have seen her at church. Anyway, she left town not too long after that."

"That must be why I never knew her," said Lew. "Because I knew those brothers. Dickie's living back up here, y'know. He was arrested in Vilas County last year for dealing coke, and I had him overnight in the Loon Lake jail when Vilas County's facility was undergoing some renovations. His lawyer got him out on a technicality of some sort. Bruce Johnson, the new sheriff up there, didn't think old Dickie was the brightest bear in the woods. He was trying to figure out who was giving orders. I wonder if it's the big sister?"

"I wouldn't put it past her. I wouldn't put anything past that woman. If Parker Steadman shows up, you should ask him about her, Lew."

"How long were they married?"

"Don't know. And what I do know was told to me by Mary Lee so I'm sure the details were more than a little twisted. But keep in mind Catherine, as I said earlier, was a very pretty young woman in those days, very attractive."

What Osborne didn't say was that the girl was too at-

tractive. There had been moments in the office when he
had had to remind himself that she was seventeen and he
was a married man, a father. He had never known, before
or since, a woman who could ooze sex like the young
Catherine Plyer.

"It was that same summer of my run-in with her that
she started dating Parker Steadman and got pregnant.
They were married pretty soon after that and moved to
Minneapolis, if I remember right. Maybe it was
Chicago . . . anyway, wherever it was, he had a job in the
family business.

"The next thing we heard was the baby was born and
the couple split. Only they didn't just split—this is Mary
Lee's version now—Catherine *assaulted* Parker. His family was so horrified, they paid her off. They paid her to
file for divorce. We heard it was a lot of money, which she
took—and disappeared."

"Until today."

"Until today."

"What do you mean she assaulted him? Like what—
beat him up?"

Osborne looked over at Lew. "She shot at him. With a
deer rifle. Obviously missed, but the story was she tried to
kill him. But see, this was all rumor. Who knows if that's
what really happened. I mean, there aren't that many
women who can handle a deer rifle."

"Unless you grow up hunting with your brothers. And
those two boys were pretty proficient with firearms, I can
tell you that. They were a dangerous duo, Patty Boy and
Dickie, people you don't want to tangle with if you don't
have to.

"Hey—enough of that. Here we are."

Lew slowed the truck. At a small sign reading BIRCH
LAKE, she turned right. As Nellie bounced along, Osborne
stole glances at Lew's face. He really enjoyed watching
her demeanor change as they neared a fishing spot. It hap-

pened every time: The worry lines dropped away, her brow lightened, fatigue disappeared, and by the time she parked, she was grinning like a kid.

Osborne knew the feeling well—happened to him, too: sixty-something going on sixteen.

eight

*"Modern fishing is as complicated as flying a
B-58 . . . several years of preliminary library and desk
work are essential just to be able to buy equipment
without humiliation."*

—Russell Baker

Lew pulled the truck into a small clearing. Out his window, Osborne could see tire marks indicating other vehicles had been there recently, but no one was around.

Holding her door open, Lew paused for a moment to look over at Osborne. "Hey," she said with a questioning lift of her eyebrows, "ready to go play with some fish?" She shook a finger at him. "Now just you remember Birch Lake is a secret—don't you *ever* tell a soul about this place."

"Cross my heart and hope to die."

Hopping down and out of the truck, Lew gave a quick look in every direction, stuck both her arms straight out, and waited. She had rolled up the sleeves of her khaki fishing shirt, so plenty of bare skin was exposed. But no insects took the bait.

"So far so good," she said after a moment. "Last time I

was here, the mosquitoes dive-bombed us. Better bring your Deet just in case, Doc."

Walking to the back of the truck, Lew yanked down the tailgate and reached inside. Osborne hurried back to help. "First we unload this stuff." She pointed to his gear bag and the little cardboard box. "You don't wear a fishing vest in a float tube so what you'll need on the water, you want to pack into your tube."

"Really?" That worried Osborne. It had taken him hours to pack the damn vest. Hours that had convinced him that fly-fishing vests were a diabolical plot orchestrated by the same miscreants who designed 3,000-piece jigsaw puzzles. The goal was the same: torture. The only difference was the weapon of choice: pockets. Pockets of all sizes—small, large, horizontal, vertical, square, oblong, tubular, zippered, Velcroed, buttoned, zippered *and* Velcroed.

Add to that the fact that each pocket was destined for some particular tool, line, or other mysterious fly-fishing gadget. Of course there were no directions: you had to figure that out yourself. You could go mad managing the pockets on your fishing vest. Not to mention the strange hunks of fake sheepskin stuck here and there.

Osborne had worked slowly, carefully, packing and repacking until his vest looked not only like he knew what he was doing but, more important, *so he could remember where the damn stuff was.*

Now he had to take it apart and do it all over again? Jeez Louise. Maybe Ray was right when he needled, "Listen, Doc, stick with bait fishing. All ya need is a rod in one hand, tackle box in the other, doncha know." He had a point there. After all, when you open a tackle box, you can see every lure lined up neatly under clear plastic—they aren't hidden behind zippers, flaps, and goddam Velcro *barricades* for God's sake.

While Osborne agonized, Lew bustled. Her anxiety

over Roger's ability to monitor the drugged-out girl had
given way to cheery enthusiasm. "Take just what you
need, Doc, and we'll stick everything else back in the
truck. Oh, and we have to pack in a mile—so keep it
light."

"Got it," said Osborne, still without a clue. Following
the first set of orders, he moved his gear bag, box, and rod
case from the truck down onto the grass. Lew did the
same, setting her stuff off to the other side of the truck.
Then she pulled out the two float tubes and shoved a red
one at Osborne.

It looked like a monster doughnut, only it had a seat instead of a hole in the middle. Shallow, zippered pockets
ran up both arms. He was happy to see a deeper pocket
running across the back. The mesh seat with its straps resembled a child's high chair. Osborne shrugged. He
couldn't imagine how this was going to work, but plenty
of men he knew did it so it couldn't be rocket science. Behind him, Lew's hands flew as she tucked what she
needed quickly, expertly, into the zippered sections dot-
ting her tube.

Feeling lost and late and knowing he was going to hold
up the show yet again, Osborne decided to get at least one
thing accomplished. Turning his back so Lew couldn't see
what he was doing, he opened the cardboard box. Thank
God for Ziplocs and his own foresight. Quickly, he
shoved the three bags, which included some cutlery and
paper plates, into the large pocket across the back of the
tube, then grabbed the tablecloth and napkins and pushed
them in on top. He was just pulling the zipper shut when
he felt a hand on his shoulder.

"What are you doing? What's that?"

"Oh, nothing." Did she see the tail end of the tablecloth? "Extra shirt in case I get wet."

"You won't get wet," she said in a tone that made him
feel like a numbskull. "And who cares if you do? It's

sixty-five degrees—you're not gonna freeze to death. And you don't want to carry any more weight than you have to. . . ."

"Okay." Ignoring the criticism, Osborne reached into a pocket on his fishing vest to grab his box of trout flies. He studied the contents. Irv Metternich, a good friend and former patient who had fly-fished for years, had just given him two Deer Hair Hoppers, size twelves, that he had tied himself—and a larger Grizzly King. Osborne wanted to try those just for friendship's sake. Earlier, he had also tucked in two size fourteen stone flies and his favorite, a size twelve Adams.

Lew snorted whenever she came across a fly fisherman with boxes and boxes of trout flies stashed in his vest pockets—"You never need more than five at a time if you have any idea what you're doing." Osborne was getting better at listening to what other fly fishermen were saying, which clued him into the current hatches at least. Today he thought he had good excuses for four of his six selections.

"Oh, gosh no," said Lew, leaning over to peer into his box. "Those won't work, Doc. We're supposed to have a hex hatch—but I don't know if they'll be emergers, duns, or spinners. Listen, put those away. I'm going to give you the right flies tonight after I see what the hatch is. We might have to nymph with sinking lines and I know you don't have any. You just get your sunglasses, your rod, and your waders. I'll take care of the rest."

Oh, great, thought Osborne, a hex hatch. He struggled to remember what the hell kind of mayfly that was. He knew he should be able to conjure an instant image to which he could match a trout fly but it totally escaped him at the moment. Sometimes he wondered if he would ever master the basics of this sport.

"Look, Doc," said Lew, her voice softening at the confusion on his face. "You haven't float-fished before so take it easy. Here"—she shoved a pair of rubber flippers at him—"these are for you—boot fins."

Ten long minutes later, Osborne had managed to locate and pack his polarized sunglasses, floatant, clippers, forceps, Ketchum release, two new leaders, some 4x and 3x tippet, an extra pair of reading glasses, a packet of Kleenex—everything except his water bottle, waders, boots, and fins. Not only that, he had a shot at remembering where everything was. And he had his reel safely on his rod with the fly line threaded through the guides. He relaxed ever so slightly.

Lew handed him one of two small backpacks that she had pulled out of the truck. "Put those boots and waders and that bottle of water in here, Doc, then we'll hook the float tubes and the fins onto these packs."

"Okey-doke." Helping each other, they rigged up. Lew locked the truck, hid the keys behind a bumper, and they started down the path into the woods.

"I feel like a little kid getting ready for my first day of kindergarten," said Osborne. The float tube was annoying, bouncing off the back of his legs as he walked. He decided not to let it bother him.

The hike took them into a light-filled forest of white birch and hard maple. Splashes of sun sprinkled down through the canopy of spiky maple and serrated birch leaves. It bounced off the baby maples, bright green and leafy, that blanketed the ground in every direction.

The sun, just beginning its descent, chose that moment to soften the air with a golden sheen. Osborne loved this time of day. He let his eyes wander through the woods, which were luminous and deep. Dark brown trunks of maple etched black lines against the brilliant white of the birches. Everywhere was leaf and light.

"Trout live in beautiful places," said Lew, her voice low and soft as she trudged along before him. It was her favorite expression. She stopped for a moment to inhale and look about with pleasure. Osborne said nothing. At this moment, the forest cast a spell so magic, so infinitely peaceful, that no words were necessary. Maybe this was why he loved fishing with Lew: He never had to say more than he wanted to.

As they resumed their walk, Osborne studied his companion from the back. She had rigged her float tube, her fish net, and her flippers with such precision that she strode soundlessly along the path while he bumped along, the float tube banging off the backs of his heels. He couldn't have felt more awkward than if he had spilled an entire box of fishing tackle.

Another fifty yards and Lew stopped short, a look of annoyance on her face. "For heaven's sake, Doc, let me rig that higher for you," she said, turning him by the shoulders to adjust his straps. That helped. On they went.

As they walked, Osborne was reminded of Lew's home, where everything, like the rigging of her back pack, had its place. Just a week ago, when they had decided to fish a trout stream thirty miles west of Loon Lake so it made more sense for him to pick her up for a change, he finally had a chance to see where and how she lived.

She owned twenty acres bordering tiny little Lake Tomorrow and lived in the original farmhouse. Once upon a time the place had been a goat farm; now it was a jewel. At least that's what he thought. Built of weathered planks, inside and out, and with rooms whose walls were hung with silver-framed fish etchings interspersed with trophy fish mounts—including a muskie nearly fifty inches long—the farmhouse was quite small, picturesque, and comfortable.

Arriving ten minutes early that day, he had caught her still in her apron with flour up to her elbows. She was pulling four loaves of bread from the oven of an old ceramic and iron gas stove. Over her head hung a rack of pots, all sizes and blackened with use. On a wooden table behind her sat two dozen freshly frosted cinnamon rolls. The aroma made him hungry even though he had just wolfed down a ham sandwich.

"Lewellyn! I didn't know you cooked."

"Bread and rolls—every Saturday." She spoke with the same crispness she used to assign a jail cell to a drunken ATV rider.

"Every week? How do you eat all that and not get fat?"

"Oh, this isn't for me. I cook for my nephew and his family. And my daughter's family when she visits. Here, have one."

She handed him a roll on a piece of paper towel and waved him toward the living room. The room held a wood-burning potbelly stove, an old wood and leather chair with a leather ottoman, and an oak bookcase. It was a place that made him feel like putting his feet up and staying awhile. A long while.

Careful not to drop crumbs, Osborne leaned over the bookcase, curious to see what she read. The shelves held a collection of books on fishing muskie and trout, a stack of old Orvis and Cabela catalogs, one book on shotguns, and a couple on tying trout flies. There were several children's books, which he imagined she read to her grandchildren, some cookbooks, and oddly, a well-thumbed paperback edition of *Zen and the Art of Motorcycle Maintenance*. The top of the bookcase was covered with framed photos.

Lew walked in, drying her hands on a towel, just as he was examining the pictures. She pointed to one. "That's my nephew and his wife and these are his children. . . . And this is my daughter, her husband, and my two grandchildren. Aren't they cute?" And there were more pictures—of her parents, aunts, and uncles—and her son, the one that had been killed. "He lived hard and it's good he did for all the time he had, Doc." Once again that crispness. What a funny woman, thought Osborne. Rarely did he catch her in a moment when she wasn't no-nonsense.

Then she had shown him the rest of her place, including the bath with its old claw-foot tub. Her bedroom held an antique iron bed painted white and covered with an orange-and-white patterned quilt—"My great-grandmother made that." Over the bed hung a wood carving of an eagle in flight. A beat-up vanity, well on its way to losing all its paint, was angled into one corner. Her holster hung off the side and the .40 caliber SIG Sauer rested beside the telephone.

Can't beat *that* as a quaint setting for communications and firepower, thought Osborne. He still found it hard to believe he had a crush on a woman who packed heat.

A second room held a small workshop. Neatly organized like the rest of the little farmhouse, two countertops held boxes of tools and supplies for woodworking. "When the weather is too rough to fish, I relax in here," said Lew. "I make walking sticks, wall sculptures, pins—that kind of thing. Nothing special."

"Did you carve that eagle in your bedroom?"

"Yep—that's one of my favorites. These walking sticks over here in the corner? These are my own designs, too." Then she pulled out a wooden box and opened it to show him more of her work: little wooden grouse pins, lots of leaping trout, and Christmas angels.

"Lew, these are good. You should sell these."

"Actually"—she paused and for the first time ever he saw her blush—"I do. A shop up in Boulder Junction carries my stuff. Everything I make on these I save in a special account that I plan to use to buy fishing equipment for my grandchildren when they're old enough. And

travel—I want to take them fly-fishing in Colorado someday."

Osborne had the feeling that he was one of the few people who knew this about her. "So that's that," Lew had
said, shutting the box. Excusing herself then, she had
changed into her fishing clothes.

While he waited, Osborne had felt a little sad. What a
full life she had. Too full. No room for him, that's for
sure.

The sun was still high as they walked. The light dappling
through the leaves, a gentle breeze, and the fragrance of
some wild bloom did its best to make all the cares of the
world seem far away. They were three quarters of a mile
into the maple and birch forest when the path took a turn
into a stand of virgin hemlock.

Ancient trees towered over them, shutting out the sun.
Dark shapes hunkered behind splayed, dead stumps. The
trunks of the living trees were so tall and bristled with
dead branches that Osborne felt as if he were creeping
under the legs of giant spiders. The change was typical of
a northwoods forest: in less than ten feet, these woods
could turn on you—from hallowed to haunted.

Off to his left, through the shadows, he saw jagged
branches clawing at the air. The sight jolted him back to
the morning—to Erin, the fear in her eyes and the terrify-
ing memory they had revisited.

Stumbling suddenly, Osborne grabbed for the spindly
branches of a young hemlock to steady himself. The float
tube didn't help. It swung around, catching in the over-
hanging brush. Leaning back to tug it loose, Osborne
hoped like hell the damn thing wasn't punctured. He was
still leaning when it came free with a snap that sent him
lunging backward. Grabbing at air with one hand and trying desperately to keep his rod free of branches with the

other, he went down on his butt—and the tube. It was a soft landing.

"Need a hand?" Lew hurried back to help him.

"I'm fine, I just tripped on something."

"You didn't *just trip*, Doc. You weren't watching where you were going. What is up with you anyway? You haven't been yourself all afternoon."

Really? He thought he'd been doing just fine.

Before he could answer, Lew said, "You're preoccupied. I know you well enough to know you've got something on your mind. You want to talk about it?"

She yanked his float tube around and adjusted the straps again. Osborne brushed pine needles off his hands and knees.

"You don't have to if you don't want to," she said. Her tone implied the exact opposite. She gave him a sharp look, then started down the path again.

After a few steps, she called back over her shoulder, "Are you worried about the fishing?"

Again he felt that sting behind his eyelids. "No . . . I'm worried about my daughter."

Lew stopped and turned around. "So tell me about it while we walk?"

"I was hoping I didn't have to ruin the evening with this."

"Trust me, if there's a hex hatch, nothing can ruin my evening. C'mon, get it off your chest, Doc. I may be able to help—after all, I've raised one, too, y'know."

And so he told her everything, starting with Erin's surprise visit that morning and ending with the vision of the decomposing body, the bones fighting their way out of the burlap sack. The only thing he forgot to mention was the mysterious appearance of the peach pie.

When he had finished, Lew nodded. "Feel better getting it off your chest?"

"A little. No, a lot better. I feel much better, Lew. Thank you."

"Good. Now we'll go fishing and we'll both think about it."

That struck Osborne as not quite fair, but he had to admit he was up for sharing the burden.

nine

"The very mechanics of fly fishing are restful and re-laxing. The act of rhythmically casting one's rod and line to and fro slows one's mood to the tempo of the gentle winds and undulating currents."

—Martin J. Keane, *Classic Rods and Rodmakers*

At the end of the path, a pool full of sky broke the gloom of the forest. Though it was already past six, the July sun hung high enough in the west to send shards of glitter rippling across the surface.

Ready to launch in boots and waders, Lew stood with her hands on her hips, eyes raking the water. "I see slurps . . . some jumping. But those are little dinks." She waited. "We oughta see some *big* brook trout in this lake, Doc—planted, of course. This is one place that doesn't get overfished because very few people know about it. I've seen plenty sixteen to twenty inchers—caught one nineteen inches last time I was here."

An impish look crossed her face. "If I get one over twenty-two inches tonight, I might have to keep it—and you might not have to tell anyone."

"To mount?"

"Yep. How many times do you see a twenty-two-inch brookie in this neck of the woods, huh? Ready, Doc?"

"I think so," said Osborne. Boots on over his waders, he was standing in water up to his knees, one hand on the float tube, the other holding his rod. He watched as Lew stepped into the mesh seat of her tube, sat down, then leaned forward to strap the fins on over her boots.

"Be sure you clip the ankle strap on," she said. "If the fin slips off, it's gone and you will be floating forever. Hook the stripping basket across your lap like so," she demonstrated, "and you're set." She pushed off from the bottom. "You want to kick nice and slow and don't let your fins break the surface or you'll scare the fish. Just like this—keeping it slow and rhythmic."

"Lew, it'll take forever to get anywhere," said Osborne a few minutes later as he tried to follow her out. They didn't have far to go. The lake was quite small, maybe five acres at the most, a perfect oval ringed with hemlock, balsam, and white pine. Feeling like a human bobber, he did his best to follow Lew as she worked her way toward the center in a silence broken only by the trill of an occasional bird.

At first, Osborne found the boot fins awkward and ineffectual—propelling him nowhere fast. On the other hand, he had an immediate sense of being one with the water and that was good. He could see sneaking up on a loon or joining a family of ducks with no one noticing—not a bad crowd if you needed new friends. To his surprise, in less than five minutes they were a good distance from shore and Lew was bouncing with excitement, switching her tube around so he could catch up.

"We got a hatch!" She pointed off to the southern shore as she held a thermometer in the water. "Definitely a good hatch, too. See those little dinks leaping off to your left, Doc? But this water is too warm on the top for the big guys—we have to go down. I figured we would. They're feeding on the emergers on the bottom. Whoa, look at that! This is a *fine* hex hatch."

"Maybe I should use that Hairwing Dun that I've got?"

"No, not yet. I know this water real well. We need weighted flies with a touch of split shot on a sinking line. That'll sink your fly down to where it can drift through the feeding zone and reduce the vertical drag so you're less likely to spook the fish."

She reached for his fly rod. Fingers moving deftly, she clipped and tied. "Because this lake is so clear, I'm giving you fluorcarbon tippet for the sinking line and I'm tying on a rabbit fur strip nymph."

"So no dry flies. . . ."

"Not if you want a big fish."

"Lew, whatever you say—I definitely want a big fish." Given his track record, Osborne hoped for *any* fish. Even a dink would do.

She handed his rod back and began to work on her own. "Maybe after dark you could try an extended body deer hair." She spoke through the line in her teeth. "That's when that Hairwing Dun might work, but only if we see hexes all over the surface. This is just like fishing muskie, Doc—by this time in July, the thermocline sets up so those big fish go deep. Kinda like the Packers: 'Go-o-o Deep!'" She flashed a big grin as she mimicked a crowd cry. "But if you do decide to use a dry fly, be sure it's a size six—"

"I know, I know—better the wrong fly in the right size than vice versa."

Lew knotted, then spit, then tested her knot. "Good. Okay, let's fish."

Osborne raised his rod for a backcast. He could move easily in the float tube, which was a good sign.

"Oops, no, Doc, you don't *cast* a sinking line. You have to troll, letting the line drop and keeping the slack out so you can feel a strike. Watch me."

That he was happy to do. Sometimes he thought he fly-fished not for the challenge but just to see the sheer enjoyment on her face.

Feet moving under the surface, Lew positioned herself about twenty yards from shore and thirty feet from Osborne. With a simple roll cast, she had the fly line out, let it sink, and then, kicking slowly, she trolled.

Bam! A trout slammed the line.

Osborne's adrenaline skyrocketed as he watched Lew work the fish: rod bent, line taut, letting it run then stripping in her line. He loved to watch her—every move fine-tuned to the action of the trout. Her whoops of excitement and the shine in her eyes were so infectious he had to laugh out loud as he shouted encouragement. Soon she had a fourteen-inch trout, which she deftly measured against the ruler diagrammed on the stripping basket, then released.

"See how easy it is, Doc? Hey-y-y, did you hear my rod *sing*?"

"Sure did." God, he was happy he was here. While Lew checked the condition of her leader and trout flies, Osborne paddled off to troll on his own.

In less than two minutes, he had a strike.

"Set that hook!" shouted Lew.

Yanking too soon and too hard, he lost the fish. Ten minutes later, another strike but no fish. No mistakes on his part, however. That strike was a signal that he recognized from his years of bait fishing for muskie and walleye and bass: Something big was down there, nibbling, testing. What a night this might be! Holding still to hang in the same general area as that second strike, he suddenly felt the fin slipping off his right boot. Darn!

Cradling his rod against his left shoulder, Osborne paid no attention as the line sank, the fly drifting down and down while he reached with his right hand over the side of the tube to rank on the strap holding the fin to the heel of his boot.

"C'mon, Doc, what are you *doing*?" Lew sounded exasperated. "You can't catch fish that way." Just as she spoke, something hit his fly and zoomed.

"Whoa!" Osborne grabbed his rod at the last minute and held on.

"Set that hook!"

"I did!"

"Let it run . . . don't let that line go slack!"

"I won't, I won't, ohmygod. . . ."

The fish was running deep and it was strong—it had to be big! Lightly grasping the stripped line with his left hand, Osborne let it out, watching it speed away. Suddenly the fish turned, heading in the direction of Lew— then it was under her. The two of them burst into excited laughter. This was amazing! Then, just as suddenly, the line went slack.

"He broke it," said Lew, "that son-of-a-gun. I'll bet he bit that fly right off."

She was right. But even as Osborne examined his decimated tippet, he was happy. He grinned over at Lew. "Do you believe I'm as excited now as I was when I was six years old catching my first fish—it was a ten-inch rock bass."

"Yeah," she said, "doesn't it always feel that way?" She looked around. "I hate to say it, Doc, but this hatch is over."

"We got in a good half hour."

"A *great* half hour. Let's head back. I need to grab a bite before heading over to the hospital to check on Roger and that girl."

"See the point over there?" said Osborne, indicating a spit of land not too far off. It looked conveniently sandy with a few fallen logs that could serve as seating. "Since it isn't dark yet, why don't we go ashore for a minute—I have something I want to show you."

"Oh? All right. I need to see a man about a horse anyway."

While she was in the woods, Osborne set up quickly: tablecloth, napkins, cutlery, paper cups, and with a couple quick squeezes on the Ziplocs, the plates were filled with slices of roast lemon chicken and cones of orzo, gleaming with olive oil and herbs. The menu was limited but he was pleased. Years of camping, in spite of Mary Lee's disparaging remarks and refusals to come along, had paid off: His al fresco table technique looked great in the twilight.

Oh, right. He reached deep into the back pocket of the float tube for one last item. By the time he could hear Lew striding through the brush behind him, the candle was lit.

"For me?" She was dumbstruck. "You did all this for me?"

"Well, you're such a good cook yourself, I didn't want to show up with tuna fish."

"You silly man." She leaned up on her tiptoes, one hand resting lightly on his shoulder, and brushed her lips against his cheek. He was happy.

"Everything is delicious, Doc," said Lew, "but this peach pie is the best. Umm. I can't believe you made this yourself!"

Osborne looked at her. "I didn't . . . I thought you made it."

"Me? I bake bread, not pies. What do you mean you thought I made it?"

"Someone left a warm pie on my deck this morning. At first, I thought it was Ray. When he said it wasn't him, I thought for sure it must be you."

"Not me. Maybe a neighbor?" Lew pushed the very last crumb of pie onto her plastic fork with her finger, swallowed with a look of intense satisfaction, then waved her fork at Osborne. "About that Schultz case—I would appreciate it if you would take the time to look over the file for me. All that happened just before John Sloan took over as chief of police from old man Raske and you *know* what a razzbonya that guy was."

"Yes, I do," said Osborne, the naming raising an ugly memory. "Raske was a real nogoodnik. I always felt sorrier'n hell when he got his hands on some of those young Indians from the reservation. The man was merciless—he went too far and there was nothing you could do to stop him.

"He was a patient of mine, too. Never paid his bill, of course. I finally told his wife I didn't need their business, which was none too smart on my part. That arrogant son-of-a-bitch. I just kept my fingers crossed that no one in my family would need help from the police so long as he headed up the department."

"He wasn't just a bully—he was lazy as hell," said Lew. "The state of the files from those days is pathetic. If he had a crime scene and no easy answers, or if it involved a friend of his—hell, he wrote it off as a misdemeanor. That man had the cleanest desk north of Wausau and south of the Canadian border. I'll tell ya, Doc, if you're up for it? When you finish looking at the Schultz file, I've got a half-dozen more we can check out. Chief Sloan was always going to get around to it but he never did.

"Plus, it'll take your mind off the other situation." Lew scrambled to her feet to help clean up.

"I hope so. I sure don't know what to do about that."

"Hey, Doc, when we get over to the other shore, I've got a little camp stove, some plastic mugs, another bottle of water, and a couple of those one-cup coffee bags in my pack. I can make us each a cup of coffee if you like."

"I thought you needed to get back."

"No more than you needed to make me this lovely dinner." She grinned.

Osborne knew full well he had fins on his boots but he could have sworn they were wings—his float tube seemed to fly back. And when he and Lew reached the other shore, which had western exposure, they were just in time to enjoy a peach and periwinkle sunset.

And so they sat, shoulder to shoulder against a fallen log, sipping their coffee in silence. The lake so still they could hear the flutter of a loon's wings from the far shore.

"About your daughter," said Lew, her voice low and her eyes on the glowing sky. "She has to work this out herself, you know."

"I know, I just worry so."

"She's a big girl."

"I don't want her to end up like her old man."

"How's that?"

"Alone. Alone with three kids to raise."

"You're not alone." Lew cocked her head and looked at him in mock disbelief. "You have Ray."

He threw her a look.

"C'mon, be real, Doc—you are *not* alone."

She looked around. "Where's your pack?" Spotting it, she jumped to her feet, zipped it open, and pulled out the checked tablecloth. She waved it in front of him as if she were a magician about to perform: "You may call it a tablecloth, Dr. Osborne, but I call it. . . ." She shook it open, then spread it on the sand and grass in front of the log. Dropping to her knees in the center, she smoothed the edges, then sitting back on her heels, she reached for his hands and said, "I call it a bedspread."

The invitation in her eyes was something he had never expected to see again in his lifetime. But given the opportunity, he did not hesitate.

ten

"You can't say enough about fishing. Though the sport of kings, it's just what the deadbeat ordered."

—Thomas McGuane, *Silent Seasons*

The sound of footsteps crashing through the forest brought them upright in an instant, grabbing for clothes. Osborne made a snap decision to forgo underwear, yanking his khakis up both legs even as he had one arm in his shirtsleeve. With seconds to spare, he was able to buckle his belt and shove the tablecloth into the pack along with his jockey shorts.

"I thought you said no one knew about this place," he said, keeping his voice low as he reached for his boots.

"I didn't say *absolutely* no one," muttered Lew, moving fast herself. "Must be coming in to fish a late hatch."

By the time the noisemakers had emerged from the woods, he and Lew were tucking away the final few items of fishing gear. The sun had set but the sky was streaked with backlit clouds, making it easy to see the intruders.

The first of the two approached—instantly recognizable as the type that Osborne's McDonald's coffee crowd nicknamed a "Jack pine savage"—jack pines being the ugliest trees in the northwoods and *savage* a word that needs no explanation.

The man was medium height, thickset, somewhere in his thirties or forties, and wearing the "savage" uniform of grimy jeans, a faded green-and-white-plaid flannel shirt with sleeves rolled up to expose the elbows, and the shirt front mashed down into his waistband. The latter was belted in a fruitless attempt to restrain the droop of an expansive beer belly.

A soiled Green Bay Packer baseball cap was crammed low on a head of hair that looked like he cut it himself, which was very likely as there was no doubt as to who chopped at the beard hiding his face from the sideburns down. Beer belly was carrying a spinning rod and a box of tackle that looked like it had been slamming around in the open bed of a pickup for years. A wad in his cheek hinted at the state of his teeth: black-brown with tobacco stain.

His companion was a little more sartorial, having selected his wardrobe to match his five o'clock shadow. He was shorter in stature than the first man, and his slumping shoulders sported a well-worn black corduroy jacket decorated with a large red stain on one shoulder. Unbuttoned, the jacket framed a black T-shirt emblazoned with a garish Harley-Davidson logo—all the more visible because it stretched taut across the man's barrel chest.

His pants, also black, looked like they could stand up by themselves and were complemented with matching black tennis shoes, though on closer examination Osborne could see they were actually *white* tennis shoes: filthy white high-tops with rubber soles and no support, the old-fashioned kind. He carried a spinning rod and a six-pack of MGD.

Something about the second man made Osborne uneasy. He made a mental note to keep his can of Deet close at hand. A little of that in the eyes can stop you in your tracks. Osborne finished sliding the sections of his fly rod into their canvas sleeves, then folding the sleeves lengthwise to slip into his rod tube, all the while watching the two from the corner of his eye. Nothing too remarkable about beer belly, but that other guy . . .

Meanwhile, the two men had paused about twenty feet away, set down everything they were carrying, and strolled down to the shoreline. They didn't appear to be aware of Lew and Osborne, who were screened from the winding path by a small stand of young balsam. That was odd. Hadn't they seen Lew's fishing truck?

Osborne continued to puzzle over the appearance of the shorter man. Granted he was wearing all black, but even so he looked unusually pale. From the side, his face appeared soft and pulpy and oddly dimpled—as if someone had taken a fork to his cheeks. The man stopped at the water's edge and turned his head away to look south. As he did so, it dawned on Osborne: The guy's hair grew in the wrong direction.

Actually, it wasn't growing at all. Instead, it was brushed up, forward and down over the top of the head. But unlike many baldies, who nurse their hair forward from the top of their skull, this guy was more inventive. He started all the way from back of his neck at a spot that was just below his ears. As he turned to face west, Osborne was fascinated by how the hair flattened out, mat-like, over his ears to end in a hunk plastered low on the forehead. Probably literally plastered—you'd have to do something to secure that floating bog.

Just then Lew hoisted her pack up onto her shoulders. The rustle of her movements caught their attention and the two turned to peer past the stand of trees. They took a couple steps in the direction of Lew and Osborne.

"Where the hell *you* from?" said beer belly, his manner a little too abrupt.

"Loon Lake," said Lew, unfazed. "Wisconsin."

No one said anything for a few beats.

"Where are you from?" said Osborne, keeping his voice low, cool, and professional—the tone he found effective while administering root canals.

Beer belly backed off. "Up near Manistique. My buddy here is from Mercer over in yer neck of the woods. How the hell you find this place?"

"I fish here pretty often," said Lew. "How'd *you* find it?"

"A fishing guide over in Marquette, cousin of mine. He told me about it. Big trout, he said. How many you get?"

"Not a one," said Lew. "No luck tonight. This is a tough spot, y'know. Fish here are too damn smart." She turned so Osborne could hook her float tube onto her pack. Then she did the same for him. He could see she wanted out of there as soon as possible.

"Yeah, Loon Lake, huh? I been hearing 'bout that tournament you got goin' down there next week. That bass tournament? Big purse, huh? A million bucks? That's a lotta dough."

While beer belly talked, Osborne watched the guy with the bog on his head walk over to pick up his rod and six-pack. He didn't look so good from the rear either—the black pants so baggy in the seat that it looked like he had a frying pan stuck down there. Real cute these two.

"Yep," said Lew, agreeing with beer belly as she moved backward to exit the clearing and the conversation, "we expect quite a turnout."

"Might see you folks around next week. I'm hoping to hang out and see how the pros do it."

"Oh, yeah?" said Lew, pulling at her straps as she headed toward the path. "Well, enjoy the evening." Beer belly moved off to let her by.

"How long *you* been livin' in Loon Lake?" he said as Osborne walked past.

Osborne resisted the impulse to pretend he hadn't heard

the question. He wanted out of there as badly as Lew, but once courteous, always courteous.

"Little over thirty years."

"Yeah? I'll bet you know a friend of mine." Beer belly rocked back on his heels. "Dickie Plyer—ring a bell?"

Osborne saw Lew stop and turn slightly.

"Oh, sure, I knew his father. I'm retired from a dental practice in Loon Lake and Dickie's father and I had some patients in common. I remember Dickie growing up. Haven't seen him in years. What he's doing these days?"

Beer belly chuckled. "You mean when he's not in the hoosegow? Last I heard, he's into boats." The hoosegow? Osborne wondered if that's why bog hair was so pale.

"Boats?" said Osborne. "Well, isn't that interesting. I ran into his older sister the other day. She's in the custom dock business—"

"Docks, boats, you name it," said beer belly. "They're always into something, those two, that's for sure."

Lew gave Osborne a slight nod.

"Boats, huh? So Dickie is building boats. Well, I'll be," said Osborne, trying his best to sound like a benign grandfather type. Then, not to seem too curious, he said, "Y'know, when you live in a little place like Loon Lake with all of three thousand people, you end up pretty familiar with the comings and goings of folks. His sister told me she's living up in Presque Isle. I wonder if Dickie isn't up there, too."

His speculation was met with silence. Bog hair watched his friend. Beer belly shrugged. "Dunno, just heard he's into boats."

As if to change the subject, bog hair spoke up. "I know someone in Loon Lake—ever hear of Ray Pradt?"

"My neighbor," said Osborne without thinking. Then he kicked himself, hoping he hadn't just made a horrible mistake.

"Oh yeah?" The man set down his six-pack and spinning rod and shoved his hands into his jacket pockets. "I owe Ray. Now you talk about a good man. . . ."

"He has his moments," said Lew. "But I'll tell you, when it comes to the hoosegow, Ray Pradt's seen every one in a four-county region." She watched beer belly kneel to open his tackle box, then walked back to look over his shoulder. "You might try that bass popper"—she pointed—"the Frenzy. These big trout go for flash and I've had luck with a Frenzy myself." Beer belly picked up the lure.

"I mean it—that Ray's a good man," continued bog hair. "I was up ice fishing on Trout Lake couple years ago and my ATV went out on me. I was about froze to death trying to get it started, when Ray pulled up in that old truck of his. Almost ran me down! Does he still have that big walleye leaping off the hood?"

Osborne laughed. "That's our Ray, door's been jammed closed on the driver's side so he has to crawl in the window of the damn truck—but he's got himself an expensive, custom-designed hood ornament."

"He gave me a ride into town. My feet were so cold, he had me wear his Sorel boots. Made me take 'em with me. You know how much those things cost? You say 'hi' from Bert Kriesel, will ya?" Smiling, bog hair stepped forward to shake hands.

"Will do. Paul Osborne." He took the man's hand. As if bad hair, bad shoes, and baggy pants weren't enough, Osborne couldn't help but note that the guy's upper jaw sported two of the longest canines he'd ever seen. Too bad some dentist somewhere hadn't offered to file 'em down—would take only a few minutes and would make the poor guy look a hell of a lot less like a carnivore.

Beer belly jumped to his feet and walked down to thrust a hand at Osborne. "Harold Jackobowski, pleased to meet you both." He turned to Lew, who had followed him down.

"Lewellyn Ferris," she said as he pumped her hand. She glanced at her watch, then started toward the path again. "Tight lines, boys." She waved.

"Say, you two," said Harold, "we got a nice rig parked back there. Feel free to take a look if you want. Cold beers in the fridge, help yourself."

Lew and Osborne marched through the darkening forest in silence. The float tube was rigged higher this time and bounced much less, so Osborne kept up with Lew's pace easily. What a day this had been. His heart was so full, he didn't know what to say, much less where to begin. He opted for silence. They both did. It wasn't until they'd reached the bend that took them into the birch and maple woods that Lew paused for a moment.

"Goddam worm fishermen," she said, looking back down the path toward their new friends. "They're gonna catch a couple big trout and eat 'em, goddamit."

Osborne shifted his pack slightly. "You think so, huh." It was a rhetorical question.

"I know so. I checked out their equipment—all they got are lures with barbed hooks. I can guarantee old Bert and Harold are not into catch-and-release, that's for sure."

It was nearly pitch black when they reached the parking area. Lew's truck was still the only vehicle in the small clearing.

"What the—I wonder where those two parked?" she said as she unlocked the truck. Working fast with the help of a flashlight, they stowed the float tubes first, then loaded the rest of their gear. Once inside, they hadn't driven fifty yards down the rutted narrow lane when they discovered why the two men had been so surprised to see them.

The latecomers had parked before reaching the end of

the lane in a wider clearing and for good reason—they were driving a huge brand-spanking-new RV.

Osborne whistled. "That bus must cost at least a hundred thousand dollars."

"How the hell can those two cheese balls afford a rig like this?" said Lew.

She turned off the ignition, but left the headlights on as she reached for the flashlight. Osborne followed her out of the truck and around the RV. Lew ran the flashlight across the clearing where the RV was parked. Sure enough, a path led off in the direction of the lake. Not only that, but the beam picked up signs of other vehicles having parked there previously as well.

"Looks like that fishing guide from Marquette is taking over the place." Lew was not happy. "I'm going to ask Ralph to give him a call—tell him to back off with the worm fishermen."

"Good luck."

"No, Doc, if he gets a call from someone like Ralph, someone who owns a sporting goods store and could potentially send clients his way—maybe he'll listen. Worth a try anyway. This *was* a good place to fish. Jeez, this thing is at least forty feet long!" She walked around the front of the RV.

"What'd I tell you?" She pointed to a deluxe gas grill set up on the grass outside the door leading into the RV. "Dammit!"

A metal canopy had been pulled forward from above the door to the RV. Alongside the door, it appeared that a section of the humongous vehicle had been pushed out from the inside to expand the interior space. An inner door stood open behind the closed screen door. Lew tried the handle—it was unlocked.

"Harold invited us . . ." she said, opening the door and stepping back for him to go first. "After you, Doctor. . . ."

"Would you leave a vehicle like this unlocked? I sure

wouldn't," said Osborne, hesitating on the top step. He felt uneasy entering but Lew was determined to see the inside of the RV.

"Keep going, Doc, and don't worry. I would break the lock if I had to—hard to believe this belongs to those two jokers. I have to wonder if it's stolen. . . ."

"I doubt it. I mean they introduced themselves. Would they do that if they had a stolen vehicle sitting here?"

"Doc, you need to spend more time in my line of work—you won't believe the level of stupidity, but you could be right. Still, bears checking out."

Once inside, Osborne groped along the wall for a light switch. "Holy cow," said Lew as light flooded the interior. "Do you believe this?"

The small entry, floored in granite, opened to a full living room suite furnished with a curved sectional sofa and a matching armchair and ottoman—all upholstered in buttery, pale yellow leather. Scattered across a dark hardwood floor were several small Oriental rugs, giving the room a rich, expensive look. Gleaming brass light fixtures hung from the ceiling.

Osborne thought of Bert's black pants. "Those guys not only do not own this, they don't even get to *sit* here," he said.

Lew chuckled. "Like I said—something isn't right."

She opened a door off to the left. It was the room that had been pushed out from the interior and it served as a bedroom. Clever design of a double Murphy bed along with a narrow table and one lamp made it easy to see how the room could fold in for highway travel.

A beat-up duffel, unzipped, rested on the floor beside the bed. Lew knelt and rummaged through it quickly. Pulling out a checkbook, she flipped it open—"Belongs to Mr. Bert," she said as she paged through the check register. "Interesting—small deposits and just two days ago he put in six thousand dollars. Six thousand bucks?" She looked up at Osborne. "Bert? That's a lotta loose change for a guy who looks like he can't afford to get his clothes cleaned."

She flipped back a couple pages. "Here's another one— an eight-thousand-dollar deposit on June twelfth. Then ATM withdrawals drawing it down real fast . . . lives in Mercer, all right." She shoved the checkbook back in the duffel.

Next to the duffel was a large cardboard box, the flaps folded closed. Lew pulled them open and peeked in. "Chrome parts of some kind, Doc." She pulled one out. It was cased in clear plastic with a sticker on the outside: "Gear Shift Control Cover—for a motorcycle maybe?" She shrugged and put it back, then pushed around the contents of the box. "More of the same."

"They must be delivering this RV for someone," said Osborne.

"That makes sense. Let's look fast before they drink that six-pack and head back here."

Moving quickly to the back of the living room area, Lew opened a door leading into a small hallway. At one end was a stainless steel kitchen with a bar area for dining. A door off the hall before the kitchen opened into a bathroom, long and outfitted with ceramic tiles, gold-plated fixtures, a Jacuzzi, and a skylight. Bert's dop kit sat on the counter along with a can of hair spray.

"This place cost money," said Osborne. "Lots of money."

"Listen." Lew cocked her head.

A faint gurgling came from the rear of the RV. Opening a door at the back of the kitchen, they found another hall-way with a door to a bedroom—this one also pushed out the side of the trailer and was furnished with collapsible twin beds and zoo patterns on the wall, obviously designed for children. A well-scuffed dark brown Samsonite suitcase, overflowing with worn socks and underwear, stood half open against the wall.

"Harold," said Lew. Again, she rummaged through quickly. "Just clothes and these." She held up two birthday cards. "Looks like Harold's got a girl."

"Or a mother."

"No-o-o, not these cards."

A small bathroom also opened off the hall, this one with a shower. Still, the gurgling noise continued to come from somewhere farther back in the bus.

"Don't tell me they travel with a washer and dryer," said Lew. A utilitarian-looking handle to what appeared to be a small closet was all that remained unexplored.

"You can try that," said Osborne, "but that's where the spare tires are usually kept. I'll bet the noise is coming from underneath—sounds like an air-conditioning unit, doesn't it?" Lew tried the handle. The door slid open easily.

"It's a closet all right," she said, "but these are the strangest-looking tires I've ever seen."

The space behind the small door was surprisingly deep. Approximately four feet by eight feet, the room held two livewells running the width of the RV. Barely enough space was allowed at each end and between the two for an adult to squeeze through. The gurgling came from the tanks. Lew got between the two and lifted the lid on the first livewell. "Take a look, Doc."

As he peered in, she opened the top of the second tank. "Same."

"What do you figure?" said Lew, "about thirty fish here? Well over the possession limit of Wisconsin and Michigan combined."

"Good-sized, too. I see a couple must be close to four, five pounds. You don't find smallmouths much bigger than that," said Osborne. He squatted to look under the tanks. "They've got a good aeration system going—that's what we hear—and from the looks of the refrigerator coils running along the base of both tanks, they're keeping them plenty cold."

"Which means these fish will stay healthy for quite a few days, don't you think?" Lew reached in and lifted one of the fish up by its gills. She examined it closely: "One hook mark, almost healed."

Returning the fish to the tank, Lew stepped back to look overhead. Shelving above the livewells held rolls of chicken wire, a tool box, and an empty minnow bucket. Osborne pulled the minnow bucket down and peered in. One dead crayfish floated in a puddle at the bottom.

"Let's check out the driver's area," said Lew. "Boy, would I like to know who's taking delivery of a very expensive RV and way too many smallmouth bass."

"Being driven by two guys who can't afford the tires," said Osborne.

"Right."

"But who might plant a few fish for the right price."

"Right again. 'Course we can't prove that, can we?" Lew shook her head. "They could always say they're planning a fish fry. This is gonna be a rough week, Doc. I've never known anyone to cheat by planting fish during a tournament. . . ."

"You've never had a national tournament in Loon Lake—much less one with so much money at stake."

The door to the driver's seat was also open. The interior was spacious, nicely appointed with wood and leather, and held two bucket seats spaced quite a distance apart. On a table unit between them, anchored under two oversized paper cups from Burger King, was a partially folded map. Clipped to one corner of the map was a handwritten note. Lew scanned the note, then handed the map over to Osborne. While he read the note, she reached for a vinyl briefcase jammed into a pocket on the door on the passenger side.

"Take Highway 47 south to Rhinelander," Osborne

read, "at the juncture with Highway 8, take Business 8 into town, take a left on Highway 17, and follow that past McDonald's to the Best Western Motel on the right. Park the RV there, check in to Room 58, and let the desk know that the vehicle is with you. Harold—*be there by Wednesday noon.*" The last sentence was underscored. The note was unsigned.

"At least we know they didn't steal it," said Lew. "Check this out." She held up one of the papers from the briefcase. He recognized the logo, FISHING HOT SPOTS. It was a hydrographic map of the structure, holes, and other features found in a body of water. Someone had taken a pencil to mark various sites.

Lew sorted through the papers quickly. "Looks like they've got maps for all seven lakes that'll be fished in the tournament." She shoved the packet back into the briefcase and stuck the case back in the door. "Wish I had more time to see what they've marked on these and why, but I'd just as soon not be in here when they get back."

"And there is absolutely nothing illegal about two dedicated fishermen planning ahead," said Osborne.

"I almost wish I hadn't lined Ray up on that other job," said Lew. "He could come in quite handy with these two."

"Maybe he'll have a few minutes. Loon Lake is such a small town, I wouldn't be surprised if he happened to run into those boys, would you?"

"Give him a call tonight, Doc? I'd love for him to chat up old Bert—enough to find out who he's working for." She backed out of the RV cab. "I guess when you own a rig like this, you can afford a professional driver, huh?"

"Last I heard you have to have a commercial license to drive one," said Osborne.

"These razzbonyas? I'd be surprised if they had a *fishing* license."

"I'm with you, but do you intend to press them on it tonight?"

"Not right this moment, and certainly not when I'm standing in another state. Nah, time to let some line out and see where old Bert and Harold run with it. That's what I want to see. And I doubt I'm alone. I'm sure a certain game warden I know and the tournament officials will be very interested. Doc, let's see if we can find the registration for this vehicle."

"We better hurry," said Osborne as Lew moved the paper cups and started to open the lid of the table between the seats. "Those boys may get lucky and be back here pretty darn soon."

"You're right." She let the lid drop. "I'll do a search on the license plate first thing tomorrow."

eleven

". . . the good of having wisely invested so much time in wild country. . . ."

—Harry Middleton, *Rivers of Memory*

Just past ten-thirty Lew swung her truck into Osborne's driveway. She had pushed the speed limit all the way back. For a brief moment, as they hurtled down Highway 45, Osborne considered inviting her to stay the night. But one look at her face and he thought better of that idea: She was all business.

Maybe she knew what was on his mind because she reached over to where his hand rested on the seat between them and gave it a friendly pat. "We have to talk," she said. "Not tonight; I have too much on my mind. But soon."

That was good enough for him.

"Doc, mind if I use your phone to check in?" said Lew, leaning toward him as he opened the door to get out. She had called in once already from a small gas station just over the state line. That was over an hour ago and the only news was that Roger was still at the hospital and that the girl had not regained consciousness.

"Go right ahead," said Osborne. "Door's open." He grabbed his rod case and gear bag from the back of the truck and tucked the empty cardboard box under his arm. "I'll see you inside. I'm going around to let the dog out."

"Thanks." Lew bounded up the stairs to his back door while Osborne let himself in the rear gate and hurried through the yard to open the dog run.

"Sorry, Mike," he said to the hyperenthusiastic dog bouncing off the back of his legs, "I know you love me unconditionally but I need the Achilles. Sit." He raised his right arm. The dog sat. "Good dog—heel." Mike obeyed, tail wagging happily.

Running up the stairway in the dark, he flicked a switch on the outside wall that spilled light onto the deck behind him. As he did so, he heard a familiar scuttling in the bushes off to the lakeside of the deck. Mike gave a warning bark and Osborne turned toward the sound, but all he could see was the light reflecting off a foil-covered package set in the center of the patio table.

The parcel was safe from the inquiring nose of the black Lab—but only the dog. Some other critter had nosed its way under one edge of the foil. Osborne paused. He didn't remember leaving anything on the table. Certainly not something that would draw raccoons.

"Well, Mike, what have we here?" As he lifted the foil, a toasty aroma floated up from a basket of golden fresh-baked dinner rolls: two, well-gnawed. They must have been set there still warm from the oven. No wonder that raccoon was hanging out. Now who on earth? Osborne shook his head. This was getting absurd.

Balancing the basket on top of the gear bag and backing his way in, he managed to elbow the patio door back far enough to let both himself and Mike through without dropping anything. Lew was already on the kitchen phone.

Osborne set his gear and rod down, then walked through the living room toward the kitchen, turning on lights as he went. He set the basket on the kitchen table. Just as he reached the door to the utility room where he kept Mike's food, the headlights of a car swung across the kitchen windows. Erin?

She was out of the car and running before he could open the back door.

At the sight of Erin's tearstained face, Lew excused herself from the phone conversation. With a quick wave of her hand, she indicated things were fine as far as Roger was concerned, then raised her eyebrows as if to ask if she should leave.

Erin answered for him, "No, Chief Ferris, please— don't go. Dad, I'm sorry, I don't mean to interrupt, but—" She pulled out a chair and plunked herself down at the kitchen table. Osborne finished scooping food into Mike's dish, then walked over to his daughter. He put a hand on her shoulder and squeezed gently. He could feel her whole body trembling, like Mike with a face full of porcupine quills. Erin reached up, putting her hand over his. He sat down beside her.

"I told Lew what the situation is, kiddo," said Osborne. "I hope you don't mind."

"Oh, God, no, anything, anyone who can help me figure this out."

Lew said nothing. Instead she crossed her arms and leaned back against the counter, her eyes fixed on Erin.

"Any news today?" said Osborne. "I tried to reach you earlier—"

"I was gone with the kids all morning. When we got back, I had a letter from Mark. He told me where he is, Dad. He's at the hunting shack."

"Thank God." Osborne sat back. Only when he relaxed did he realize how tense he had been since Erin's visit that morning. This sounded a hell of a lot better. Mark was hardly the first man to demand time out in the woods.

"And he's *borrowed* twenty thousand dollars from our savings."

"Twenty thousand dollars? You're kidding."

"To buy a motorcycle."

"How can you spend that kind of money on a motorcycle?"

"A Harley-Davidson." The expression on Erin's face was a little too familiar.

"Better than another woman," said Lew with a shrug. Osborne thought he saw a twinkle in her eye.

"You don't think this is outrageous? That is money we have been saving for our children's education," said Erin, an edge of hysteria in her voice. She leaned forward on her elbows, both fists clenched.

An old bad feeling clutching at his chest, Osborne pushed his chair back from the table, away from his daughter. How many times had Mary Lee struck that identical pose? Angry with him, so *very* angry with him.

"Please, Erin, don't be like your mother. Don't do that to Mark."

His daughter looked at him, stunned.

Osborne couldn't believe what he had just said. Too late. She burst into tears.

"Oh my God, Dad. This is so bad. I'm really awful, aren't I? My husband hates me, my kids hate me." Face in her hands, she sobbed.

Lew reached for a box of Kleenex on the counter and set it on the table by Erin. She leaned back against the counter, crossed her arms again, and waited. She seemed quite unperturbed by the drama taking place around the table but then again Erin wasn't her child.

"Now hold on a minute," said Osborne. "No one hates you. . . . That's not what I said." He looked over at Lew for help.

"Erin," said Lew, "how old are you?"

"Thirty, almost thirty-one," said Erin, sniffling. She looked more like a tearful eight-year-old than a grown woman. She grabbed a hunk of Kleenex.

"How old is your husband?"

"Thirty."

"How long have you been married?"

"Eight years."

"Have you had blowups like this before?"

"Never." As Erin spoke, she took a couple deep breaths. Her hysteria eased.

"So maybe all this is just a wake-up call—time to deal with things you've both been ignoring. Have the two of you seen a counselor or a therapist?"

"I did this afternoon."

"And Mark?"

"He won't, I don't think. He said he knows all the shrinks in town because of his work and he hasn't much respect for any one of them."

Lew chuckled. "He's got a point there."

"And I know he's been so stressed out at work, too."

"I know a psychologist over in Minocqua who might be right for Mark," said Lew. "A man. A northwoods type— he hunts, he fishes; who knows, he might even ride a motorcycle. Why don't we try to get Mark an appointment with that guy? I'll get you his name and phone number tomorrow. He does couples therapy, too."

"Okay, if I tell him you like the guy, that might help. I know Mark has a lot of respect for you, Chief Ferris." Erin wiped at her nose and her eyes. "Dad, why did you say that about Mom? That's not fair. I'm not like her."

Osborne looked at his daughter. "Do you want me to be honest?"

"Yes . . . I think."

"Given that you grew up in this house, you got the best and the worst from both of us. So did your older sister.

Erin, your mother felt cheated. She always felt that I should have made more money, built a bigger house, had more things. Maybe she was right. The choices I made: to live in a little town, to go fishing on Wednesdays instead of scheduling more patients—"

"Dad, I know all that. I'm not that way. I wouldn't be here if I was."

"But you want a great deal from life."

"What the hell is wrong with that?" Tears brimmed again.

Lew spoke up. "Nothing is wrong with that, Erin. Why don't you take it easy on both you and your husband and just try to figure out what it is that each of you needs right now."

"But a *motorcycle*?"

"Well, okay, when was the last time he went fishing?"

"He doesn't fish."

"Has he ever ridden a motorcycle?"

"Oh sure, he had one when I met him. He sold it to buy my wedding . . . oh . . . oh, my gosh."

Osborne reached again for his daughter's shoulder. "So maybe he finds on a bike what some of us find in the boat?"

"Maybe you're right," said Erin, sniffling. "Oh, Dad, and I was going to write a really angry letter."

"I'll bet you were," laughed Lew. "But you didn't, did you?"

"No, thank goodness," said Erin.

"A Harley-Davidson can be a very good investment these days," said Lew. "They sell for more used than new." She saw the look of surprise on Osborne's face. "Doc, I know these things. My son-in-law works in marketing for Harley-Davidson in Milwaukee." She looked back at Erin. "You want some advice from a woman who's been around the block a few times herself?"

Erin nodded.

"Start by making your mind up that whatever you do, whatever you say to your husband—you will be kind."

"Okay . . . how do I be kind about a motorcycle?" Erin still had that set to her jaw. "How do I be kind about spending my children's college money?"

"By not jumping to conclusions until you know the whole story, Erin. Maybe he has made a mistake or maybe he has a very good reason for doing what he's done. Can you give this some time? Do you have to have all the answers right this moment?"

"No . . . I guess not." Erin took a deep breath. She seemed to sit up a little straighter.

"The big rally in Tomahawk starts this weekend. Instead of criticizing Mark—why not ask if he'll have the new bike in time for the rally. And would he be willing to take you on the back?"

"Whoa," said Erin, her face brightening, "that would amaze our friends."

"Did you ride on the back of his bike before you two got married?"

"Oh, yeah, that's one reason I thought he was so sexy."

"I rest my case," said Lew, raising her hands, palms out, and smiling. She glanced at her watch. "Oh brother, it's late. I have to be in Park Falls at eight tomorrow morning and I still need to stop by the hospital on my way home. I have got to go—"

Erin jumped to her feet. "I've got to get back, too. But hey, thank you, Chief, that's a great idea. Dad, I feel so much better—this is like a positive approach. And you know," she threw her father a wicked glance—"Mom would *never* have done anything like this."

"C'mon, let's walk out together," said Lew, putting her arm around Erin's shoulders as they headed toward the back door. She looked back at Osborne. "Don't forget to call Ray. I hope it isn't too late to try him tonight?"

"It's never too late to try Ray."

• • •

As Osborne reached for the phone, he saw the blinking light on his answering machine: "Ray here. I'll be by for coffee at six, Doc. And say, I need to borrow your car."

That wasn't the only message.

"Paul, this is Brenda." The voice was breathy, excited. "I hope you like the rolls. Bye. I'll be by for the basket in the morning."

Oh no, thought Osborne. Please, God, not Brenda Anderle. He lifted the basket of rolls from the kitchen table and tipped them into the trash. Before making the call to Ray, Osborne went through the house closing curtains he seldom closed. He hated the sense of being watched.

An hour later, he was still awake. Awake and more content than he had felt in years. He loved this room. Yes, in some ways the house was still too much Mary Lee: too many decorative gewgaws and color schemes so tightly woven a room could look more like a magazine instead of a home.

But he never felt that way in the bedroom—*his* bedroom. After Mary Lee's death, he had retired the expensive bedspread, replacing it with an old quilt made by his mother. Hand-stitched squares of patterned reds, blues, greens, yellows, lavenders, and oranges spilled across an ivory background like the dots of candy on Christmas cookies. The old quilt was as warm on top as it was underneath.

He had designed this room himself, giving it windows on the east and the west and placing his bed against the north wall. Since it was on the second floor, it was high enough that he could watch the sun rise and set and—he had double-checked—no one could see in. Tonight, with the windows wide open, the room was at its most pleasant. Breezes whispered off the lake and moonlit shadows danced on the walls, taking him back to childhood.

Childhood and confession. Osborne let his mind wander back to the moment that Lew unbuttoned her blouse and everything that followed. Vindicated at last.

It had started in fifth grade when Sam Gilbert arrived back from vacation with a small, thin booklet he had stolen from his older brother's underwear drawer. The brother had left it behind after being home on furlough from an Army base overseas somewhere.

Osborne never knew what country the book came from but the story was set in early Roman days and, fortunately, was printed in English. He and Sam spent so many hours reading and rereading the pages that it fell apart and they had to tape it all back together. Unlike the tomes they were assigned for class, this riveting manual was chock full of adventures that made for tense Friday afternoons as the boys awaited their turns for the confessional.

"Father, forgive me for I have sinned. . . . I have had many impure thoughts. . . ." Osborne was always honest and the priest was wise enough or jaded enough not to inquire as to the exact source of the recurring misdemeanors. Following confession and with his psyche lightly slapped by an understanding Jesuit, Osborne would return to his pew and say the requisite Hail Marys required to cleanse his soul—until the next time he borrowed the little blue book from Sam.

He had always assumed that these delightful scenes were similar to what happened between a man and his wife. When he first laid eyes on Mary Lee, he couldn't help but imagine her as a willing player in the fantasies of his youth. Not long after their vows were taken, he realized that he'd said way too many Hail Marys—he had a good account in heaven that he'd never be able to use.

But today it all changed. What had always been so enticing in that little blue book wasn't just the action—it was the reaction, the joyful enthusiasm of a willing partner. No indeed, he did not regret all those Hail Marys. He just had to use them up before it was too late. Not a bad night of nymphing. No sir-e-e.

And with that happy thought, he fell asleep.

twelve

"We have other fish to fry."

—Rabelais, *Works,* Book V, Chapter 12, 1552

"But, Ray, the question is—how do I keep from hurting the woman's feelings?" As he waited for an answer, Osborne wondered if he was crazy to be asking Ray for advice.

After all, Ray was the one who still harbored hope that he was the right guy for his old high school sweetheart, the New York fashion model who was now on her third divorce, ratcheting up from millionaires to billionaires. Ray seemed oblivious to the fact that life in a rusting trailer home with a lurid leaping fish painted across the front might hold minimal appeal for the lovely Elise.

On the other hand, while Ray might be disappointed in love, he was a free man. A free man with a great excuse for not committing, an excuse that kept other women on the hook for a long, long time. How long does it take to get over a broken heart? Yep, Ray knew how to drag *that* line all right.

For reasons that Osborne could not fathom, at least half a dozen (if you believed Ray) hardworking northwoods females had offered to support the guy's fishing habit. One promised to build him his own bait shop! Even Mallory, when she drove up from Lake Forest, maintained such a high level of interest in Ray's comings and goings—and laughed so delightedly at his dumb jokes—that Osborne still had occasion to worry his neighbor might graduate to son-in-law. An alarming thought.

If experience with females counted, Ray was definitely the man to ask. Success was another story, and Osborne's question had nothing to do with success.

Mulling over Osborne's dilemma from where he sat at the kitchen table, Ray sipped his coffee. It was his fifth cup. He was so excited about the job Lew had dropped in his lap that it had been hard to get him to focus. Not only a new client but a television star! He had spent the previous evening glued to the Fishing Channel, prepping for his first meeting.

When Osborne finally managed to work in news of the encounter with Bert and Harold, he'd had to settle for a trade: Ray would do his best to intercept the two at the Best Western in exchange for the use of Osborne's new Subaru station wagon.

"My first impression will be critical, Doc." Osborne agreed. They both knew the beat-up old pickup with the door frozen shut was not going to inspire confidence.

"But planning to wear that fish on your head?"

"Now that's different," said Ray, raising both hands, palms out, in protest. "That's signature, Doc. That's style." Ray never hid the fact that one of his chief goals in life was to have his own fishing show on ESPN. This could be just the break he needed. He was going all out.

"Hey, it's not the big time, it's only the Fishing Channel, but it's a foot in the boat, doncha know. You never know what they need on air, Doc. Gotta give 'em something *different*. Like I said, something with style. You watch, they'll be *begging* me."

"Firing's more like it."

"C'mon. I'm a natural. You know that."

Osborne waited as Ray continued to sip, deep in thought, eyes scanning the road beyond the driveway. The maple armchair could barely hold his lanky six feet five inches as he leaned back, feet thrust out in front and crossed at the ankles. A light drizzle had kept them from having their coffee on the deck, which was fine for a change. Together they could contemplate the view out the kitchen window: all the comings and goings on Loon Lake Road.

Finally, Ray set down his coffee cup. "I think the best thing is to let it run itself out, Doc. The one time I tried to tell a woman I didn't want to see her anymore, she slugged me. So don't do that."

"But I haven't been *seeing* her! Can't I just say, 'Thanks, but no thanks'?"

"You can. You can do that. But she lives right down the road, you use the same post office, you go to the same gas station, the same grocery store . . . how many times a week would you say you run into Mrs. Anderle?"

Osborne thought hard. "Half a dozen at least but—"

"Doc, do you want to have this hurt puppy look ev-v-cry time you see her? No-o. My advice is to let it fade away. Let her be the one to lose interest. The way you do that is very simple: *stay busy*. If she invites you to dinner, you've already made plans. You of all people—you've got excuses up the wazoo. Ask Mallory up for a visit. Use this trouble with Erin—say you need to baby-sit. The secret is to be specific so they don't hear it as an excuse."

Osborne perked up. "Lew asked me just last night to look at the file on the Schultz murder and suicide. That could turn into a full-blown investigation. I might have to go down to Wausau, maybe Madison. . . ."

"There you go. Perfect excuse and no one gets her feelings hurt. Uh-oh," said Ray, looking past Osborne and out the window. He unlocked his legs and straightened up. "He-e-re's Brenda."

"You're kidding."

"No siree—it's Mrs. Anderle with the hourglass figure . . ." Ray winked at Osborne. "But the fair lady's sands of time have shifted."

Up and out of his chair, Osborne was too late to the back door. His visitor had entered.

"Paul, you dickens." Brenda Anderle's flushed, cheery face hung in the kitchen doorway like a morning moon. "I tried surprising you two times yesterday. Honest to Pete, you leave early and get home late, don't you."

She bustled into the kitchen, clearing the way with a plate of something held out in front like a leaf blower. It was covered with a blue-and-white-checked cloth, which she whipped off with a Houdini flourish to expose a chocolate bunt cake drizzled with white icing.

"Cup of coffee, Mrs. Anderle?" said Ray, gazing hungrily at the cake.

Osborne could have killed him.

"I'd love one—got any cream?" Without waiting for her host, who was reaching for a mug on the rack beside the coffeepot, Brenda bustled her way into his refrigerator, turning her back to them as she scanned the shelves. Ray gave Osborne a big wink.

"Okay, Doc, I'll be by at eleven. See ya."

Osborne was speechless. Ray was leaving him alone with Brenda Anderle?

"No, wait, Ray—" Osborne followed him out the back door.

"Sorry, I gotta shower." Ray dropped his voice. "Hey, you're a big boy, you can handle this."

"Okay, okay, but one more thing—did that woman you know at the law firm say anything about Mark?"

"Oh, right. Nothing unusual that she's aware of except he's been getting a lot of calls from someone named Cheryl."

"Cheryl?" Osborne didn't like the sound of that. "A client maybe?"

"Umm, she didn't seem to think so." Ray squinted slightly and turned away. It was a look he had when he knew he was delivering unwelcome news.

"What's that all about?" said Brenda as Osborne walked back into the kitchen. She had parked herself at the kitchen table, where she took up a little too much space.

As a young wife and mother, Brenda had been quite striking with porcelain skin that looked all the more delicate framed in vermilion curls. And her body in those days was as generous as her laughing mouth. Married to Harvey Anderle, a veterinarian, the family had built their home on Loon Lake Road about the same time as the Osbornes, using the same builder, and they had daughters the same ages as Mallory and Erin.

But while Brenda was invited to substitute in Mary Lee's bridge game, she never achieved the status of full-time membership. Nor was she ever invited to join the Garden Club. Whatever the reasons Mary Lee and her friends had excluded Brenda, Osborne had always found her to be pleasant and appreciated that she had always been good to his girls even if she did wear too much lipstick.

As far as Harvey went, he was a fly-fisherman in the days when Osborne was devoted to muskies and spinning rods, so the two men had never fished together. When Harvey succumbed to cancer in his mid-fifties, Brenda was left with enough that she could keep their home, which was four mailboxes down the road. The family had been patients of his, of course, and he had, in turn, always used Harvey as a vet.

The problem was that since Harvey's death, Brenda had continued to cook for two—and eat accordingly. Where once her height carried her full figure well, she now resembled a side-by-side, freezer included. The effect was heightened by her habit of wearing what appeared to be chenille bedspreads festooned with either fruits or animals. Today, she was draped in strawberries.

Osborne reminded himself that she meant well. Still, he could not help noticing that age and weight and lack of exercise were causing her face to fold in on itself. And she still wore too much lipstick. When she smiled, smears ran across her top front teeth. Osborne looked away quickly, realizing he hadn't heard a word she'd said.

". . . So I was thinking maybe this Friday we could try the fish fry at the Pub? They just started serving bluegill."

"Gee, I'm sorry, Brenda. I'm afraid not. Not this Friday. I'm expecting Mallory—"

"Next Friday then."

Osborne faltered. He hadn't given any thought to what he was doing ten days down the road.

"Good. I'll mark my calendar," said Brenda as she rose to leave, a satisfied smile on her face. "And don't you be surprised if you're surprised a time or two between now and then," she warned, wagging a finger at him as she poured out her remaining coffee in the sink, then rinsed the cup. She had a way of being in his house as though she belonged there.

"Paul"—she paused at the back door—"I am so happy this is working out. You know, with Mary Lee and Harvey gone—we should do more together. Nothing serious; we'll just have a good time." She raised her eyebrows invitingly, giving him another lipstick-streaked smile as she opened the back door and stepped out.

Osborne watched her move her body across the driveway to the road. She stopped to look back and caught him watching her. He waved, she waved, he felt trapped.

• • •

Osborne hurried through the breakfast dishes. Before heading into town with Ray, he wanted to check his office files for anything he might have on Jack Schultz. Granted they were dental files, but looking at the records of Jack, the wife who left him and their three daughters might jar some other memories. A final cup of coffee in hand, Osborne made his way across the yard to the garage.

On the side of the garage that faced the lake, he had screened in a small porch for cleaning fish. A door in the back of the porch opened into a long, narrow storage area, separated by a wall from the main garage and protected from sunlight and fumes. It was the one space Mary Lee had forgotten about after their home was built. The day she had insisted he deliver his office files to the landfill, he had waited until she left for the grocery store, then carted them up from the basement to this space.

And thank goodness he had. They were proving to be more important than even he had imagined. For one thing, when he opened his practice, he had acquired the records of the retiring dentist whose practice he had purchased, so his files held dental records dating back to the early 1920s. Even though he was retired, Osborne still subscribed to the leading dental journals, which kept him well aware of advances in DNA research and genetic coding, advances that made dental records such as these valuable in ways that dentists of his generation had never anticipated.

The archives worked for him on an emotional level, too. The smell and feel of the triple-folded cards with their pale green grids made him feel like he was in the company of old friends, people for whom he could do something that mattered.

He pulled Jack Schultz's record. It was as if the man were in his dental chair at that very moment: The dates, the smudged ink notations, the diagram of Jack's mouth conjured an image as potent as human flesh. They had always talked fishing, of course.

Jack had been a carpenter whose first love was bass fishing. He might not have been the most outgoing of men, but he sure could argue live versus artificial bait. When Jack had run into financial difficulties after his wife left, he had paid his bill with two bookcases he made from trees he'd cut on Osborne's land. The bookcases still stood in his living room.

Osborne pulled the files on the Schultz girls. He didn't have the ex-wife's in this cabinet. Hers would be in a file drawer with those of other patients who had long ago moved away from Loon Lake. But the girls were there with their father: Evelyn, Edith, and Esther. Old-fashioned names today, but popular back then. Evelyn and Esther had both married and settled in Loon Lake. But whatever happened to Edith?

He looked over the Polaroids he had taken of each of the girls from their junior high days. They all had that same genetic crowding of the lower front teeth. Though he'd sent them to Wausau for their orthodontics, he had kept current with their cleanings, with an eye out for any signs of decay on the enamel under their braces.

The expressions on the faces of the younger girls were open and relaxed, if slightly embarrassed. But not Edith's. Her eyes were so old, too old for a girl barely into her teens. She was the oldest and possibly the one that was most aware of the reasons for the breakup of her parents' marriage. She was also the one who took her father's death the hardest—and stepped in to take his place.

Her photo had been taken a year after his suicide when the girls were living with an aunt. Edith was only fourteen but her expression was so tense and knowing that she might have been at least ten years older. The eyes were too solemn. There was no youth in that face.

Osborne walked over to the doorway to examine the

photo better in the natural light streaming into the cleaning porch. He knew Jack didn't murder that teenager. A man who cared so deeply for daughters nearly the same age as the victim? Whose concern for their health and well-being drove him to work late nights in order to have something to barter for their dental care? It didn't make sense. He could understand Jack murdering his ex-wife—but a child like one of his own?

The victim—her file should be in there, too. Osborne pulled open the drawer holding the files from A to E. As his fingers walked through the B's, he could recall the sight of the corpse but he couldn't remember ever hearing how Jack was supposed to have killed her.

Ah, here she was. Gloria Bertrand. Her last visit was for a school checkup. Osborne looked over the dates: she was fifteen when she died. His receptionist had noted the date of her death and that she was interred in St. Mary's Cemetery. Bertrand . . . Osborne stared up at the ceiling as he sifted back through his memory. Yes, she had an older brother, Tim. That would have been an active file when Osborne retired so Dr. Frahm, the dentist who had purchased Osborne's practice, might have an updated address for Gloria's brother. If Osborne was lucky, he might still be living in the area.

Osborne checked his watch—nearly ten-thirty. He had less than an hour before Ray came to pick him up. As he stacked the records to carry them back to the house, he heard the low roar of an inboard motor. It grew louder. Loud enough that Osborne decided to call the warden—that boat was too big for Loon Lake. Damn these tourists who want to race all the time. Big boats and jet skis—some days he wished there were a bounty on their heads.

The boat drew closer and closer until the old oak file cabinets started to shake. It sounded like it was in his driveway. Osborne banged shut the screen door of his cleaning porch and headed toward the offending noise.

Then it dawned on him. Of course, it must be Mark on the motorcycle. Relieved as he would be to see his son-in-law, he knew he had to have one question answered right away: Who the hell was Cheryl?

The motorcycle in the driveway, white and gleaming with chrome, was larger than any Osborne had ever seen. Mark, dressed head to toe in black leather, had swung himself off the bike and was just removing his helmet. Osborne was struck by how much shorter his son-in-law looked when he wore all black.

But the rider who turned a stricken face to Osborne was not Erin's husband. It was Lewellyn Ferris.

thirteen

"See how he throws his baited lines about,
And plays his men as anglers play their trout."

—O. W. Holmes, *The Banker's Secret*

"Doc?" Looping the strap of her helmet over one of the handlebars, Lew bent forward to shake loose the curls clinging damply to her temples. "Got a minute? Whoa, it's hot under that helmet."

"I didn't know you rode a motorcycle."

He must have had a funny look on his face because Lew chuckled as she looked up at him. "You never asked. Of course I do. We all do. Myself, Roger, the other deputies. It's just part of the job, Doc."

"*Roger* rides?" Osborne found that hard to believe.

"He tries to avoid it, but it's a requirement of his position. I won't be surprised if he calls in sick next week during the rally."

Osborne leaned back on his heels, studying the bike. He knew nothing about motorcycles. Lew was hardly a small woman but this was a lot of steel and chrome for anyone to handle. "That thing must weigh a ton, Lew. Is it *yours*?"

"Heavens, no. It belongs to the department," said Lew, peeling herself out of the leather jacket. She was wearing a short-sleeved T-shirt, which matched the khaki color of her summer uniform. Osborne couldn't help but notice the shirt was damp against her chest.

"We get a new one every year from Harley-Davidson. They lease us the bike for a dollar, then take it back after one year and sell it used. Some community program they have; I'm sure they get a tax break. And it doesn't weigh a ton, more like seven hundred pounds. It's an Electra Glide model, nice bike."

Jeez, she was offhand about something that huge. "Seven hundred pounds, two thousand pounds—what difference does that make if it tips over?"

"Doesn't happen—not to me anyway," said Lew. An edge in her voice signaled she hadn't come to discuss motorcycles.

"Is something wrong, Lew?" A rush of tenderness laced with concern tightened his chest. Was she here to say she had made a big mistake last night?

"I didn't ride out here to show off. I have to put some time in on this machine because it's brand new and I'm not sure that I won't need to patrol the motorcycle rally later this week. You don't go into a crowd on one of these babies unless you are *real* comfortable. So I rode it up to Park Falls for my meeting this morning and *that* is what I've come to see you about."

Whew, thought Osborne.

She threw the jacket over the seat, tossed her gloves on top, and hands on her hips, looked him over as if she were measuring him for a new suit or, he would think later, a casket.

"I need you to help me out, if you can. But we need to talk so you are fully aware of the risk before you agree."

"Coffee?"

"Love a cup."

Osborne shifted the stack of dental records he was carrying onto one arm and held the gate open. "You want to sit inside? Outside?" He checked his watch as he beckoned toward the deck at the rear of the house. "Ray's picking me up at eleven and we're going into town. He agreed to stop by the motel and see if he can intercept our friend Bert."

"Good," said Lew. "One thing I learned this morning—Bert Kriesel is up to his ass in something much bigger than a livewell of smallmouths."

Minutes later, coffee mugs in hand, they strolled out onto the deck. The drizzle had let up and a hazy sun coupled with a light breeze had dried the puddles off the plastic deck chairs. Osborne did a quick check of the patio table: no unexpected baked goods, thank the Lord.

Sitting down, Lew checked her watch, then took a quick sip of coffee. She leaned forward, elbows on her knees as she waited with anxious eyes for Osborne to get settled.

"Llewellyn, you look like you've been slugging Mountain Dew."

"Bad for the teeth." She managed a slight grin. "But I can probably use some. With what happened this morning, I'll need that or No-Doz to make it through the next week. Doc"—she inhaled deeply—"my workload has just quadrupled and I'm not sure how to handle it.

"Here's the deal. Our meeting this morning was with two DEA undercover agents out of Chicago. Over the last six months, the DEA has seen a three hundred percent increase in the amount of Ecstasy coming in from Canada and funneling south via commercial traffic—like UPS and FedEx. They have word that a large shipment is due to enter just north of here so they are setting up a bust to take place sometime next week."

"Not this week, but *next* week?" said Osborne. If Lew

asked him to help out in some way, he would have a great excuse for canceling Brenda. He felt better already.

"Right. They know the source in Canada but they want to nail the couriers down here. One of those couriers, a major player, happens to be headquartered in our backyard, Doc, and my job is to provide undercover backup here."

"Just when you've got the motorcycle rally and the fishing tournament. Do these people understand that Loon Lake doesn't normally see fifty thousand people all in one four-day period?"

"Actually, Doc, that is exactly why it's happening at this time. The information is that dealers from Indiana, Iowa, Minnesota, Michigan, not to mention southern Illinois, are coming in for the Tomahawk rally and to pick up their merchandise. But"——Lew raised her hands as Osborne started to speak——"let me finish because there's more to the story.

"The agents have been watching a small farm not far from Loon Lake. They are pretty sure that this is where the drugs are being delivered, sorted into smaller loads, and shipped downstate. They want me to put someone near that location to observe traffic patterns and level of activity. It's no coincidence that a major shipment is due in because the people behind the drug ring know that every law enforcement team in north central Wisconsin will be stressed over these next ten days."

"Where exactly is the farm?"

"Back in on Willow Creek. The owner has been using an import-export business for his cover, alleging that he's a private dealer in fishing antiques like bamboo fly rods, wooden muskie lures, rare trout flies, that kind of stuff. The business allows him to receive and ship internationally with few questions from his shippers."

"I know the woman who manages the Loon Lake UPS

office," said Osborne. "Her mother was a patient of mine."

"Oh?" Lew's face fell. "That's not good. I was hoping those people wouldn't know you. Well, let me finish because there's one more wrinkle to all of this. Turns out the gentleman in question, before adding Ecstasy to his inventory, had been and still is a fence for stolen Harley-Davidson bikes and parts. That's been his bread and butter, not the antiques—and he's been doing this, they think, for a number of years."

"And you didn't know any of this?"

"Nope." The edge was back in her voice.

"One reason I didn't which I *can* understand is that the only Harley-Davidson dealership in this area is in the next county and has only been open a year. They filed their first complaint last week. They had a customer bring in a bike and asked one of the mechanics to file off the VIN number. With permission from the dealership owner, the mechanic did what he was asked. Later, over beers, the customer told the mechanic he could get him a good deal on a 'new' bike. A few more beers and the mechanic had the address."

"Same place where the drugs are coming and going?"

"Right. And, Doc, I probably don't have to tell you the second reason I know nothing. . . ."

"Wausau?"

"Yep," Lew snapped the word. "Our time-honored tradition of the Wausau boys refusing to share information with the rest of us. They've known about the Ecstasy route for several months now, but they've never said a word to me, to Eagle River, to Mercer, to any of us. I find that inexcusable and I plan to bust their chops."

"So you're telling me they knew about this guy operating up here and didn't tell you?"

"Well . . . not exactly. They've known Ecstasy was being moved down Highways 45 and 51, but they thought the deliveries were being made in Stevens Point near the university. I have to be fair—no one knew until last week about the size of the operation here in Loon Lake. A UPS driver got suspicious of too many cash COD deliveries and boxes that rattled."

"What else do you know about the farm?"

"The main house is built right on the ridge above the creek, just past Hagen Road. A newer barn is where the inventory is kept. The problem is the house, which is known to the DEA as being a 'safe house' with cameras installed in the eaves. The ridge makes it possible for them to see anyone coming in by road. The one attempt the agents made to search the place, someone was well warned—both house and barn were clean."

"I know that area pretty well," said Osborne. "It backs up to state land where I used to deer hunt. Willow Creek does not have any public access but it does have trout. You might be able to find a logging road that's been cut in recently and follow that back to the creek, then fish your way down. Who cares about some elderly guy casting Woolly Buggers?"

"That's not a bad thought. You get in there from the back, you'll have a good view of the place," said Lew. "But guess who owns the property in question?" She paused for dramatic effect: "Patrick Baumgartner."

"Never heard of the guy."

"AKA Patty Boy Plyer. Seems he put together a false ID and moved back up here a few years ago. He's been so respectable, he's the local fire warden."

"But if he's been living up here, why haven't we seen him around?"

"Does all his business in Eagle River. Never comes into Loon Lake or Rhinelander. And he's careful how he travels—keeps a private plane in Land o' Lakes."

"That's smart," said Osborne. "He's close enough in to

have access to major highways, but far enough off the beaten track to ensure his privacy."

"Yep," said Lew. She didn't have to add what they both knew: Patty Boy could count on the fact that little towns in Wisconsin, like little towns anywhere, are very parochial. Twenty miles could be a thousand, so seldom does one community know much about the other, much less interact.

"If Patty Boy and Catherine are operating within a hundred miles of each other, I can't imagine that Dickie doesn't fit into this whole routine. Family traditions die too damn hard for that crew."

"Doc, that is the first thing I mentioned to the agents. You want to nail Patty Boy, I said, then you just sit back and wait for a good old Plyer family reunion.

"Something else I learned this morning. Remember Harold Jackobowski saying that Dickie is into boats? That's how Ecstasy is sold to dealers: a thousand pills equals one boat. And a pill can go for anywhere from ten to fifty bucks, so one boat is worth a hell of a lot of money. No wonder Dickie is into boats."

"Hence you are more interested than ever in Harold and Bert."

"You betcha."

Osborne thought back to his encounter in the Loon Lake Market parking lot. "I don't know if this means anything, Lew, but when I ran into Catherine and her husband, they sure looked like bikers—leather vests, tattoos."

"But driving a van, you said, not riding, which is odd. Bikers don't usually dress that way unless they plan to ride. It's just too damn hot."

"Speaking of driving, any news on that girl?"

"I stopped by the hospital on my way to Park Falls this morning and had a little chat with her and her parents. She was in much better shape than yesterday."

"Was Ecstasy the cause of the convulsions?"

"Definitely related, but the doctors aren't positive she was convulsing. What we saw could have been convulsions caused by heat exhaustion or it could have been muscle spasms caused by an excessive release of serotonin, which is another side effect of Ecstasy. She told me she paid twenty-five dollars for two pills she bought from a boy she met at the rave. Name is Danny and he's cute. 'Curly blond hair, medium height . . . cute.' Not exactly Miss Observant, this girl."

"Cute," said Osborne. "Well, we've both raised daughters so I guess we know what that means."

Lew gave a quick glance at her watch and leaned forward, elbows on her knees. "Doc, you can see I need help, but if you say no, I'll understand. This is risky stuff."

"But can you find someone else if I say no?"

"It'll be tough. I should never have alerted Ray to that other job. Dammit, he would be perfect for this."

That was it for Osborne. Lew thought Ray would be better at this? Oh, she had another thought coming if that was the case. Without even hearing the details, he decided right then and there that he was the man for the job, whatever it was. Ray, for God's sake.

"The rally in Tomahawk will draw over thirty thousand bikers," said Lew as she poured out the last of the coffee into both their cups. "And it's anticipated there will be more than a few finding their way to Patty Boy's place. A DEA informant said the word is out that he's hosting a flea market of stolen Harley parts and accessories for his nearest and dearest. That plus a few boats of Ecstasy."

Osborne was confused. "As much as I want to help, I'm not sure how I fit into this picture, Lew."

"Nor am I . . . yet. But one thing I do know, Doc—you aren't going to get close to that place, not even to fish, unless you're on a motorcycle."

"Now, w-a-a-it a minute. You want me fly-fishing in Willow Creek *and* riding a motorcycle?"

"Peter Fonda does it." Lew shrugged. "Look, forget it, Doc. I knew this was too much to ask."

"No, no, I can handle it, but you have to show me how to ride one of those things."

Lew grinned over at him. "I knew you'd say yes. I called Marlene from Park Falls after the meeting this morning and asked her to enroll you in the motorcycle safety class at Nicolet College over in Rhinelander."

"Why don't I just take a few private lessons?"

"Better this way. The classes start tomorrow and run all day for three days. You'll be like any other middle-aged man going through a midlife crisis—and people will believe you. Nights this week, though, I also need you at UPS."

"What the hell am I doing at UPS?"

"You're the new quality control official. I haven't had time to make the arrangements but I will later today. The DEA has learned from UPS that Patty Boy's cover, Webber Tackle, has scheduled a series of pickups and deliveries over the next week. We need someone to 'observe' a few of those shipments before they leave the loading dock. The top brass at UPS are cooperating fully with the DEA so the support is in place."

She tipped her head in thought. "It would be better if that UPS manager didn't know who you were but maybe that's just as well. Retired dentist turned biker, that works."

"How about *widowed* retired dentist turns biker to pick up chicks."

"You won't be the first, Doc," said Lew. "Seriously, I think this will work. Now I need to get back to the office."

She started down the stairs, then stopped, "One more thing, Doc. See the Harley-Davidson dealer later today if

you can. He's expecting you and he'll have everything
that you'll need—boots, chaps, a jacket, a helmet, goggles. . . ."

"Whoa, now wait a minute——"

"Safety first, Doc. It's risky, riding a bike this size. If
you go down, you do not want road rash."

"Okay, okay. One last question, Lew. If the DEA knows
so much about Patty Boy, why don't they just arrest him?"

"Because if they time it right, they hope to make one of
the biggest Ecstasy busts ever in the Midwest. Raises and
promotions, Doc. Doesn't matter which side of the law
you're on, it's always about the same thing: profits."

The dental files sat in a neat pile on the kitchen table.
Waving his hand toward them as Lew headed for the back
door, Osborne said, "Well, darn, I guess my looking into
the Schultz murder case is moot? That's too bad. Just before you came, I pulled my dental records for Jack and his
family; I even had the victim as a patient."

Lew paused. "I doubt if you'll have time, Doc. But I'll
ask Marlene to pull that file for you."

From his kitchen window, Osborne watched and listened as Lew roared off on the motorcycle. She made it
look easy.

Expecting Ray to walk over from his place any moment, Osborne waited out in his yard, throwing the ball to
Mike and thinking. Peter Fonda, huh. He made a mental
note to check out *Easy Rider.* It had been years since he'd
seen that movie.

Peter Fonda . . . fly-fishing and motorcycles . . . Osborne
wasn't sure if he should feel flattered or frightened . . . or
both.

fourteen

"I object to fishing tournaments less for what they do to fish than what they do to fishermen."

—Ted Williams, 1984

Again and again Osborne snapped the heavy rubber band holding the accordion folder shut as he stared out the window of the Loon Lake District Library. His gaze was fixed on the entrance to the Kankelfitz Best Western Motel across the street, where nothing changed no matter how hard he looked at it.

Not even a car drove down the street between the motel and the library. He checked his watch for the seventeenth time. Dammit. He should have known better.

What had possessed him to rely on Ray to show up on time in the first place? Anyone who ever had dealings with the razzbonya knew the man was accountable to only one schedule: "Raytime."

It was a word coined by the McDonald's crowd, a word that could be uttered with a chuckle or a curse, a word that referred to a schedule outlined not by the hands of a clock but by any opportunity to chat. Could be one of the good nuns out for her morning walk was happy to entertain one of his cleaner dumb jokes. Could be he decided to stop for gossip and a bag of fresh shiitake mushrooms at Hank's Citgo. It was no accident that Raytime rhymed with "waste time."

Osborne covered his eyes with his hands. He gave up. Moments like these were when he understood why Lew was always reluctant to count on Ray. You could never be certain he would be where he said he'd be, do what he said he'd do. Ray meant well but he never met a straight line he didn't have the urge to bend, twist, or snap.

Still, Osborne absolved himself of total stupidity; this morning's arrangement had seemed free of hazard for the simple reason that Ray's future as a celebrity was at stake. Osborne couldn't imagine him running late for fame. So what had gone wrong?

Osborne snapped the rubber band again.

"Sshh!" whispered a young woman from across the room where she was trying to read a magazine. She threw him a dirty look.

Just forty-five minutes earlier, he and Ray had parted, heading in opposite directions but with the clearly stated objective of meeting on the steps of the library, across the street from where Osborne's car was parked, *no later than noon.* That would allow plenty of time for Ray to drop Osborne at Erin's home, then take the car to the airport to meet his client, whose plane was due at twelve-thirty.

According to Ray, his client was going to provide a car for the remainder of the assignment as he was to be her driver/protector for the week. All that was needed this morning was for Ray to arrive in a decent vehicle, make a good first impression, and return to town with Osborne's car.

Upon agreeing to that plan, Ray had ambled off, intending to intercept Bert and Harold in the Best Western parking lot. That gave Osborne just enough time to walk four blocks east to Lew's office in the Loon Lake Court House, where he hoped to pick up the Schultz file.

So far so good. Lew was on the phone when he got there but she had pulled the file and set it on Marlene's desk. Marlene, in turn, handed the file to Osborne, who then hurried back four blocks to the library, where he had been sitting now for over thirty minutes.

So much for plans. It was now twelve-seventeen and still no Ray. The airport was only eight minutes out of town but this was pushing it. And Erin, who was expecting Osborne for lunch, did not need the frustration of a no-show father on top of a no-show husband.

Frustration mounting by the second, Osborne stood up and tried to peer around the curtains to see farther down the street, nearly putting his eye out on a decorative rod as he did so. Darn, the car was right where he had left it. He had the keys so he knew Ray couldn't leave without him.

"Yo, Doc."

Osborne whirled around. "Dammit, Ray!"

"I know, I know," Ray raised both hands and feinted as if to ward off blows. Osborne knew he had deliberately snuck in the back way to surprise him, too—which did not add to his happiness.

"Better hurry, Doc, or we'll be late." Osborne rolled his eyes.

Out the library doors, down the stairs, and across the street they ran, Osborne handing over the car keys as they approached the car.

"Too late to drop you off, I guess, huh?" said Ray, yanking the door open and throwing his body inside. He shoved the driver's seat back, way back. Osborne looked over at his friend. Had Ray planned this little maneuver?

"I'll call Erin from the airport," said Osborne. Reaching back from the passenger seat, he set the large brown accordion file on the back seat. "I'll get a cup of coffee in the restaurant while you talk to your people, how's that."

Ray waited for a red light. "Hey, don't you want to hear about old Bert?"

"I would love to hear about old Bert," said Osborne, "but you know darn well I promised Erin I'd be over there for soup and a sandwich—so you better have a good reason for running so late."

"You won't believe it," said Ray, checking to his left before making a right turn on red. "Yours truly . . . saved the day. . . . No one was in that RV when I knocked on the door. Now . . . had I stopped there. . . ."

"But you didn't."

"No, I did not. I checked with Pam at the front desk, cute girl, used to date her sister. She said the boys had parked it there over an hour ago, left the keys with her, and walked off in the direction of the phone company. So I said to myself . . . what . . . would . . . you do in Loon Lake at eleven in the morning?"

"I wish you had asked *Pam* who owns the RV—"

"I did that, I'll get there, Doc, hold your horses, will ya? One of the pros fishing the tournament owns it, a guy named Bruce Duffy out of Lansing, Michigan. He flew in last night and stayed at the Kankelfitz. Okay?"

"Okay, I'm sorry." Osborne didn't mention that he was sure Lew would have the same information from DMV records by late afternoon if not sooner. "Go on, sorry I interrupted."

"So, like I said, I asked myself . . . what . . . would . . . you do in Loon Lake at eleven in the morning?"

"And—?" Osborne knew it was futile to hurry the man along but he was in the mood to try. Either that or beat him to death.

"Pancakes." Ray gave Osborne a knowing look. "Can't beat the Pub's pancakes."

"That's true." Osborne knew he sounded like a one-man Baptist choir.

"So I took myself over to there and sure enough doncha

know those two jabones were up to their ears in maple syrup. And fritters—they had corn fritters, too."

"Ray, I know the breakfast menu at the Pub. Can we skip to the action? Were they surprised to see you?"

"Maybe, couldn't tell. I told 'em you told me they might be around. Next thing, though, I shook 'em up a little. 'Hey, big Bert,' I said, 'I hear you boys are lookin' to plant some fisheroonies!'"

"You said that." Osborne looked out the window again. He was too old for this. This and motorcycles. Jeez.

"Yep, and did those two look unhappy."

"For God's sake, Ray."

"C'mon, I told 'em I was just kidding. Then I told them that you told me they were working for one of the pros in the tournament and that's when I asked who that was and they told me what I just told you—the Duffy guy.

"He's a big deal, Doc. Won the Bass Classic two years ago and was Angler of the Year a while back, too. Looks to me like he's putting a lotta pressure on the boys. He wants the top prize."

"Ray, why on earth would a professional fisherman of that stature hook up with a couple of dumyaks like Bert and Harold?"

"I asked that question . . . kind of. Actually, what I said was I envied Bert the gig because he must be making some re-e-e-ally good dough on it. And if there's a pro tournament up here *next* year, I said I'd sure as hell appreciate it if he would put me in touch with the right people. That's one list I'd like to have my name on! And I mean that, Doc. Technically speaking, as an 'amateur co-angler,' which is what he calls himself, all those two have to do is help the guy scout good fishing holes during the qualifying rounds."

"What'd he say to that?"

"Y'know Bert did time in the pen. . . ."

"No, you never told me that," said Osborne.

"I'm sure I told you that." Ray looked at Osborne in surprise.

"Okay, I forgot—but finish the story, we're almost there."

"That night I met Bert on Trout Lake when his ATV broke down and I gave him a ride? Maybe I didn't mention that I had a little altercation with the game warden as we drove off the ice."

Of course he didn't; that's why Osborne hadn't heard this part of the story.

"My fishing license had expired and my truck was . . . full of sweet air because Bert and I had just shared one. In fact, the only good news was I hadn't had any luck that night; otherwise I'd 'a' been in the hoosegow with the warden eating my catch. So ol' Bert had a front row seat for my moment of distress. After the warden read me the riot act and we were driving into town, Bert volunteered that he'd done some time back in the eighties for growing weed on his mom's property up in Mercer. So this morning when I asked him how he connected with this professional bass fisherman, all he said was—and I quote—'a friend from the old days' put him in touch.

"It was the look he gave me when he said it that reminded me he did time in Marion. Now"—Ray raised a hand as if to block an argument—"you can say I'm leaping to conclusions but intuition tells me that's what he meant, okay?"

Osborne nodded. He believed.

While intuition was one talent of Ray's that no one sneered at, he also entered the Pub fully informed. Before asking for advice on Brenda Anderle earlier that morning, Osborne had filled Ray in on the encounter at Birch Lake, every detail from Bert's dirty pants right down to the traveling fish fry held hostage in the RV's livewells.

"It adds up," said Osborne. "Your intuition plus three dozen expertly aerated smallmouths in an expensive RV parked in the middle of nowhere. All that *and* a first prize purse of a million bucks? Works for me," said Osborne.

"Doc, get your numbers right. First Prize is actually a measly half a million bucks. The purse goes up *another* five hundred thousand dollars if the winner is fishing in one of five Ranger Boats with Mercury motors that are awarded by lottery on opening day," said Ray. "I'd say the million dollars is a long shot even for the pros. But it's still one mother of a fishing tournament. I can see why someone would try to cheat."

Osborne checked his watch: four minutes to the airport.

"Little more to the story, Doc. I think Bert's working a scam on that pro. He has no idea what he's doing. I doubt he's fished more 'n two or three times in his life and Harold's no better.

"No wonder they were happy to see me. The minute I sat down for a cup of coffee, they had those fishing maps spread out all across the table and not a clue for the hot spots in any one of those five lakes. They're not gonna help Duffy win a half-million bucks, he'll be lucky if he's not excommunicated. And you want to know how I know?"

Osborne waited. Three minutes to the airport.

"They actually asked me to show them my honey holes for big bass."

Osborne looked over at Ray: "Are you *serious*?"

"Just like that."

Ray slowed behind an elderly woman in the car ahead. Oncoming traffic was too heavy to pass. Neither of them said a word, well aware they knew exactly what the other was thinking: An experienced, dedicated fisherman does not tell anyone, ever, the location of his best fishing holes. Nor would anyone who ever fished for any length of time expect him to. Not even blood relatives expect to share such sacred information.

Osborne caught the look on Ray's face. "Oh no, you showed them, didn't you."

"Yep, and I made it simple so Lew can put Roger on this one. But . . . one thing I need you to make very clear to Police Chief Lewellyn Ferris . . . *this is not entrapment.* These boys have a choice."

Ray knew and Osborne knew that the last thing Ray needed was to be perceived as being on the right side of the game wardens. In one fell swoop, his reputation would be skewered. Never again would he get a good tip on fishing private water (water belonging to someone other than the tipster, of course).

Ray turned the car onto Airport Road. "That sunken island on Cranberry Lake?"

"Yep."

"Well, I showed 'em on the map where it is. And I gave them a strategy. I said, 'Look, don't even try to guarantee finding big fish for the guy, he's a pro, he should be able to do that. What he needs from you is a good haul of decent-sized smallmouth that'll add up to a healthy qualifying weight limit. Make that your goal. No red flags that way, either.'"

"So you did not encourage them to plant fish."

"Hell, no. My suggestion was simply that they put some minnow bait down in there to draw fish. Of course, given those boys are pretty dim candles, I had to explain that fish have a lateral smell organ, which means they will find those minnows. Who doesn't know that? If baiting with a bucket of minnows is against the rules of the tournament, that's their worry. I don't know if it is or not. On the other hand. . . ."

Again Osborne waited.

"Knowing they didn't have a clue as to how to get bait out there, I suggested they use leech traps . . . *my* leech traps."

"The ones behind your trailer?"

"Yep, I gave them directions to my place, told them they could use however many they want—but I need 'em back when they're done."

"You think they'll forget the bait and put those smallmouths from the livewells in the traps?"

"You betcha. The minute those traps disappear from my place? That's the signal for Roger to stake out the island. All he'll need is binoculars and the phone number for the tournament officials. I heartily suggest, however, he better be damn sure they're putting big fish down there before he calls."

Ray pulled Osborne's car onto Airport Road. "I hate to see Bert shoot himself in the foot with this. He's not that bad a guy. He even . . . offered . . . to do me a favor in return. . . ." The sudden change in cadence signaled something Osborne should have been expecting: Ray's punch line.

"Could you wipe that smirk off your face and get to the point?" said Osborne.

"After what you told me about Lew wanting you to check out Patty Boy Plyer's place? Well, as we're leaving the Pub, ol' Bert asks me if I have a motorcycle, which of course I don't. But I said my girlfriend, Rosemary, has her eye on getting herself a used Harley."

"Who the hell is Rosemary?"

"Doc, I made her up."

"Oh."

"Bert said forget used, he's got a buddy in the area doing business shipping Harleys north to Canada and out of the country. If I want one, I should let him know and he can get me a good deal on a *new* bike—like an eighty percent discount."

"Eighty percent?"

"Right, and I said I might be very interested because Rosemary's birthday is coming up."

"Wow!"

"So he said his friend has a kind of swap meet/party planned for early next week when the rally opens. I can find out when it's happening if I tune in to *Help Your Neighbor* starting this Friday."

"No, they're advertising?"

"Not exactly. It's a coded message. They'll broadcast the time and place the same way they do the raves. That's how he said it, too—'the same way they do the raves.'"

"Amazing." Osborne leaned back in the seat. "Brazen enough that no one would even notice."

"First commandment of the profession," said the man renowned in the northwoods for his ability to eschew the cover of darkness ("that's when they're waiting for you") and do his best poaching in broad daylight.

"Lew was wondering how the word got out to all these kids in such a short time. *Help Your Neighbor*, huh?"

Osborne had to admire the chutzpah. *Help Your Neighbor* was heard every morning at eleven on the Loon Lake AM and FM stations as well as being picked up by other stations across the region. Popular with locals and tourists, it served as a bulletin board for anyone with something to sell. No businesses were allowed to advertise, strictly individuals.

You want fresh raspberries? Home-grown tomatoes? A baby-sitter for Saturday night? Sell your boat? Wife throw you out and you need to rent a room? *Help Your Neighbor* had it all. For twenty-five years the radio program had been one of the most popular morning minutes of listening in the region. Who would have thought it would serve as a clearinghouse for drug dealers?

"Bert said to listen for someone looking to sell 'boats and bikes' and I'd be able to figure it out from there."

"Boats and bikes? Sounds pretty damn innocent, doesn't it."

"Last thing, Doc? When I walked out of the Pub with them, over to their vehicle—a rented pickup with an extended cab—I could see two cased guns in the back seat. Shotguns or rifles, I couldn't tell, but I warned 'em. I said, 'You want a smashed window, boys, you just keep a gun or a good fishing rod right out in the open like that.' Honest to God, Doc, I wonder how they got this far in life."

"You didn't happen to get the license number on that rental?"

Ray handed Osborne a scrap of paper.

Osborne studied the number on the scrap of paper, his mind elsewhere. "I find it hard to believe a professional would risk fishing a major tournament with a couple dumyaks like those two."

"It doesn't make sense, does it," said Ray, his eyes much more serious than usual.

The car neared the airport entrance, then nosed its way into the *No Parking* zone.

"Unless. . . ."

Osborne waited, hand on the door handle.

"He *has* to use those guys."

"Ah-h-h," said Osborne.

"And they *have* to work with him. Could be someone else is giving orders?"

As Ray turned off the ignition, Osborne checked his watch. They were five minutes late. He reached for the accordion file; Ray reached for his hat.

fifteen

"She was now not merely an angler, but a 'record' angler of the most virulent type. Wherever they went, she wanted, and she got, the pick of the water."

—Henry Van Dyke

She came at them like an oak tree in a forty-mile-an-hour wind. It took Osborne a hazy few seconds to locate the human beneath the shivering foliage, but as she got closer, he could make out two eyes, rimmed white as a black squirrel's and just as determined.

"Oops, I think that's my client," said Ray, a look of chagrin on his face. It had to be. The only other people in the small lobby, besides the Northwest ticket agent, stood behind rental car desks.

"Client, hell, it's a walking duckblind," said Osborne under his breath.

They were trapped, the baggage carousel behind them blocking any attempt to back up. Skidding to a stop, the figure reached up to fling off the leaf-hung hood obscuring its face, then planted its feet wide apart as if ready to take on all comers. Fluttering oak leaves spilled down the legs and onto the matching boots. She wore more camouflage than Osborne had ever seen on one person—obviously expensive and quite out of season.

The exposed face was lush and full with a mouth slashed red-brown over very white teeth. So white they had to be capped. Her hood had hidden the rich russet of her shoulder-length hair, which she swept from her forehead with a dramatic flourish of her right hand.

The airport lighting was not kind, and two circles of blush caught Osborne's eye. He knew from years of having excess makeup from the faces of female patients wind up on his sleeves that it was a failed attempt to add bone to chubby cheeks. Half-handsome, half-garish, the face reminded Osborne of the prosperous tourists who came north in the summer with their faces full of money, faces whose size and extravagant coloring had often reminded him of overripe fruit. But fruit or duckblind, this woman sure knew how to make an entrance.

She stared at Ray, saying nothing, her eyes measuring, calculating, arrogant. Osborne watched her take it all in: the jaunty angle of the stuffed trout hat, the crisp, smooth-fitting khakis, the height, the laughing eyes, the sheer handsome friendliness of Ray Pradt.

Then she laughed. A loud, delighted laugh. Osborne might be ignorant of many things about women but he was the father of two daughters and he did know the meaning of that laugh: she liked what she saw.

This could be dangerous. Unlike some women who come on like nibbling, gentle bluegills, this one was different. He would warn Ray to make sure he got paid early and often. Then again, maybe he didn't need advice—what kind of fishing guide doesn't know a shark when he sees one?

"Hayden Steadman," she said, moving in so close she brushed Ray with her shoulder. "You must be Ray Pradt . . . my security manager."

Ray beamed at the unexpected title. Their eyes met and they were nearly level as Hayden Parker was one tall woman. Tall, big-boned, and overflowing. From where he stood slightly behind Ray, Osborne could see that the camouflage jacket had fallen open to expose a matching shirt, minus fluttering leaves. The shirt was unbuttoned one button too far. Hayden had very nice breasts, large enough to match the rest of her, including her voice. And she knew it.

"Hey, who are you?" She poked her head around Ray to stare at Osborne. Her manner was so abrupt and challenging that Osborne was caught off-guard. He didn't know what to say.

As he stammered, Ray said, "Oh, this guy? He's my assistant, Dr. Paul Osborne." Hayden looked confused. "He works for me in my guiding business," Ray added. "Doc is retired and likes to help out."

Osborne extended his hand and tried to smile graciously in spite of the fact Ray made it sound like he spent his days filling minnow buckets for Grand Pooh-Bah Pradt. He'd take it out on Ray later. For starters, he'd let him pay for the damn parking ticket they were sure to get.

"I, ah, were you planning to wear *that* during the tournament?" said Ray, watching her leaves flutter.

"Heavens, no. But isn't this stuff great?" Hayden executed a quick spin, flinging the jacket over her shoulder as if it were a mink coat and the airport lobby a high-fashion runway. "I'm celebrating our new sponsor for The Fishing Channel and my husband's newest venture, which debuts in October, The Hunting Channel. This is their product."

"Ray, Miss Steadman, excuse me a moment, will you?" said Osborne. He took cover at the pay phone twenty feet away, set the file down between his feet, and quickly punched in Erin's number. She answered on her remote phone from where she was sitting in her backyard.

"Don't worry about it, Dad," she said after he explained

why he was so late. "I'm fine. Mark called an hour ago and we had a long talk. He's coming in for a visit with the kids and me tonight. And he's bringing his new bike! Chief Ferris was right, Dad. Her approach is working—oops, gotta go. Cody just fell off the swing."

Osborne hung up the phone and retrieved the file from between his feet. He was anxious to take a look at the contents. But to get to the restaurant, he had to walk past Ray and the human duckblind.

Two people who appeared to be members of Hayden's entourage had straggled up during his phone call. One was a young man whom Osborne guessed to be in his late twenties, head shaved and wearing baggy black shorts and a Red Hot Chili Peppers T-shirt. He looked in serious need of a nap and a shower.

The other was a young woman, slight, thin, and nondescript-looking with black hair caught back in a limp ponytail. Her olive complexion couldn't hide the circles under her eyes. She wore a simple white T-shirt and jeans and also looked like she needed a good night's sleep—possibly due to the large black purse and heavy briefcase she had slung over her shoulder.

As he walked past the group, Osborne glanced more closely at the girl's face. Something about her seemed familiar. Ray caught his eye and signaled. Osborne paused mid-stride and started over toward Ray.

"Where's Parker?" said Hayden, whirling around. It was less a question than a bark directed at the two young people. She made no move to introduce them to Osborne. Obviously, they weren't important. He wasn't important.

"He's making sure all the luggage is here," said the young man. "Shouldn't be long." His manner was calm and polite and Osborne hoped he was paid well.

"That's why we have our own plane," said Hayden in a petulant voice. "Of course everything is here."

The young man shrugged.

"We've been to seven cities in twenty-one days," said the young woman in a soft voice. "Things can go wrong." She appeared to be apologizing for Parker Steadman's absence.

Eyes back on Ray and ignoring the woman's comment, Hayden twirled again. "For only eight hundred and fifty dollars you, too, can entertain turkeys in L. L. Bean's Total Illusion 3-D Camo with patented odor-eliminating technology. State of the art."

She paused mid-twirl and looked at Ray. "They'll be doing forty million dollars in advertising on our channels. *I'll* be featured in the ads—*and* I'm doing the entire lake house in their '*camo*' patterns." She gave "camo" a special emphasis as if to imply that the jargon of the hunt was her second language. Ray gave Osborne a quick wink, then looked at Hayden with a questioning expression on his face.

"The house? You mean that place on Lake Consequence where you folks are staying? How do you wallpaper logs?"

"Oh, Mr. Pradt, now don't be silly," said Hayden, teasing. Osborne shifted from one foot to the other. Forget the restaurant; all he wanted now was a sign from Ray that he could take his car and leave.

But Ray's eyes were on Hayden, whose voice kept getting louder as she spoke. Listening with half an ear, Osborne studied the profile of the young woman with the black hair. What was it about her?

He heard only snippets of Hayden's chatter: ". . . ten thousand square feet . . . full-log construction with the lodge-style décor throughout . . . we have a million five into it so far. . . . the *furniture* is what we're covering in camo . . . my interior designer flies in from Manhattan tonight. . . ."

Just then, Parker Steadman entered the baggage claim

area. Or rather his stomach entered and he followed. The former was new to Osborne; the latter was not. Parker had always been extraordinarily tall with a long, bony frame. His face, under a shock of prematurely white hair, was flushed. Whether from exertion or booze, Osborne couldn't be sure. The stomach, on the other hand, carried credentials.

This was not a Harold Jackobowski beer belly, a slovenly mass adding girth to an already pudgy human frame. No, this was an insouciant protuberance, an emblem of a life lived well. This was a belly primed with martinis, succored with beef tenderloins and oysters on the half-shell, and lavished with single-malt twelve-year Scotch whiskies. No cheap brass buckle restrained this specimen; it appropriated the airspace over sterling silver double G's by a good six inches—and that was diameter only. Osborne chose not to consider the volume.

Parker walked toward the group, slightly pigeon-toed and knees straight, the jacket of his business suit open to ease the forward progress of all body parts.

"Almost home," he said, looking around with a wide, jovial smile creasing his face. He looked like a big happy teddy bear. "Everything made it here, too." He thrust a hand at Ray. "You the new security guy? Pradt's the name, right?"

"Parker the Predator, how are *you*?" said Ray, pumping the man's hand.

Parker just laughed. "They usually call me that behind my back, son."

Osborne shook his head and looked off in the opposite direction. Ray had a way. Boy, did he have a way. At least he didn't ask Parker if he was expecting.

Hayden looked amused.

"Now what the hell do you call *that*?" said Parker, leaning back on his heels to get a better look at Ray's head where the stuffed trout was surveying the attempts of the two to short-circuit one another. "That's the damndest thing—you make that yourself?"

"Hardly, Mr. Steadman, hardly." Ray smiled modestly, though Osborne knew he had planned all morning for this moment. Ray removed his hat and tipped it back and forth so everyone could get a good look. The antique muskie lure draped across the front glinted silver in the light.

"Made for me by an el-der-ly Ojibwa woman, the very same woman who taught me the secrets of birch bark canoes. I traded fresh walleye for wisdom, best deal *I* ever made."

Hayden looked more than amused as she motioned to the black-haired woman, who promptly pulled a notebook from her purse.

Once again, Osborne looked off into the distance, hoping his grin didn't show. Ray could really lay it on. Just then he heard his name. ". . . You remember Dr. Paul Osborne?" Ray was pointing at him.

Parker gave Osborne a blank look. Obviously not. Osborne extended a hand. "You had an appointment in my office one summer when you were in your teens. I'd be very surprised if you remembered that."

"No, I think I do. Wasn't your office over the bank? Did Catherine Plyer work for you that summer?"

"Why, yes, that's right."

"Then you must have known my late father-in-law."

"Dr. Plyer hunted with us one year."

Parker motioned to the tired-looking young man who was standing nearby. "Rob, check and see if our cars are out front yet, will you?"

Osborne noticed that a flight must be due in as a small crowd was gathering in the lobby area. A number of people appeared to recognize Hayden and had stopped to stare.

"So"—he turned back to Osborne—"is Ray your son?"

"Oh, no. No-o-o, nope. We're neighbors and we do a

little muskie fishing together." Osborne hastened to change the subject. "I want you to know that everyone in Loon Lake is looking forward to your tournament. This is a big deal for us—great for the economy."

"Thank you, Doctor. If all goes well, I'd like to see it become an annual event; Our advertisers love the location. By the way"—Parker turned to the black-haired woman, who seemed to be doing her best to hide off to the side—"Edith, where are you? Edith is from Loon Lake. She's Hayden's executive producer. Edith, do you know Dr. Osborne?"

The small dark head turned soft eyes to Osborne. She smiled shyly, giving him a questioning, beseeching look, almost as if she prayed he wouldn't recognize her. But the jaw, the configuration of her teeth, the unmistakable central incisor—identical to the mouth she had at fourteen. All that had changed was the face: Now it was old enough to carry those eyes.

"Edith Schultz, of course," said Osborne. "I thought I recognized you."

"Excuse me, everyone. Have you forgotten I have ties here, too?" Hayden's bleat made it sound like she was about to cry.

"Kitten, I didn't mean to leave you out. I thought you met everyone." Parker reached a long arm around Hayden's leafy shoulders and pulled her to him. She nuzzled in like a hurt child. Looking up at Ray, she said, "I went to summer camp in Eagle River."

Osborne watched as her expression changed to one of petulance as she pushed herself away from Parker, thrusting his arm off her. "Parker, you haven't said a word about what's happening to me!"

The level of tension in her face and body and voice had ramped up so fast, it reminded Osborne of the day Erin's three-year-old Cody, while in his care, had burst into unexpected tears.

"What on earth is wrong, little guy?" Osborne, the be-fuddled grandfather, had asked.

"You hurt my *feelings*," sobbed the toddler.

Well, Hayden had thirty-plus years on the kid but her technique was the same. As was its effect: She got every-one's attention.

From the corner of his eye, Osborne could see from their faces that Edith and Rob had been here before. Parker, however, looked worried: "Oh, kitten—"

"Our safety, Parker. *My safety* —"

The trill of a spring robin cut her off. Another trill. Hayden's mouth dropped open. Ray grinned and, hands cupped to his mouth, gave another bird call.

Rob looked like he was going to explode. Edith turned her face away.

Hayden gave Ray a baleful stare that eased into a con-fused smile. "Why? What?"

"Too many people around. Better to discuss this later," said Ray with just the right air of warning and authority.

"Oh, you are so right," said Hayden, throwing looks of extreme annoyance at the poor souls who had made the mistake of stopping to watch after recognizing her.

Osborne had to hand it to Ray. He had just outdressed *and* outperformed a national television personality. And left her charmed. This would make a great story for the McDonald's crowd.

"Hey, the cars are here," said Rob.

The last Osborne saw of Ray that afternoon was his neighbor folding all six feet five inches into a condensed version of a Range Rover.

"A Mini Rover, and not just any," he heard Hayden say-ing as she threw her camo jacket into the back seat and prepared to ride out to the house with Ray at her side. "This is a Paul Smith Mini, a limited edition of fifteen hundred cars."

"I know Paul—he owns Smitty's Bar up on the river," said Ray.

"You jerk, I mean Paul Smith the British fashion designer." Hayden giggled and fastened her seat belt.

"I feel like a sardine," said Ray, handing the car keys out the window to Osborne.

Meanwhile, Parker had climbed into a Chevy Suburban with Edith and a great deal of luggage. A second van, to be driven by Rob, was parked behind that one and loaded with video equipment.

Osborne was happy to have his own car back. Once again, he stashed the accordion file on the back seat. Reaching down to adjust the seat back to where he could reach the brake pedal, he was startled by a rapping on his car window. Parker's head with its preternaturally white hair loomed over his left shoulder. The man might be a good twelve years younger than Osborne but he sure as hell didn't look it today.

"I want to apologize for Hayden's behavior back there," he said after Osborne had rolled down his window. "She's been terrified by these threats and has a tendency to overreact."

"Entirely understandable," said Osborne. Mistaking a tantrum for terror? Parker had obviously not raised children.

"But this business is almost over—the threatening calls, I mean. We'll only be needing Ray for a day or so."

"Oh?" Lew would be happy to hear that; she could certainly use Ray's help.

"Yes, I just hired a firm that has the technology to monitor all incoming and outgoing phone calls—on cells, remotes, everything. They're pretty sure they'll be able to pinpoint the source of the threats by tomorrow sometime."

"That'll be a relief."

"You bet it will. Hayden is convinced it's someone up

in this neck of the woods. Someone who knew her when she was at camp and has gone off the deep end now that she's a celebrity."

"Well . . . that's always possible, I suppose."

"If I've learned one thing in life, Dr. Osborne, anything is possible. Say, I'm hosting some of the fishing pros and sponsors who are coming in for the tournament at my home Saturday evening. I'd like for you and your wife to join us if you would. Be nice to mix some Loon Lake folks in with the out-of-towners." Parker smiled his jovial smile again.

"Thank you," said Osborne, "but—"

"Edith will be in touch with the details," said Parker, waving as he walked off.

"Excuse me," Osborne called after him. Parker stopped and Osborne waved him back toward the car. Osborne kept his voice low as he said, "How does Edith feel about being back in Loon Lake?"

"What do you mean?" The look of surprise on Parker's face answered Osborne's question: He knew nothing about the circumstances of her father's death. "I think she's pretty happy to be back, to see her family. Why?"

"Just asking," said Osborne. "I'll check with her about Saturday, then."

sixteen

"There's no taking trout with dry breeches."

—Cervantes, *Don Quixote*

Osborne made it up to the Lake of the Woods Harley-Davidson dealership in less than thirty minutes. The owner, Gary Skubal, was so happy to see him, he practically pushed Osborne back to his office.

"I had a long conversation with that Ferris woman this morning," said Gary, rapping a business card on his desk as he spoke. "I don't know." He pulled open the top drawer of his desk and studied the interior as if an answer were lurking there. Finding nothing, he closed the drawer and picked up the business card again.

"Women police officers, women riding motorcycles. It's a new world out there." He squinted at Osborne as he rapped away. "She fishes, too, doesn't she? She was interested in that new pontoon I got sittin' out in the drive. Takes all kinds, I guess. Sold four bikes to gals in the last month." For the life of him, Osborne couldn't tell if Gary was positive or negative on the subject of women or just revved on coffee.

He could, from the flat vowels, tell that the man was a

transplant from Milwaukee. Gary appeared to be in his late fifties, of medium height, slightly overweight and balding. But even with a Harley-Davidson leather jacket open over his khakis and striped shirt, he looked more like an insurance salesman than someone who sold sin on wheels. He also looked worried.

"I've had thirty thousand dollars in orders for chrome and leather accessories canceled in the last five days, Doc. That's never happened in the eighteen months that I've been open. That's not the half of it. I had two V-rods, two Fat Boys, and a Heritage Classic sold—and those were just canceled. People gave up deposits of a thousand dollars so they have got to be getting some incredible deal somewhere.

"The thing I told Ferris that's got me convinced we can nail somebody if we act right now is that every one of those customers is coming up for the Tomahawk Rally. I had so much business booked, I put on extra mechanics to work over the weekend. Now this." He tossed the business card over his shoulder. "She has got to do something."

"Chief Ferris told you the Illinois authorities just informed her that they have known there's a chop shop operating up here, right?"

"So? Why didn't she know before?" said Gary. "What's she been doing all summer—ticketing crossing guards?" Osborne said nothing, figuring the belligerence was just a cover for worry. Gary picked another business card out of the plastic stand sitting on his desk.

"My mechanic who got the tip was told to get in touch with a woman named 'Cheryl' if he wants anything. He was told she shows up now and again at The Two Sisters bar over in Eagle River. I'm parkin' my butt over there all night tonight, tomorrow night, the next night . . . Will you be there?"

Osborne ignored the question as he stood up. Cheryl.

That was the name of the woman calling Mark at his office.

"Excuse me, may I borrow your phone?" he asked.

"Sure." Gary handed over a remote. Osborne punched in Erin's number. Disappointed when all he got was her answering machine, he knew his voice was more than a little terse as he left a message. "Erin, when you see Mark tonight, ask him who he bought his bike from. Get as much detail as you can. Please, *don't forget*." God, he hated sounding like a father.

"Something ring a bell, huh?" Gary looked hopeful for the first time since they had been chatting.

"Worth a try," said Osborne. "How do you think people hear about this place?"

"That's easy. Word of mouth through the H.O.G. chapters for one." At the confused look on Osborne's face, he explained: "Harley Owners Group. And the different clubs. A lot of the people who come to a big rally like this will ride in a group; all it takes is one person to get the news out to hundreds. Ferris said you don't ride but you're taking the class starting tomorrow, right?"

Osborne nodded.

"You'll see what I mean when you get there. Harley-Davidson stands for more than just a bike, it's a lifestyle. Everyone who rides a Harley is your friend, and friends do friends favors. Come on, let's get you all set up."

Out in the shop, Gary had set aside what he called "leathers" for Osborne to try on. Chaps, a vest, a well-padded jacket. The clothing fit okay but it was heavy. Osborne looked at himself in the dressing room mirror. Not bad. With the boots, a leather headwrap, and goggles, he barely recognized himself. But he liked what he saw.

The leather headwrap combined with his black eyes and the Meteis cheekbones that he had inherited from his grandmother to give him a lean, dark profile. The silvering sideburns and his black hair that had looked so distinguished in the dental office now looked . . . dashing. What would his grandchildren say? Better yet, Lew?

"Ferris was worried you would look too clean-shaven," said Gary, back in his office with Osborne's leathers draped over his arms. He seemed determined not to use her title. "But that deep tan of yours works. You look like you've been riding for a month. All you need is a little windburn and you'll get that over the next couple days. How'd you get so tan? You golf?" As he asked the question, he reached for a box sitting on the floor.

"Fishing. I get out almost every day. Fly-fishing, a little muskie fishing. What kind of fishing do you do off that pontoon boat of yours? Walleye?"

"Yep. That reminds me. . . ." Gary, in the midst of pulling a helmet from the box, stopped and walked over to his desk. Leaning over a laptop computer that stood open, he punched a few keys.

"I thought I remembered that right. Two of those canceled accessory orders were from guys coming down from the UP to fish as amateurs in that bass tournament next week. Mention that to Chief Ferris, will you? Tell her we have a strong crossover market with bait fishermen. Many of the guys who ride Harleys fish—walleye, bass, muskie, panfish. Our consumer base is so similar to the big boat manufacturers and the inboard and outboard motor companies that I buy their mailing lists for my winter promotions."

"So they're not all Hell's Angels chugging beer?" Osborne was joking. He knew better. Joel Frahm, the dentist who bought his practice, owned a Harley. He and his wife rode every weekend the weather was good.

"Bad to the bone in their dreams," said Gary. "My bikes average twenty to thirty thousand *before* they're chromed up. A huge percentage of my customers are professionals—doctors, engineers, businessmen, you name it.

The one thing they have in common is they love to ride: the wind, the sun, the absolute freedom of the road."

He reached again for the box holding the helmet. As he pulled it out, Osborne could read the price on the box. "Wow, four hundred bucks?"

"Most expensive in the shop. Ferris and I decided you should look like you spend too much money on your appearance and not enough on your bike," said Gary. "That's typical of a certain type of new Harley owner. They want to look the part, but they don't know that much about motorcycles yet."

"I'm supposed to look rich and stupid, is that it?" Osborne wasn't sure he liked this role.

"No, we want you to look like you need help getting your bike chromed to the max. We want you to be a target, someone who appears to have easy access to cash and, with a bare-bones bike, is an excellent candidate for accessories like chrome front wheels, fringed saddle bags, parts that might interest you—especially if they're cheap."

As he spoke, Osborne remembered the open box by Bert's bed in the RV. Those carefully packed chrome parts were beginning to make sense.

Minutes later, Osborne was standing out in the sunny driveway. The shop door went up and Gary emerged, wheeling a black and green monster. "I'm riding *that*?" Osborne backed off ten feet.

"Electra Glide Ultra Classic," said Gary, leaning the big bike on its kickstand. "Black and suede green. Twenty-one thousand dollars. We chromed up the front just a touch, but you still need lots of accessories on this baby. My average customer for this bike would have put on an extra five thousand dollars without flinching. See these chrome nuts here on the wheel—those go for ten dollars each."

"And I thought a dental chair was expensive," said Osborne. "You do realize I've never ridden a motorcycle. What if I tip this over?"

"You don't 'tip it,' you 'drop it,'" said Gary with a rueful chuckle. "Don't worry, I put engine and bag guards on so you won't damage the engine if that happens."

"It's not the engine I'm worried about," said Osborne.

"Look, that won't happen. That's what your motorcycle safety class is all about. Wait till you see how many grandmothers take it."

"Really?"

"You'll be surprised. It's a two-day intensive course; they start you out on small Japanese bikes and you get plenty of riding to build your confidence. Ferris told me you can handle it."

That helped . . . a little. Gary grinned at the look on Osborne's face.

"C'mon," he said. "Forty-eight short hours from now, you'll have the basics down cold. When you get on this bike, the only difference will be size and stability. You won't *believe* how stable this bike is—impossible to drop unless you're on sand or gravel. Trust me."

"Trust me." The words echoed in his mind all the way back to Loon Lake, but they didn't do much to keep second thoughts from crowding in, too. That was one big motorcycle. It wasn't until Osborne turned into his own driveway that he realized it was after four and he hadn't had any lunch. Boy, was he was hungry.

Mulling over the contents of his refrigerator and with Mike bumping at his knees, Osborne almost missed the note taped to the screen door.

Written on a sticky note bordered in light blue and highlighted with daisies, the note read: "Thought you might enjoy one of my yummier hot dishes—put it in your oven on warm. Freezes great, if necessary. Happy day! B."

Osborne shut off the oven with an angry twist, then

pulled out the covered casserole. Chicken potpie. The same recipe Mary Lee used to make from the St. Kunegunda Women's Auxiliary Cookbook. Not only that, it was baking in a good ceramic casserole dish, which he would have to return, of course. The woman was not subtle.

In spite of his irritation, the creamy dish with its golden crust was too seductive. A ferocious sense of hunger overwhelmed him and he lifted a fork. She was right; it was yummy. Within minutes he had made a large dent in the small pie.

Loading up a third helping along with a big glass of milk, he let himself and Mike out onto the patio. Setting the plate and glass down on the table, he went back for the accordion file. He tipped the papers onto the table and started to sift through as he ate.

A lot of the documentation was faded and difficult to read, mainly reports filed by the two police officers working for the little town at the time. Finally, he found what he was looking for; the coroner's report. Osborne knew better than to expect too much.

Irv Pecore had been the Loon Lake coroner for thirty-three years. That was thirty-three years too many for residents like Osborne and Lew Ferris, who kept hoping he would retire from the appointed position. Unfortunately, as the son of one of the most powerful dairy farmers in the northwoods, he had a sweetheart deal that was too good to give up.

Not the most respected pathologist, Pecore had a habit of letting his golden retrievers roam his office and lab areas, a habit that many Loon Lakers found so atrocious that on the few occasions an autopsy was necessary, they went along to be sure the canines didn't get too close to their beloved family member.

But twenty years ago, Pecore's reputation was more respected. Questions were seldom raised. It was Lew's predecessor, John Sloan, who blew the whistle on Pecore after too many inconsistencies in his reporting. Sloan couldn't remove Pecore, but he did his best to get cases requiring solid analysis into the hands of the crime labs in Wausau or Madison. The Schultz case predated Sloan, and it appeared, as Osborne reviewed page after page, that Pecore was the only coroner to be involved.

His plate clean, Osborne took his dirty dishes into the kitchen, then returned to the deck. Putting his feet up, he settled back in the chaise longue to look through the file again. The late afternoon sun threw a soft haze through the tops of the pines. Light filtered down onto the deck, a fly droned over the crumbs on the table. An outboard motor throttled low across the water. A lazy, hazy, drowsy afternoon.

Osborne turned to what appeared to be the last report from Pecore in this file. On the line requesting "Cause of Death" was scrawled one word: "Undetermined." A few more handwritten squiggles on the page seemed to indicate where Pecore was filing the physical evidence "until further review." And there was a date.

That was all? Osborne leaned back and closed his eyes. Something was missing. There must be another file or at least another report from Pecore somewhere. Jack Schultz did not commit suicide over a cause of death ruled "Undetermined."

The date, what was it about that date? Ah, yes. That was Mary Lee's birthday. It all came back now. In the days following the discovery of the body in the woods across the road from their home, dozens of curiosity seekers had parked up and down their road. He and Mary Lee had invited friends for barbecue the afternoon of her birthday. She was quite upset when everyone had had difficulty parking, so upset she had called the police.

Osborne raised his head to check the date on Pecore's report. This *was* Pecore's final report. With the girl dead and her alleged assailant dead, that jabone had simply quit working on the case. Dashed off the report and headed up the street for a beer. That would be Pecore all right.

Osborne leaned back. The sunlight was soothing on his forehead.

A phone shrilled. Up out of the lounge chair and through the sliding screen door into the kitchen, Osborne bumped his way with Mike at his heels. The unexpected nap left him feeling a little groggy.

"Doc," said Lew. "Did you forget about our meeting?"

Osborne looked at the clock. "Oh, gosh, Lew. I'm so sorry. I'll be there in five minutes."

seventeen

"Yet fish there be, that
Neither hook nor line
Nor snare nor net, nor
Engine can make thine."

—John Bunyan,
Pilgrim's Progress,
1678

Osborne swung around the corner and into the UPS parking lot. As he pulled in, he was shocked to see the big green-and-black motorcycle parked near the entrance to the building. Caressed by the setting sun, the big bike gleamed with all the flash and dazzle of a silver spoon muskie lure. And the sight of it had the same effect on Osborne's heart as the strike of a big fish: life-threatening heart fibrillation.

Lew was waiting for him in a tiny cubicle behind the receiving desk at the UPS station. She was in uniform but wearing the black leather jacket he'd seen her in that morning. Leaning up against the wall, arms crossed, she motioned for him to take the stool beside her.

Osborne sat down. Smiling over at him from where she

sat on a folding chair next to a well-worn card table was
Lucy Priebe. Actually, the prim, tight line of Lucy's lips
was an attempt at a smile. While her mother had been a
patient up until he sold his practice, Osborne hadn't seen
Lucy since she was in high school. She hadn't been happy
to see him then, either.

"Hello, Dr. Osborne." Lucy glanced back over her
shoulder as she spoke, an eye on the door that opened
from the parking lot to the receiving area. In her late thirties now, Lucy was small-boned and a little too thin. Her
features were delicate under a cloud of graying brown
curls. She wore wire-rimmed glasses and no makeup. A
Goody Two-Shoes just like her mother.

"I was explaining to Chief Ferris that my husband in-
sists I have no part in this even if I am the night supervisor. He wants me off the premises by seven o'clock."
Osborne looked over at Lew. She caught his eye with a
slight nod. Fine with Lew.

"Lucy," said Lew in a reassuring tone, "that's fine. I
want people to think that Doc is taking over for you these
next three nights. Following your directions, he will su-
pervise the drivers and the delivery schedule. You have no
drop-offs from the public after six, is that correct?"

"Yes, and I will take care of all the paperwork," said
Lucy. "People will wonder why you're working here, Dr.
Osborne." That prim snottiness again. Of course, what
Lucy was dying to ask was why he was working with
Lew.

"Tell them I lost money in the stock market." Osborne
thought that sounded darn good given the condition of his
retirement portfolio at the moment. "I need the benefits."

"I don't care what they think so long as you don't tell
anyone he's working undercover for me," said Lew.

"Not even my husband?"

"Especially not your husband, Lucy. Now would you
take a minute to update Doc on everything we've dis-

cussed, please? I want him to hear your version, every detail."

"Excuse me, one minute," said Osborne. "Before I have a heart attack, Chief Ferris, would you explain why that motorcycle is out front. You don't expect me to ride that tonight, do you?"

"Heavens no," said Lew, dismissing the idea with a wave of her hand. "Don't you worry about that. I'll explain later. I need Lucy to fill you in before our visitor arrives and we don't have much time. Lucy?"

"Our first inkling that something was not quite right with this particular customer was about two years ago," said Lucy. "A UPS station in upstate New York had several shipments stolen—an inside job, we think. The stolen packages were overnight shipments of very expensive, custom-made bamboo fly rods. At first, the boxes disappeared. Then later—this was months later—we found that they had indeed been shipped but the labeling had been altered. The boxes were delivered to this station. To a regular customer of ours—the Webber Tackle Company up on Hagen Road."

Osborne looked at Lew. Patty Boy's operation.

"The owner of Webber Tackle is Patrick Baumgartner," said Lew. "Right, Lucy?"

"Yes, my understanding is that Mr. Baumgartner runs Webber Tackle Company and he is a dealer in antique fishing equipment of all sorts. Until recently, he moved quite a few shipments through here daily—sending and receiving. One of our best customers in the area.

"When we checked with Mr. Baumgartner about that lost shipment, he insisted those boxes were never delivered to his address, even though our driver distinctly remembers dropping them off."

"Did anyone sign for them?" asked Osborne.

"That was the problem. The driver often left boxes in their barn—without a signature. He had a signed release to do that because many times there's no one on the premises. But in this case, Mr. Baumgartner was adamant that he never saw those boxes. He said they might have been stolen or we were wrong. We couldn't prove they hadn't been stolen so we had to drop it."

"What was the value of the shipment?" said Lew.

"It was insured for twenty thousand dollars. Two antique fly rods that a dealer was sending to a collector in Scotland. Each was valued between ten to fifteen thousand dollars. And another thing—Webber Tackle Company often got shipments from that particular dealer. So it was a curious situation, as you can see."

"Were you the supervisor then?" Osborne asked.

"No, I was promoted last spring, but I was working here at the time."

"I see."

"The Chicago office got involved because the company had to pay the insurance, of course. But then things worked fine up until three months ago."

Lucy leaned forward. She dropped her voice, even though the loading area behind them appeared to be empty. The primness was gone. In its place was an edge of fear. "Our driver, the one who delivers to the Baumgartner address, became suspicious of shipments he was handling for them. He had an unusually high number of COD deliveries and some of the boxes had a funny rattle to them."

"From that same dealer with the expensive fly rods?" asked Osborne.

"No, no. These came from a variety of addresses in Canada."

"A rattle?"

"Sounded like little BBs or cookie decorations—or pills."

"We opened one finally, which we have the right to do if we suspect something illegal or dangerous is being shipped. It was very strange. The box was full of fishing lures, wrapped in bubble wrap and padded with foam—"

"What kind of lures?" said Osborne.

"Wooden. Old ones—used, you know. We took everything out. Nothing. Then I noticed that the foam units that were packed around the lures rattled. We cut one open and it was full of pills. That was pretty unsettling, I can tell you. I called Chicago right away and they called the authorities."

"That's when the DEA entered the picture," said Lew. "Right?"

"Right. They told us to put everything back together the best we could, but keep some of the pills. I glued the foam back together with Super Glue and we delivered the box."

"How long ago was this?" asked Osborne.

"Two weeks ago. I've been a nervous wreck ever since," said Lucy. "Thank goodness, we didn't have any more COD deliveries for that address until last week—"

"I checked the date and it was the Wednesday before that rave last weekend," said Lew. "I still can't believe that Chicago never said a word to anyone until yesterday. Sorry, Lucy, I interrupted."

"When that box came in, I called down to Chicago right away and my supervisor said that the authorities wanted us to deliver as contracted, that they were monitoring the deliveries and to let them know each time a shipment like that came through. Well, I can tell you I did not feel right sending a driver out there. I mean drug dealers? Forget it."

"Did you look in that box?"

"No. What I did do was call Mr. Baumgartner and tell him he had an overnight delivery that had arrived here but my driver was ill. He sent someone down to pick it up. When she came, she said that they were just as happy to pick up all their deliveries this month because they're renovating their barn and the road is a mess. That was fine with me."

"Thanks, Lucy," said Lew. "Doc, the pills were analyzed and they were Ecstasy, all right. My directions from the DEA agent in charge are to work with the UPS supervisor to monitor all incoming shipments these next few days, strictly observation only. Lucy isn't comfortable doing that, so UPS has agreed to let me bring you in. Under normal circumstances UPS personnel are the only parties legally allowed to open a questionable package, not me, not the DEA."

"They have two boxes here right now," said Lucy. She checked her watch. "That woman is due to pick them up soon. She's always right on time at seven-thirty. And that's interesting, too. The Webber Tackle deliveries are always timed to arrive so close to the pickup time that they are never on the floor more than thirty minutes."

"CODs, these packages?" said Lew.

"No, and none since last week. No rattle either."

"What time is it?" said Osborne.

"Seven twenty-five."

"I don't understand why they don't just arrest these people," said Lucy.

"The DEA is trying to corral the entire operation from the suppliers to the dealers, within the U.S. and in cooperation with Canadian authorities," said Lew. "If they shut this dealer down too soon, they'll miss the chance to put the kabosh on other major players in the network. At least"—she raised her hands—"that's what they're telling me and I have to take orders on this one.

"Doc, you and I are going to keep an eye out that window by the loading area. See if either of us recognizes the person making the pickup," said Lew. "We better hurry."

Osborne followed her past the dark plastic curtain closing off the public receiving area. Anyone walking in to mail a package would have a difficult time seeing past it.

As Osborne walked over to the window, Lew followed. He felt her shoulder brush his arm and she looked up with a slight smile. Up close, he could see lines of fatigue around her eyes. He resisted the urge to put his arm around her and pull her close.

Just as they reached the window, a silver van pulled into the parking spot next to Osborne's SUV. "Looks a lot like the one I saw Catherine Plyer in the other day," said Osborne. He kept his voice to a whisper.

"Any way to be sure?"

"Hers had rude stickers on the side window behind the driver," said Osborne, "but I can't see anything from here."

The door of the van opened and a short, squat woman hopped down. She appeared to be four feet by four feet square, an impression enhanced by what she was wearing: baggy jeans, a too-wide short-sleeved black T-shirt hanging out over the pants, and a black leather vest decorated with silver conchos and a great deal of fringe.

The brown hair framing her square face was chopped short and shoved behind her ears, the edges of which glinted in the fading sun thanks to a series of metal studs outlining each lobe. But it was her arms that fascinated Osborne. From the wrists on up, not a patch of bare skin was evident, only swirls of blood red and black. Even her elbows were tattooed.

"Recognize her?" said Lew.

"Never saw her before in my life."

"Good." Lew hurried over to the plastic curtain and whispered something to Lucy.

As the woman neared the UPS entrance, Osborne realized that he had assumed she was a woman only because of what Lucy had said. Given the sullen expression and the stocky build, he couldn't be sure she was female until she was close enough for him to make out the sagging slopes beneath her vest and shirt.

She didn't appear to be in a hurry. Instead of entering UPS, she sauntered over to where the big green-and-black motorcycle was parked. Crouching, she looked it over. Then she walked around to examine it from the front. Finally, she stuck her hands in her pockets and headed for the entrance to the receiving room.

"Nice bike," she said to Lucy, who was at the counter. "You ride?"

"Heavens, no," said Lucy cheerfully. "That belongs to our new night supervisor."

"Oh yeah?"

"Yeah, he starts tomorrow. We're training tonight. Cheryl, you've got two heavy boxes here. Let me get someone to give you a hand."

Lew shoved Osborne toward the receiving room. He walked through the plastic curtain. "Did I hear someone needs a hand?"

"Hell, no, I can manage fine," said the woman. Osborne could see a bundle of keys hanging from a belt just visible under the edge of her shirt.

He reached to pick up the larger of the two boxes. It weighed a good forty pounds. "Not to worry, save you a little time," he said.

Arms full, they walked out into the parking lot and past the bike. "That yours?"

"Yep. Some of us never grow up, doncha know."

"How much did it set you back?"

"Twenty-one big ones."

"Oh yeah? You been riding long? You don't look like you ride." She was right about that. He was still wearing his good khaki shirt and pants from the morning.

"Just starting, I'm taking that motorcycle safety class over in Rhinelander."

"You're just starting and you spent that kinda dough?"

"I've always dreamed of owning a Harley. Call me crazy, I guess. But if I don't do it now, when?"

"No, I understand, I do. Are you in the class that starts tomorrow?"

"That's the one, wish me luck."

"I'll see you there. I've been waiting all summer to get in—how long you been on the list?"

"You will?" Osborne could not keep the surprise out of his voice.

"Yeah, I'm sick and tired of riding on the back of my old man's bike. I'm getting myself a cherry red Low Rider. Cheryl Hikinnen," she said, sticking out a beefy hand. "We're moving pretty soon so I was real glad to hear I made it into this session."

"Paul Osborne."

"Nice bike, Paulie. Keep the rubber on the road and the shiny side up, man."

"I'll do my best."

She paused as she opened the van door. "You're not riding tonight, are you?"

"Gosh no, I just had it delivered here."

"Good, I saw a lotta deer on my way down Highway 45 tonight. You don't wanna hit one of those on a new bike— on *any* bike for that matter." Cheryl gave Osborne a wave as she boosted herself up into the driver's seat. The sullenness had vanished, replaced with a happy grin and a twinkle in her eye.

Osborne stepped back to return the wave. He checked the side window. That was Catherine's van, all right.

Lew pushed the bike into the rear of the loading area, where it would be locked up for the next two days. She locked it and handed Osborne the key.

"Can you give me a ride back over to my office? I rode the bike over so no one would see it in our parking lot. Gary dropped it off about an hour after you met with him today. He's desperate for us to close down the chop shop.

This went very well tonight, Doc. Better than I had hoped."

As they climbed into his car, Osborne reached for the accordion file, which he had grabbed as he ran out of the house.

"Lew, I want to show you something. I had a chance to page through the Schultz file late this afternoon, and Pecore's final report is very confusing." He handed her the sheet of paper, then put his key into the ignition.

"Doc, please, this is the last thing I want to deal with. In two weeks, okay?"

Osborne checked over his shoulder as he backed out. "Okay. It's just that Jack Schultz's oldest daughter, the one who was the same age as the victim, is back in town for a few weeks. I saw her today at the airport." He pulled the car onto the street.

Lew had tipped her head back against the headrest and closed her eyes. She was clearly exhausted.

"Oh?" she said. "What's her name?"

"Edith. She's working for Parker Steadman and his wife as a producer. I just thought that while she's in town, it might be a good time to have some questions answered."

Lew opened one eye and looked at him. "Okay . . . what's the deal? What's so confusing in Pecore's report?"

"Why did he list the cause of death as 'Undetermined'? I was always under the impression the baby-sitter had been bludgeoned and died of head injuries. Is there another file or report somewhere?"

"Wha-a-t?" Lew picked up the piece of paper she had dropped in her lap and scanned it quickly. "What time is it?"

"Eight-fifteen."

"Turn left at the next corner."

"Lew, this can wait."

"Pecore lives on this street, third house on the right. We're stopping in."

Pecore was home all right. Home and drunk. So was Mrs. Pecore. She was sitting in a housedress and rocking in a rocking chair. Four empty beer cans had been tossed onto the rug beside her. They appeared to have been enjoying their evening cocktails in the dim light of a large-screen television, which anchored one end of the long living room. It was a nice living room in a traditional kind of way, just dark and gloomy and reeking of dog.

After letting Lew and Osborne in, Pecore, glass of bourbon in hand, had dropped his own heavy frame back onto a sofa already occupied by two golden retrievers. Mrs. Pecore acknowledged their entrance with a slight nod then turned her attention back to the TV. Osborne took a chair while Lew walked over to drop the report in Pecore's lap. Then she crossed the room and sat down.

"What's this?" Pecore squinted at the page.

"Put your glasses on," said Lew.

"Why are you showing me this now?"

"Jack Schultz's daughter is in town. She wants some answers," Lew lied easily.

"This is years old! What the hell?"

"Statute of limitations never runs out on murder, Irv. Remember making out that report?"

"Well . . . yes. After Jack shot himself, we closed the case."

"Without determining the cause of death? A capital murder case?"

"We had the killer, what else do you need?"

"Am I to assume you never analyzed any of the evidence?"

"Now that's not true, I got the evidence."

"That's not what I said."

"Do you know, Ferris"—Pecore waved his drink at

her—"do you know how much it would have cost this little town to investigate that case any further? Those tests
cost money, y'know. Thousands of dollars we would have
had to spend. I had a budget to watch."

"Oh, this was a budget decision, was it?"

"Yes."

"Irv, the head of the police department makes the budget decisions, not the coroner."

"Well, that sure as hell wasn't you, was it."

Lew dropped her head. Osborne was not going to be
surprised if she slugged the lazy bum.

"I know the law," Pecore slurred. "That goddam evidence is right where I put it back then. Nice and tidy." He
might be drunk but he still had the instinct to cover his
butt.

"You didn't destroy it?"

"No, I did not."

If that was true, Osborne knew that the only reason the
evidence might still be in existence was simply because
Pecore hadn't cleaned either his office or his storerooms
in years.

"Whatever you got, I want it sent to Wausau tomorrow
morning."

"I'll check on it."

"You didn't hear what I said." Lew stood up. "I said I
want it in Wausau *tomorrow*. I will take care of sending it
down. You have it on my desk by eight A.M. or my next
budget will be minus one coroner."

"You can't do that."

"I can give it a damn good try." And she could, too.

Mrs. Pecore, during this exchange, never took her eyes
off the TV, never stopped rocking.

"Thank you, Lew," said Osborne back at the car. "Jack's
suicide has always bothered me and I've always worried

about his girls, especially Edith. She was such a sad little kid after all that happened."

"It's easy, Doc, as long as I can keep it off my desk—and those Wausau boys owe me. I'll just say I have a new witness and see if they can't work this up on an urgent basis."

"What about the budget issue? Is Pecore right?"

"He's correct that the lab work costs money, but he was wrong not to have followed through. As far as I'm concerned, this is still an open murder case and that means the budget is there. That's why I was happy for you to look into it in the first place."

She looked over at Osborne. "As far as questioning the daughter, do you think she's up for it?"

"I'm not sure. Guess I'll find out soon enough. But with everything else you've got me doing, I doubt I'll see her before Saturday."

"Saturday?"

"I haven't had a chance to tell you. Parker Steadman invited us to a dinner party he and his wife are giving Saturday night." He did his best to sound light, happy, and hopeful.

A long pause. "The thing is, Doc," said Lew, her voice smaller than usual, "you need to know something about me. Especially after the other night."

Osborne's heart fell to the floor of the car.

"I'm a 'sometime' person and I don't know if that can work for you."

"What does that mean?"

"It means I like doing things with you—fishing, getting together like the other night—but not on a regular basis. I'm not couple material, Doc. I've learned that the hard way. And I just . . . I don't want you to expect too much."

That wasn't quite as bad as he was expecting. "Does that mean you'll go to dinner with me . . . sometimes?"

"Yeah, kinda. . . . The thing is, Doc . . ." She turned her

head to look out the window as she spoke, "we have very different histories here in Loon Lake. Different lives. My little farm? I need that solitude. You have a lifestyle very different from mine, and a social life . . . I can't fit into that. Frankly, I don't want to fit into it."

Osborne thought of the chicken potpie in his refrigerator—he didn't want to fit into it either.

"Are you saying you don't like my friends?"

"Maybe it's a bit of the reverse. But that's not the point. I do want to see you . . . sometimes."

"So you will go fishing with me again."

"Of course. So long as you understand I like to fish with other people, too."

"And you'll be my date Saturday night?"

"I would like to, but that depends entirely on what happens over the next couple days. I'll let you know Friday if that's okay. What time does your motorcycle class start in the morning?"

"Nine."

"How about stopping by the office for coffee around eight? We'll take a look at what Pecore's got before I have it sent down to Wausau."

Osborne pulled up at the back door to the jail and her office. She leaned over to leave a swift kiss on his cheek. "I'm tense, I'm tired, but I feel good about us. 'Night, Doc."

"Good night, Lew." He drove home slowly. Like a wild trout, Lew belonged free. Catch and release worked for fish. Could it work for humans?

eighteen

"Fishing, after all, is still a mind game."

—Roland Martin, champion bass fisherman

"Pa-r-r-d-e-e," Ray's voice boomed through the phone.

"What?" Osborne should never have answered. He was so tired, he hadn't even called Erin to see how the evening with Mark had gone.

"Saturday night, Doc. And you are talking to the Chief Cook and Bottle Washer! I have . . . persuaded—no, I take that back. I have *demonstrated* my talents . . . to the extreme—"

"I think you mean 'extent,'" said Osborne. He knew he was being a little too curt but he was so damn tired.

"Right. To the *extent* that those good people . . . are willing to let yours truly . . . orchestrate . . . the great Loon Lake fish fry . . . right smack in the middle of their million-dollar kitchen. Walleye, American fries, and cole slaw from the Colonel. Doc, this could turn into something, something big."

Osborne could see it now: an evening of Ray's cooking seasoned with raconteurship and sprinkled with birdcalls.

Some things about the guy never changed, but the ladies would love it. Tired as he was, he couldn't resist. "Sounds to me like you're auditioning for a show on that network of theirs—'First You Fish, Then You Fry.'"

Silence for a beat, then Ray said, "Doc, that is not bad. Not bad at all. I need an angle, you know."

"Ray, I'm kidding. A title like that makes it sound like first you fish, then you burn in hell."

"True . . . I'll work on it. Say, need you to help me out in the morning."

Switching subjects, Ray dropped the happy-talk cadence. "I'm not kidding about the fish fry. I'm cooking for the party. Parker said he had invited you. I figure if we're on the lake early tomorrow and Friday, we ought to catch enough to feed twenty—"

"Sorry, Ray, no can do. Lew's got me in town for a crack-of-dawn meeting, then I start that motorcycle class." He yawned.

"Yo-o-okay—I'll think of something."

Osborne knew he would. Worst case, Ray was intimate with a couple private lakes where he could poach plenty walleye in an hour or two. Trophy fish, ones the owners would have stocked, coddled, then wondered, "Where the hell did those go?"

In spite of the fatigue pushing at the back of his eyes, Osborne made the effort to be pleasant. "How's it going with Barbara Walters?"

"Very nicely, thank you. Had a little something interesting happen today, though."

Osborne checked the clock on his chest of drawers. He'd give Ray five. Times like this, he had to remind himself he owed his neighbor. Owed him in ways he could never pay back: for his drive through the blizzard to save Mary Lee's life; and later, for being patient and strong and willing to remind Osborne that the bottle held all the wrong answers. Five minutes of listening was the least he could do.

"You know how our leading lady has been getting these threatening phone calls for the last three weeks—"

"Only three weeks? I was under the impression this had been going on for some time."

"Nope. Started with this tour and always when she's setting up to shoot B-roll: four tournaments, four threatening phone calls." Ray had the lingo down. Rather than interrupt, Osborne assumed "B-roll" had something to do with background material. He could ask later.

"At any rate . . ." Ray paused for effect. "The calls come *only* when she's outdoors, which is why she was able to convince the old man she's being stalked."

"Ah hah," said Osborne. "Do I detect a hint of doubt in your voice?"

"However . . . it so happens that Mr. Steadman didn't make his millions being stupid. He didn't hire just me, he's also lined up this high-tech operation that does contract work for the government to track those calls."

"He mentioned something about that as we were leaving the airport. How's that working?"

"That's what's so interesting. They have a system that works like an electric vacuum cleaner. Locks in on incoming phone signals, selected by monitoring key words, then they can trace those signals. I don't know the details but suffice it to say I think I'm being paid less to protect than to pick up. I offered to wear a fish locator, told Parker it could do the job for a lot less money."

"I'm sure he appreciated that."

"Same principle, though. Parker's had my belt rigged with a device like a pager that makes it possible for the tech guys to get the clearest possible signal. And he made it very clear I was not to say a word about this to his wife."

"She didn't ask why you were wearing—"

"Never noticed. The woman doesn't notice much about other people, Doc. So I'm with her in that sardine can of a car, driving to all these locations where she thinks she wants to shoot this B-roll stuff when, boom, she gets one of these calls."

"While you're in the car?"

"Actually, no. We were standing in a crowd down at the boat landing where they're setting up the tournament headquarters. A couple semis were unloading these big bass boats that are going to be used in the tournament. Man, those are nice boats. Forty thousand bucks for one of those damn things."

"Ray, it's after eleven. Can we talk boats another time?"

"Sorry. So everyone's standing around watching the boats, watching them get outfitted with these Mercury outboards that you wouldn't believe——probably another twenty thousand smackaroos. And they got the music blasting, brats cooking, people talking. All that's happening when Hayden decides to walk over to one of the boats. Now she's standing a good hundred feet from me, talking to one of the mechanics . . . and the call comes in.

"I see her give me this terrified look and she's waving like mad, so I run right over. And I'm looking around like crazy because, according to what I've been told by her, the caller always says he's in the vicinity——that he can see her and blow her head off at any given moment."

"A little unsettling," said Osborne.

"But as I'm running over, I look down at that pager thing. It has an LED light that changes color when it locks in on incoming signals. And . . ."

"And?" Osborne urged.

"Doc, I stood five feet from that woman and nothing happened to that light."

"What do you mean?"

"No . . . call."

"So the phone never even rang?"

"Hell, it was so noisy around there, I could never have heard it if it had. I don't think she could have."

"Ah, she's making it up."

"Parker wants me to keep checking on this, but, yeah. We think she's lying."

"Why on earth?"

"Get attention from the old man is what I think," said Ray. "Trouble in Paradise."

"Good reason for you to keep your nose clean," said Osborne. "That explains why she was all over you at the airport."

"Yep. But I got it under control, Doc."

"I'm sure you do, Ray."

nineteen

"Some of the best fishing is done not in water but in print."

—Sparse Grey Hackle

Osborne paused in the doorway of Lew's office and peered in. The room was sunny and airy, the windows wide open to the morning breezes. Lew was seated at her desk, head down as she concentrated on some paperwork. Sensing his presence, she glanced up and he was happy to see she looked rested. In fact, she looked terrific.

"What smells so good?" he said, walking in.

"Me, of course," said Lew with a spritely tilt of her head. "Just kidding. The lilacs across the street are in full bloom."

"What the hell did you say to Irv Pecore, Chief?" said a woman's voice from behind Osborne. He stepped out of the way of a very amused Marlene. Reaching past him, she thrust two oversized manila envelopes and a larger package wrapped in butcher paper at Lew. "He stomped in here about two minutes ago and threw these on my desk. Hey, look at you, Doc! Whoa, turn a-r-o-und."

He followed orders. The two women checked him over,

eyes starting at the thick-soled motorcycle boots, traveling up his chap-clad legs and ending at the collar of the heavy leather jacket.

"What do you think, Marlene?" Lew's eyes were teasing as she chewed lightly on the end of her pen. She obviously liked what she saw.

"He needs one of those BAD TO THE BONE T-shirts." The switchboard operator chortled. "Doc, you look the part, you really do. Oops, I hear my switchboard, excuse me."

"Yeah, well, let's hope I survive this enterprise," said Osborne, feeling a little silly all of a sudden.

"You'll do fine, Doc." Lew got up from the desk and walked over to the little table in the corner holding the coffee maker. "And since you are doing me a big, big favor, let me at least pour you a cup of coffee."

"By the way," she said as she handed him the cup, "I was looking over some of the documentation they gave me in the meeting the other day. This update on Patty Boy Plyer is pretty darn amazing." Lew looked down to read from the paper she had been studying when he walked in.

"Turns out there is a federal grand jury inquiry into—get this list, now—credit card fraud, narcotics trafficking, loan sharking, and suspected murder of his former partner in an auto theft marketplace tied to the Chicago mob. Criminal record includes arrests on charges of robbery, assault, forgery, loan sharking, narcotics trafficking, and the aforementioned attempted murder. Never convicted of the latter. Has been known to use a number of aliases. . . ."

"What is an auto theft *marketplace*?"

"Chop shop, so he's got the résumé for that biz, that's for sure." She sipped from her coffee. "Loon Lake boy makes good."

She reached for one of the envelopes that Marlene had delivered. "I know we don't have much time so let's see what Pecore managed to dig up." She chuckled, probably

at the thought of Pecore cursing while frantically searching his property room.

Opening the flap, Lew peered inside, then carefully slid
the contents on to her desk: a series of black-and-white
photos, a number of small glassine envelopes similar to
the ones Osborne had used for sending teeth home after a
youngster's extraction, and a two-page typed report. Lew
picked up the report, scanned it briefly, then handed it
over.

"Here, you read it. I can look at it later. Remember
Hugh Eversman? He was a young police officer back
then—looks like he was the investigating officer and
completed this report."

"Whatever happened to Hugh?"

"Married a girl from Milwaukee and went into the computer business. He was long gone when I joined the department. I'm sure he had aspirations beyond being the grunt in
a two-man police department, which is all Loon Lake had
twenty years ago. Not like four of us is much better, but at
least the workload is spread around."

The report was meticulously typed and single-spaced.
The man had done his homework.

"The burlap bag in which the victim was found is our
best piece of evidence," wrote Eversman. "Even my un-
scientific eye can see blood and hair all over it—enough
to convince me that the girl fought hard with whoever the
assailant was. I think we should look real close at Mr. Bud
Thornton, her employer, as a prime suspect. He had a laceration behind his left ear that resembles a bite mark
(photo enclosed). Not being an anthropologist, I don't
know what forensics can do with fingernails, but if they
have markings like you find in fingerprints or on bone, we
might have a chance here as I found what looks like a
good-sized piece of ripped fingernail stuck in the burlap.
Because of that, I got nail clippings from the victim and
from every individual who might have had contact with

the victim in the twenty-four hours before her death. A long shot but worth checking out. The best likelihood of any matches with the evidence on the burlap will be the results of the blood tests from the same group of people."

Osborne looked down the list of people from whom Eversman got samples. They included Thornton and his wife and each of their three children, even the three-year-old. Also a teenaged friend of their oldest daughter who was staying with the family. Then there were samples from Jack Schultz and from Donald Bruckner, proprietor of the little grocery predating the Loon Lake Market. The baby-sitter had been seen in his store earlier in the day.

Eversman went on to recommend an analysis of all the enclosed samples to be compared with anything the coroner might find under the victim's nails or in her mouth.

"Looks like he wasn't able to establish the scene of the crime—only where the body was dumped or hidden. Did Pecore follow up on that?" asked Osborne.

"As far as I can tell, the only thing he followed up on was Happy Hour at Marty's Bar," said Lew. "Check these out."

She slid the photos over to Osborne. The black-and-white enlargements were striking in their clarity. "Someone did a good job on these."

He handed the two-page report back over to Lew. "I'll pick up a copy later if that's okay."

Lew nodded. "I'll meet you at UPS at six tonight and bring everything with me. I want copies of the photos, too. They are good, aren't they. I'll send the originals to Wausau but keep copies for us."

She scanned the report that Osborne had handed back to her. "No wonder the photos are good; Hugh asked Dick Elke to take those."

Dick Elke had been the resident Loon Lake photographer for many years, up until his death. Family reunions, high school graduation photos, and weddings were his specialty. This would have been a little out of his league, but he appeared to have done the best he could in order to shoot as much detail as possible.

The first image staring up at Osborne was like the one they had seen that terrible day, the one that would live forever in Erin's nightmares. The others were shot from different angles. And there were photos of the site where the body was found in spite of signs of trampling from onlookers, who would have included Osborne and the two Brownie Scouts.

Then, two close-ups. Osborne leaned forward in the chair to study the first image. It was a chunk of maxillary bone with seven teeth visible against a background of pine needles, decaying leaves, and decomposing flesh. The teeth were startling in their whiteness on the page.

Stapled to the photo was a typewritten note. "Listen to this," said Osborne. "Animals had gotten to the corpse and Eversman found this section of bone a short distance from the body. He tried to preserve as much as he could, scooping it up with the dirt around it, for testing."

"That may be what we've got here."

Lew opened the larger of the two manila envelopes. Inside was another packet, made of a heavier stock and taped shut. A note was scrawled across the outside. "According to this, Eversman assumes Pecore has requested permission from the family to keep this section of bone as evidence until the investigation was completed. He saved that and soil samples in here," she said.

"Nothing in the file about that," said Osborne. "Shouldn't there be a legal notice of some kind?"

"Nothing, huh? Then he didn't do it," said Lew, shaking her head. "Why am I not surprised—Pecore is such a slob. He probably figured without an open casket who would know.

"And this"—she laid her hand on the bundle in butcher paper—"this is the burlap bag. I'm not going to open these, Doc. Why contaminate what little we may be able to salvage."

Osborne looked at the second close-up. "Lew, this is an excellent shot of Thornton's neck—and a hell of a bite wound. The detail is terrific. The forensic dental guy in Wausau will be very pleased with this."

He looked up at Lew. "I think we've got something here. May I see that report again?" Osborne scanned Eversman's remarks. "Right, here it is. Eversman says that the husband of the family employing the victim, and we know that's Thornton, had a severe laceration of the neck, below his left ear. Thornton alleged that he was adding a new section onto his pier and lost his footing, causing a dock section to gash him in the neck. Also, Hugh notes the man had scratches and cuts on his hands, wrists, and forearms. Gash, hell, that's a bite."

"Based on what Eversman says here, I can't believe Raske and Pecore dropped the case on the word of some young girl," said Osborne. "It'll be darn interesting to see what can be made of all this, Lew."

"So much time has passed, Doc. Think the DNA will be viable?"

"I know it survives in teeth—they're able to use mitochondria. That's as much as I know. How soon does this go down to the crime lab?"

"One of the boys from Wausau is sitting in on a hearing over in Rhinelander this morning. He said he would swing by on his way back—have it down there by noon. He also said they've got a new guy who *loves* working with old evidence. The older the better, he says."

Twenty minutes later, from his chair in the third row, Osborne looked around the college classroom. The motorcycle safety class was more of a mix of ages and sexes than he had expected. Cheryl, who had arrived before him, was seated in the very last row and wearing the same outfit as the night before, with the exception of her T-shirt, which was red. It matched the red in the tattoos on her arms.

The sullen expression was fixed in place. She barely acknowledged Osborne, which he could certainly understand: how uncool to know the old fogey of the class.

At least that's what he thought until a couple in their mid-sixties strolled in. Seated around Osborne were five young men, all in their twenties or thirties. When the instructor asked the students to introduce themselves and say why they were there, the five turned out to be experienced riders who had had traffic citations and were required to take the course before getting their licenses back.

Two young women, both quite a bit taller than Cheryl, looked as nervous as Osborne and said that they had never ridden a motorcycle either. And finally, there were three men in their early fifties, friends, who had decided to take the class together. All three had Harleys on order and were hoping to ride to Sturgis for the national rally in August—they were beginners, too.

Osborne relaxed slightly. He wasn't alone—trepidation was obvious on half the faces in the room. The first hour flew by, and all too soon it was time to get on a motorcycle for the first time. The instructor took them out to the parking lot, where each was assigned a bike.

Osborne's confidence level was rising. Yes, the motorcycle would require using both hands and both feet—but that's exactly what he did fly-fishing. He cast with his right, stripped with his left, and used both feet to balance on slippery rocks. Maybe he *was* cut out for this.

"Dr. Osborne, ready? Got it in neutral?" The instructor, a heavyset man in his early thirties with dark hair and glasses, stood next to Osborne. He waited as Osborne mounted the bike, then cautioned, "You're tall and you have long arms. Be careful to keep your right wrist up or

you'll roll the throttle at the same time as you pull the
hand brake. You don't want to do that."

"Got it." Osborne pulled in the clutch, pushed the ignition button, pressed down with his left foot to put the bike
in first gear, then eased out the clutch as he rolled the
throttle ever so slightly and . . . he was moving! Around
the parking lot he went, then again and again. He shifted
into second gear, then slowed. Finally the instructor
waved him in. Osborne kept his wrist high as he braked
with his right hand and foot, bringing the bike to a smooth
stop.

"Excellent," said the instructor. Osborne swung his leg
off to let the next student try. He realized he was pouring
sweat under the leather jacket. Removing the jacket and
the helmet, he stepped back to watch his classmates.
Cheryl was having problems.

For one thing, she was so short that she had to stretch
to get her feet forward on the pedals. Then, for some reason, she kept killing the engine, which caused the bike to
lurch forward, then quit. Osborne winced.

"Give it more gas," shouted the instructor. "You need
momentum or the bike will fall over." But momentum
was what she didn't want: For all her tough facade,
Cheryl was frightened. The instructor finally got her
going, but she resisted shifting into second gear. As she
put-putted around the track, Osborne's heart lifted. At
least he was doing better than that.

After another hour of instruction in the classroom, the
teacher took them out to the bikes again.

"Okay, folks, this time we practice our turns. I want
you to get the bike into second gear, ride towards me,
slowing as you look through your turn, then up and
around again. Remember, slow as you shift into first and
look through your turn."

That sounded easy enough. Osborne got going into second gear. Coming up on the instructor, he slowed, shifting

into first gear. Off to his left he heard a frightening, grinding noise. Before he could figure out the source of the roar, his bike leapt forward, missing the instructor by a fraction of an inch. Up the driveway it lurched, moving as if under someone else's control. He saw the chain link fence coming at his neck. Dropping his head, he took the chain with his helmet. A stand of birch trees was coming up fast. Too fast.

No, this is not going to happen! Osborne leaned hard to his right. The bike went down and he felt himself land on his right side. The engine cut out. Osborne moved his right arm and elbow gingerly. It had taken the brunt of the fall. Felt okay. No pain, no break. The instructor loomed overhead. "Are you all right?"

He grabbed the bike so Osborne could crawl out from under. "Are you okay?" he asked again as Osborne got to his feet.

"Yes, I am—shaky, but I think I'm okay." Shaky? His entire body was trembling.

"Take a deep breath." Osborne inhaled. "Take another one. You dropped that bike like a pro, you know."

"I did?"

"Yeah, great job. Look, bike's okay, too." The instructor looked hard at him. "You don't have to ride if you don't want to."

"What did I do wrong?"

"You dropped your wrist so when you applied the hand brake, you pulled on the throttle—then you yanked on your clutch but not enough to disengage—that was the noise you heard."

"Well, I won't do that again." Osborne looked across the parking lot to where his fellow students were clustered, all watching, all looking very worried. He reached for the bike, swung his leg over, pulled in the clutch, and pushed the ignition. Wrist up, way up, he took a deep breath and started back across the parking lot. As he neared his classmates, they burst into applause.

Later, as they headed back to the classroom, Cheryl came up behind him. She reached inside her vest for a pack of Camels and shook one out, offering it to him.

"No, thanks," said Osborne, "I don't smoke."

"Paulie," said Cheryl, pausing to light her cigarette, then inhale deeply, "I am so glad you got back on the bike. You know what they say—everyone who rides has one accident. You've had yours, you lucky stiff."

"Cheryl, this isn't easy. I was terrified."

"I am so glad to hear you say that. Me, too."

Back in the classroom, she settled herself into the chair right next to his. Osborne looked down, aware for the first time that something felt strange on his right foot. No wonder—he had peeled back the entire sole of the heavy leather motorcycle boot.

Cheryl saw it, too. "Holy shit," she said, "I can get you a new pair of those cheap. I'll bring 'em tonight when I make my pickup."

No doubt about it, he was her buddy.

twenty

"Always it was to be called a rod. If someone called it a pole, my father looked at him as a sergeant in the United States Marines would look at a recruit who had just called a rifle a gun."

—Norman Maclean, *A River Runs Through It*

Lucy Priebe was waiting outside the UPS customer entrance when Osborne drove up. Leaning against the building, arms crossed and a grim look plastered across her face, she stayed perfectly still as he parked and got out of his car.

"Jackpot, Dr. Osborne," she said, pushing herself away from the building as he walked toward her. "You've got thirteen boxes for Webber Tackle and I'm out of here. My husband is picking me up. By the way, if you need a snack or something, we have a vending machine in the back."

"Thanks, Lucy. I had a sandwich on the way over."

A twenty-minute visit with Erin after the motorcycle class had given him just enough time to down peanut butter on wheat toast with a glass of milk. It hadn't occurred to him earlier that between the time he left the motorcycle class and the time he was due to take over at UPS, he wouldn't have time to drive home and grab a bite. All he'd had during the lunch break at the college was a cup of chicken noodle soup, so when he got to Erin's, he was starved.

Since the kids were playing outside, they had a few minutes to chat. Or at least she talked while he chewed. The good news was that Mark had agreed to see the therapist and they were likely to start marriage counseling the next week.

"Mark hates his job, Dad. He's been afraid to say anything because he thought I would think he's a loser."

"And . . . do you?" Osborne watched his daughter's face carefully, looking for that familiar twitch of annoyance that Mary Lee had used so effectively to convey what she thought versus what she said. But Erin's expression was open and honest.

"Maybe I'm the one who's always wanted to be a lawyer," she said. "I guess that's why I pushed him that way. So, you may find this strange, but we're talking about me going to graduate school and Mark staying home with the kids. You know how he loves to work with his hands. We could buy old houses, and while the kids are in school, he can fix 'em up to rent.

"Dad." She leaned toward him as she spoke, excitement in her eyes. "You know I'd make a damn good lawyer. I would love trial law, I know I would."

"How would you swing that financially?" Osborne drank his milk quickly, checking his watch.

"I can apply for some grants," said Erin, a little wistfully. They both knew grants would hardly generate enough to pay for law school. Mark's parents were hardworking people of modest means so they weren't likely to be able to help either.

"Mark's determined to spend all that money on a motorcycle?"

"Dad, he's getting a fabulous deal. It's not as much as I thought. He's getting a brand-new Harley for like five thousand dollars. I want him to have it. After all the hard work he's done on this house, after these months of torture working for those creeps. The one good thing to come out of that office is this bike deal."

"How's that?"

"Mr. Kasmarek's the one who put Mark in touch with the guy who sells the bikes. He met him up at the casino a couple weeks ago. He's doing some legal work for the guy, too. I think, I'm not sure."

"Mark is?" Osborne tensed.

"No, Chuck, the boss."

"What's the guy's name—the one selling the bikes?" asked Osborne, keeping his tone casual. All that Erin knew was that he had signed on to help Lew police the motorcycle rally. She knew nothing about the chop shop, nothing about the Ecstasy. "I enjoyed the class today— might be interested in buying a bike myself." As he spoke, he hoped she wouldn't notice the shredded sole on his boot. He had pulled off the loose chunks and walked sideways on what was left, hoping to save his socks.

"You're kidding, Dad. That would be so cool. Guy's name is Patrick Baumgartner. That's who Mark wrote the check to anyway. Some woman named Cheryl is going to have it ready for us. We pick it up Sunday."

Osborne set the half-eaten sandwich down on the kitchen table and took his time wiping his mouth with a paper napkin. He had better check with Lew before saying a word to Erin. The last thing she needed was for something to go wrong before the DEA closed in on Patty Boy. But he sure as hell didn't need Erin and Mark walking into a major drug bust either.

"Sunday, huh. Can I go along? I'd love to see what they've got available," said Osborne. The next bite of his sandwich went down the wrong way and Osborne choked.

"Are you okay, Dad?" Erin watched with concern from where she stood at the kitchen sink. "Need the Heimlich?"

"No, I'm fine." Osborne waved her off as he cleared his throat. "About going back to school, hon . . ." Osborne stood up as he wolfed the last quarter of the sandwich, washing it down with a huge gulp of milk.

"Don't talk with your mouth full, Dad."

"If you and Mark are able to work things out, don't let the money be a problem. I'll help you with that." He put his arm across his daughter's shoulders and pulled her close. "Now don't you two go without me Sunday— okay?"

"Sure, that'll be fun." She walked him toward the front door. "I can't believe you're doing this, Dad," she said. "That Lew person has really changed your life. Maybe . . ." Erin stopped at the top of the stairs leading down from the big yellow Victorian house. She cut her eyes sideways, giving him a sly look. "Maybe you ought to change hers."

"Now what does that mean?" He faked a grimace to cover his embarrassment.

"You know what that means, Dad." She grinned and sent him off with a wave.

Osborne got into the car thinking how happy she looked. More than anything in the world, he wanted to keep her that way.

He called the police department immediately after checking the shipment for Webber Tackle. "Thirteen boxes, Lew. Four rattle when shaken and they've all been shipped down from different locations in Canada. Overnight deliveries. Just what your DEA agents have been expecting."

"Is there room in that loading area for my cruiser?"

Osborne looked over his shoulder into the dark area behind him. "Yep, plenty."

"Good. Have the door up and close it the second I'm inside." She arrived within five minutes.

At the sight of the boxes, Lew's first reaction was consternation. "The Canadian angle complicates this," she said. "I found out today that the reason the DEA hasn't moved on Patty Boy sooner is they are in a major dispute with U.S. Customs over who has jurisdiction. Until they sort that out, neither agency can act.

"It's all politics," she said as she studied the boxes stacked one on top of the other in the delivery bay. "On the other hand, when it comes to the Loon Lake Police Department, the fact is that Patrick Baumgartner and his Webber Tackle operation are located right here—no question who has jurisdiction."

"Lewellyn, you cannot take this on alone."

"If it were any other weekend but this, I would not hesitate to move on that goombah as long as I had backup from Oneida and Vilas County, but I've got every extra officer of theirs already assigned to crowd control." At the look on Osborne's face, she raised both hands. "Don't worry. I'm taking orders—surveillance only. Just pray the DEA and Customs guys get their acts in order before anyone gets hurt.

"Speaking of which, we better hurry. What do we have? Thirty, forty minutes before they pick these up? Let's open a couple before she gets here."

"Can we do that without their knowing?"

"Probably not. We'll make it look like they arrived damaged and you repacked the best you could."

And so they selected two boxes to open: one that rattled, another that was quite heavy. Lew sliced through the packing tape on the first box. Inside were six small Styrofoam packets wedged tightly together. She dumped out the packets, then stomped on one end of the outer box.

Repacked, it would look like it had been squashed under something heavy.

The Styrofoam units were taped shut. Dropping to her knees, Lew slit the tape across the top of one and carefully pried it open. Antique fishing lures, several in small boxes, were wrapped in plastic and packed tight inside. Lew removed the bubble wrap from around one box and read from the lid: "A Musky Wizard Minnow . . . and the dealer tag says it's from the early nineteen hundreds." She sat back on her heels as she spoke.

"This is an old Pflueger lure—unused and in the original box, too," she said. "I'll bet that's worth a couple hundred bucks." Her fingers worked opened the small faded box with the same delicate touch she used to tie on a trout fly. She held the black lure with its treble hooks and propellers out for Osborne to examine. "You know it's old when it has glass eyes."

She reached for another packet. Through the plastic, Osborne could see the lure was mottled with red-and-green spots against a cream background. Lew undid the bubble wrap. "Hey, a Chippewa Skimmer! They made these down in Stevens Point."

"How do you know all this, Lew?" said Osborne, examining the colorful lure.

"My uncle ran a sporting goods store in Minocqua. He loved old lures and would tell me about them while we were out fishing. Jeez, Doc, look at all these metal spoons. . . . Oh, gosh, and this!"

She held out a small box so he could see its contents. The lure was an exquisite pale yellow with four treble hooks so shiny they sparkled under the fluorescent lighting in the dingy room. "This looks like it's in perfect condition," said Lew. She checked the cover of the box: "Night Radiant Moonlight Bait #1000. Is this gorgeous? Ooh, would I love to have one of these, Doc."

Osborne pointed to a small white sticker on the side of the box.

"Ouch," said Lew, "two thousand five hundred dollars. I'll pass." She sat back on her heels. "I guess these lures explain the rattles, particularly those metal spoons. Still, won't hurt to check."

Using the punch on her knife, she bored into the top section of the Styrofoam container. She looked in, then handed it over to Osborne. It had a curious weight to it and he could see why: The interior was packed with pills. The Styrofoam, which appeared thick from the outside, was in fact only a thin layer. Hundreds, maybe thousands, of pills were packed around the antique lures—no wonder the box rattled.

Lew checked her watch. "Fifteen minutes left, better hurry." The second box was longer than the first and much heavier. She sliced through the packing tape, folded back the flaps, and carefully removed a top layer of Styrofoam sheeting. Beneath the sheeting, set into Styrofoam casings like those used to pack computers, were three rod tubes, each cushioned in bubble wrap. Lew reached for one.

The wrapping came off easily to expose the tube and a label banded to its cuff. Lew scanned the tiny print, then looked up, stunned. "I don't believe it, Doc. This is a Garrison bamboo fly rod." She unscrewed the top of the tube. "Not the original tube, however—the rod sits too low. See? The original tube would have been made to fit perfectly.

Let's see if this is what it says it is." She pulled out the rod sack, undid its tie, then slipped out the butt section. "Ralph has spent a lot of time instructing me on how to tell a Garrison rod," she said softly.

"I'm sure he has," said Osborne. She gave him a sharp look.

Even Osborne had heard of Garrison fly rods, mainly

because Ralph Kendall, the pain-in-the-butt owner of Loon Lake's only fly-fishing shop, never let a customer out the door without a reminder that he owned one. That was another thing Osborne disliked about Ralph, in addition to his pretentious attitude toward fly-fishing and his extreme attentiveness to Lew.

"This honey yellow bamboo and the chocolate brown silk marking these ferrules are distinctive to Garrison," said Lew as she examined the rod section. "Impossible to fake. And here, at the butt of the shaft—see?" She held it toward Osborne. The rod maker's name and other markings were clearly visible. "Value?" she answered before he could ask. "Anywhere from twelve to twenty thousand smackaroos, Doc."

"And Ralph let you use his?" Osborne's eyes widened.

"Heavens, no. But I would love to someday. They say even the worst caster can drop a dry fly seventy feet with a rod like this. To cast that distance and still be able to drop the fly with exquisite delicacy, tail pointed downstream? I'll tell you, that's the ultimate in fly-fishing, Doc. Perfect imitation of an insect in flight upstream. Jeez, just imagine what it must be like to cast with a rod like this. . . ."

Her voice had dropped to a whisper. Fingers cupped carefully around the mouth of the tube, she slipped the rod back into the safety of its container, rewrapped the tube in its plastic, and set it back into the casing. She tipped up the edge of the box.

"I wonder . . . this box is pretty damn heavy for holding lightweight fly rods."

Together, wedging their fingers down the sides, they discovered that the Styrofoam bed holding the rods was only five inches deep. Hooking their fingers under it, they pulled up and out.

Chrome gleamed beneath. Lots of chrome. Tagged with original labels, too, as if it had come right off a dealer's shelves or out of a Harley-Davidson warehouse: six chrome luggage racks, two sets of Screamin' Eagle Performance Mufflers, and a bundle of chrome fork sliders.

"I see another layer down there," said Osborne.

"Ssh," said Lew, looking up. "I hear something."

Osborne stood up and looked out the window. "Cheryl's here—parking."

"You keep her busy while I get this box in order," said Lew.

"Paulie! Hey you!" Cheryl hopped down from her van and waved to Osborne as he hurried out the entrance toward her. She slid back the side door and stuck her head inside while hollering, "Where's your bike? I got a surprise." As he approached the van, determined to keep her there as long as possible, Cheryl turned, a bright smile creasing her weathered face.

"I had to rush but I think I got the right size." She held out a pair of motorcycle boots, turning them so he could see the chrome eagle on each heel.

"Cheryl, those look expensive. You don't need to do this."

"But that's not all, man. Check this out."

She set the boots down and walked to the back of the van. Pulling open the doors, she grabbed an open cardboard box and set it down on the driveway. She stepped back with a pleased look on her face. Chrome spirals caught the late-day sunshine.

"Thunderstar Custom Wheels, man. Nine hundred bucks retail, but I get 'em for free—so don't you worry." She had seen the look of protest on his face. "Where's your bike? Let's see if they're the right diameter."

The bike was parked inside the building, right in front of Lew's cruiser.

"Oh, Cheryl, I'm sorry. It's in my garage at home. I had a friend ride it over this morning. You saw me today, I'm sure as heck not ready to ride that big bike." Osborne paused, then said, "Cheryl . . . why are you giving me all this?"

"You deserve it, man, for getting back on that bike. I wouldn't have, you know. I would've freaked. And," she added, looking up at him, "I think you're class. I like you."

It dawned on Osborne that behind that churlish, tough façade was a sweet, likable young woman. "Well, Cheryl," he smiled, "I like you, too. Thank you."

The moment embarrassed her and her voice turned gruff. "Now you take these with you and check 'em out, okay? Didn't you say you have a Dyna Wide Glide?"

"No, an Electra Glide Classic."

"Oh, shit, then you need a different wheel size." Cheryl's face fell.

But as quickly as it had fallen, it brightened again. "Hey, man, I got an idea. You come to the party we're having, kind of a big swap meet on Sunday. Know where Hagen Road is? You ride that new bike out there and I'll see you get outfitted. I'll give you directions in class tomorrow."

Minutes later, he ushered her into the UPS customer service area. At the sight of the two damaged boxes, a funny look crossed Cheryl's face. Osborne could swear she looked frightened. She reached into a pocket of her vest and pulled out a cell phone.

"Excuse me, I'll be right back—I need to check and see how they want me to file the damage report." Cheryl stepped back outside to make her call. It was obvious she wanted privacy.

When she entered again, she looked shaky. "Can you tell me what happened?" She held the phone in her hand in such a way that Osborne assumed someone else was listening.

"We had a problem with the conveyor belt here when the last truck unloaded. The safety broke and a number of boxes piled one on the other. I used packing tape to secure the outside of these," said Osborne. "I didn't see any damage beyond what you see on the outside. I sure hope nothing too valuable was crushed."

"So you put this tape on here? Did you check inside the boxes?"

"I'm sorry, Cheryl, I just didn't have the time. But I can assure you that any damage is fully insured according to the shipping agreement." The color came back into her face as he spoke.

"Anyone else handle these boxes?"

"I'm the only one working tonight," said Osborne. "I usually have someone here to help me but she asked for the night off—her husband is ill. That's where the problem started. Another pair of hands and I could have prevented those boxes from piling off like that."

When Cheryl had driven off with her thirteen boxes, which barely fit into the van, he hurried back into Lucy's small office. Lew was waiting.

"Did you hear her invite me out to a party on Sunday?" said Osborne.

"I did. That's good, Doc. Ray called today, too. He wanted us to know he heard the announcement on *Help Your Neighbor.* They read an ad saying bikes and boats for sale due to an out-of-state move. The address they gave is the same one we just saw on all those boxes—Webber Tackle on Hagen Road and the time is noon to six."

"Lew, that's where Erin and Mark are due to pick up his new motorcycle."

"Hmm," Lew snorted. "Why am I not surprised? When did you hear that?"

"On my way over here."

"I hope you didn't say anything. Does Erin know about this investigation?"

"Absolutely not. She thinks I'm helping you with crowd control during the motorcycle rally."

"Good. I need to think about this."

"Lew. . . ."

"I know, I know, we have to keep them out of there."

According to the agreement with Lucy, Osborne was required to stay at UPS until eight. Lew had to get back to the jail to take care of some frisky early arrivals for the fishing tournament, which was just as well since he was dead tired. But it wasn't until he was on his way home that he realized he had forgotten to mention that he'd dropped his bike.

He was reliving that experience as he pulled into his driveway. Mike leaped at the gate as he approached, so excited and happy to see him. Osborne felt bad about that. He hated leaving the dog alone for a full day. Letting him in through the back door, Osborne smelled the surprise before he saw the note on the door: homemade lasagna and Italian bread warming in the oven.

A place had been laid for him at his kitchen table. My god, the woman was invading his cabinets! Saran Wrap covered a bowl of green salad. And a glass of red wine had been poured, the bottle set nearby with the cork lying beside it. Obviously she had no clue he was a recovering alcoholic. At least he had one secret from her. Jeez.

Osborne picked up the wineglass and walked over to the kitchen sink. He corked the bottle and put in the refrigerator. He could return it tomorrow—after he locked his doors. A light blinked on his answering machine. Two messages, the first from Brenda, of course. The sound of her voice so chilled the air that he inadvertently canceled her message before she had finished. Oh well, enough was enough, dammit.

"A-a-ny chance you can help me out tomorrow morning, Doc?" Ray's voice was next. "I'm taking the girls out at six and we'll be wrapped by eight. I really need you there; I think I've convinced them to do some B-roll at my place."

Osborne picked up the phone and left a message for Ray. Yes, indeed, he would be there. A perfect opportunity to ask Edith a few questions. He just hoped she wouldn't find it too disturbing.

Half an hour later, as he slipped under the quilt, he remembered the boots in his back seat. Motorcycle boots, chrome wheels, and homemade lasagna—could this be one and the same problem? Oh, dear God, he hoped not.

twenty-one

"There is no substitute for fishing sense, and if a man doesn't have it, verily, he may cast like an angel and still use his creel largely to transport sandwiches and beer."

—Robert Traver, *Trout Madness*

Osborne woke just as the alarm went off. He fed Mike, showered, and laid out his motorcycle leathers. On a hunch, he skipped breakfast. Instead, he reached for the St. Croix spinning rod, heavier than his fly rig and his favorite for bass, threw a couple bass poppers in the smaller of his two tackle boxes, and ambled out the door to the deck.

Leaving Mike in the yard, he decided to take the lake path over to Ray's. As he headed down the hill toward the shoreline, a stiff breeze off the water felt cool against his face. Ray would be pleased: "West is best," he liked to preach when persuading a nervous client to fish on a windy day. This might be just a breeze, but it had promise.

Two loons cruised toward the center of the lake. Squirrels chucked as they scuttled across the pine boughs over his head. Felt like a good day. Even Henry and Mollie were out early, feet working the paddleboat as they inched along about fifty feet out from shore. They waved and Osborne waved back. Silence—no one wanted to break the spell.

His hunch was right: An aroma of bacon frying filled the air around Ray's place. The Mini Rover was parked beside Ray's pickup and the morning sun sparkled off the neon muskie welcoming guests to the house trailer. Osborne stopped to examine the lurid fish. He could swear Ray had glued on some sequins.

"Hey, old man." Ray waved a spatula at him as he opened the screen door. "Grab some coffee."

Hayden acknowledged his arrival with a quick nod from where she sat at the kitchen table sorting through a stack of photos. Ray made a few extra bucks shooting winter scenes for a local calendar printer and it appeared he was holding her hostage to his art form. As Osborne poured himself a cup of coffee, he could hear Hayden making cooing noises.

He had to admit she had presence. With her long legs, large head, and solid figure, she seemed to occupy a good half of the table. Still wearing camo, too, although the morning's featured garment was a tight-fitting T-shirt that emphasized the fact she did not believe in underwear, at least on the upper level. And while she had opted for simplicity when it came to her shorts—they were plain khaki—her face was pure Kabuki. Osborne couldn't recall the last time he'd seen a woman wear so much makeup so early in the morning. Poor fish, they'd die of fright before they were hooked.

It wasn't until he turned around with a full mug of coffee in his hand that he realized someone else was in the room. The girl with grave eyes: Edith. She sat against the far wall, hunkered down behind Hayden as if trying to fade into the background. Hair pulled back from her face, she wore no makeup whatsoever. Once again Osborne was struck by the supplicant look on her face: the look of someone too anxious to please, too quick to apologize, too vulnerable.

He took the chair next to Edith. As Hayden chattered at Ray, Osborne grasped that the order of the morning was to give her a private lesson in bass fishing. "We're going out in your boat, Ray?" asked Osborne as a steaming platter of scrambled eggs, crisp bacon, and triangles of buttery toast was handed around.

"Homemade thimbleberry jelly from the good nuns at St. Mary's," said Ray, plopping down an open jelly jar. "Berries from up around Lake Superior—picked 'em myself. Nope, I borrowed the pontoon from Henry and Mollie, Doc. They're tickled pink that we've got a TV star on Loon Lake."

"Ah," said Osborne. "Wondered why they were out together and so early."

"The pontoon boat gives us a steadier platform for taping, Dr. Osborne. . . . May I call you 'Doc'?" said Hayden, waving her fork. She pointed the fork at Edith. "You got the equipment ready, right?" Edith responded to the brusque directive with a gentle smile.

"Doesn't your cameraman do that kind of thing?" said Osborne, feeling an inexplicable urge to defend Edith.

"Rob's shooting Parker this morning. Big get-together with all the pro-am teams as they start the qualifying rounds. No, Edith shoots B-roll." She could have said "Edith does all the work" and Osborne would have believed her. Jeez, the woman was irritating.

"Oh." Osborne took a sip of his coffee.

"Listen up, folks—I have a ma-a-a-velous idea," said Ray, bringing his own plate to the table and sitting down with a look of sublime satisfaction on his face, obviously convinced everyone would be as pleased as he was with his brilliance. "I will . . . call the publisher . . . of the *Loon*

Lake Daily News and ask him to send a reporter out to do a feature story on . . . our expedition this morning."

"Right now?" said Hayden. "Isn't it a little early?"

"When we get back with our catch. It's just doggone high time they do something on our Edith here. Think about it. We've never had a Loon Lake girl hit the big time in TV. Here she is shooting B-roll on little old Loon Lake. I'll twist that jabone's arm, doncha know. I guarantee we'll get front page."

Ray crunched a piece of bacon as he dug into his pile of eggs, blissfully unaware of the silence in the room.

"Edith?" Hayden looked like she'd swallowed a pickle whole.

"Excuse me, everyone," said Edith, jumping to her feet. "I'm going down to the boat and get set up. Thank you for the thought, Ray, but I think maybe we should do that another time, okay?"

She darted a look at everyone around the table as if needing permission to leave. Again something in her expression stirred Osborne. Was it her eyes? Avoiding contact, betraying the look on her face. Black around the edges.

He shuffled his chair up to the table so she could pass. As she did, she laid a hand on his shoulder. He could have been mistaken but he thought he felt a squeeze. It was slight but a squeeze nevertheless.

When she was out the door, he looked over at Hayden, who sat with her arms crossed, a pout on her face. It might be wise to change the subject, decided Osborne, maybe generate a little sympathy for a change? Not that he expected Hayden would understand. Some people led charmed lives.

Sitting forward in his chair, elbows on the table, Osborne assumed the authoritative tone he had learned to use when informing a patient they needed teeth extracted and dentures.

"Is Edith experiencing any difficulties with her return to the area? I believe this is her first time back in years."

"Not that I'm aware of," said Hayden, looking uninterested. "Why? She saw her sisters last night and seemed okay with that. Why do you ask?"

"Well, the circumstances of her father's death, you know."

"Oh . . . right." A sharp look flashed across Hayden's face. Her features tightened and she sat up a little straighter. Ray busied himself picking up plates. "Fill me in on the details, Dr. Osborne. Edith says very little. I've always wanted to know more."

"I'll know more in a few days, Hayden. Our local police chief, Lewellyn Ferris, has just reopened the case. Since I have a smidgen of forensic experience from my student days when I served in the Korean War, she's asked me to consult. The family doesn't know this yet, so I'm speaking to you in confidence."

"I'll respect that," said Hayden.

"Edith's father, Jack Schultz, committed suicide. He had been accused of murdering a young girl who was baby-sitting for a family up from Chicago." Osborne swiveled in his chair and pointed toward Ray's driveway. "They found the victim right up the road there—my younger daughter and a friend discovered the body."

"*Your* daughter found the body?" said Hayden, sounding more surprised by that coincidence than by the fact the murder may have occurred so close to where they were sitting at the moment.

"A tragedy for Edith's family. I don't know that anyone ever heard Jack's side of the story aside from what the authorities said at the time. It all happened so fast. Some people feel he may have been falsely accused. I'm one of them. So I'm planning to ask her—"

"Oh, no, I would not do that, Dr. Osborne. Definitely not. You see, one condition of her employment with us is that we not bring up the subject of her background, of her family."

"How's that?" said Osborne, feeling himself start to vibrate with irritation. What the hell made this woman think she could give *him* orders?

"Edith came to us two years ago with an excellent résumé—except for the previous year. She was honest, she told us she had been hospitalized with severe depression and other emotional problems. We agreed to hire her on the condition that she continue with her medications and her therapy. We also mutually agreed not to discuss any family history or issues unless we were in the presence of one of the psychiatrists treating her."

"That was very good of you to be so understanding."

"Selfish, really," said Hayden with an arch smile. "Parker insisted we hire Edith because of her years of experience with the competition—you know, the other outdoor sports channels. But please, we have so much on the line with this new Fishing Channel, I cannot risk having her upset or disturbed right now. She's our nuts and bolts, Doc. Without her, nothing happens."

"So you're saying I should wait until the tournament series is completed."

"Oh, at least. Frankly, I think you should drop any thought of reopening those horrible emotional wounds. Don't you?"

"Hayden," Ray interrupted, "we're ready to go. Do you need to use the rest room? No facilities on board."

Ray was busy on the pontoon stowing away fishing gear, more coffee and soft drinks. Edith had been fiddling with her videocam and battery pack. Then, deciding she needed extra batteries, she ran back up to the Mini Rover. Osborne, meanwhile, lingered on the dock. He would be the last to board and untie the boat.

In her heavy-footed way, Hayden came charging down the path from the trailer. Behind her by about fifty feet came Edith. Osborne watched as Hayden jumped onto the pontoon, forcing it, even with Ray on the opposite end, to swoon under her weight.

"Get *that* on tape," he whispered with a grin as Edith passed by. And for the first time since he had seen her at the airport, Edith's eyes lit up. She turned aside to give him a smile. That smile and the look in her eye told Osborne everything he needed to know.

"Oop, oop," said Ray, coaching Hayden, who had just cast out over a rock bar. He had her using a Ninja Jig tipped with a small plastic crawfish. "Let that jig fall right down the side of that big boulder you see. When it hits the next shelf of rock, let it sit for just a second, then let it fall down to the next rock. As soon as you pull that jig off the shelf is when you'll get hit."

He stepped back and adjusted his fishing hat against the sun. Hayden cast again. She was not a graceful woman and the lure thunked into the water without gaining much distance. Edith was taping, back to the morning sun. Osborne sat on a padded bench, feet up and another cup of coffee in hand. The light was crisp and the lake could not have been lovelier. He said a quick Hail Mary in gratitude. He took nothing for granted these days.

"How do I know when I have a bite?" asked Hayden.

"What do you mean?" said Ray. "Don't you fish with Parker? Haven't you caught a fish before?"

"Actually," Hayden laughed, "not if I can help it. I'm anchor talent, not a fishing pro."

Anchor talent, huh. Osborne could think of another spin for that phrase. He banished the thought; too nice a day to be so mean-spirited.

"Just flip the jig against the rocks and hold the rod perfectly still as the bait falls. When one bites, you'll know it. No, stay by the rocks, Hayden; you lose the rocks, you lose the fish."

An eagle spun high, high overhead, then dove. The women gasped. "Ray taught him how to do that," said Osborne.

"Oh sure," said Hayden.

"I'm only half-kidding. Most of us who've fished for years can sight fish pretty darn well—but Ray's got the eye of an eagle, he can see fish you never knew were there."

"Damn," said Hayden as her next cast plopped short again.

"Okay, Hayden," said Ray, "relax, don't work so hard. I want you to learn to think like a bass. Here's an assignment for when you're back in the city. Rent some snorkel gear, then jump in a pool and have someone reel lures over your head. . . ."

"Forget that, you're putting me on."

"I kid you not," said Ray. "The pros do it."

"Screw the pros. I'm getting too much sun."

Hayden wiped the sweat from her forehead, then set down the rod and took a seat under the pontoon's awning. Osborne poured her a mug of coffee as Edith turned off the camera. Putting her feet up on the opposite bench, Hayden leaned back. She gazed across the lake at the shoreline that ran along Osborne and Ray's property. To the north of Ray's trailer, a small orange-yellow cottage blazed with light from the morning sun.

"That's one of the Greystone Lodge cabins, isn't it?" said Hayden.

"Yep," said Ray. He bent down to reach for another lure in his tackle box and let his foot nudge Osborne's. "When were you there?"

"Never," said Hayden. "I just heard about it. You know, from friends when I was growing up."

"Yep," said Ray, "pretty well known hereabouts. Edith, your turn." He held out the spinning rod that Hayden had set down.

"Oh, no," Edith protested.

"Edith," said Ray, "did I ever tell you that when I was just seven, eight years old, your father showed me some of the best honey holes for bass? I'm still fishing 'em today. Actually"—Ray looked over at Osborne—"I think old Bert and Harold are fishing 'em."

"No," said Edith, "he did? I used to fish with my dad a lot."

Hayden turned away to look hard at Osborne. Her eyes drilled his: Hadn't Ray gotten the message?

"Yeah," said Ray, "my dad was a surgeon, never had time to fish. Didn't really like it. I learned from a lot of folks, but your father was a re-e-al fisherman. I remember he'd be out before dawn and long after dark. Here—" Ray pushed the rod at her. "Give it a try."

"Oh, okay then." Edith stood up. "Would you mind terribly if I used Dr. Osborne's instead. His is just like the one my dad gave me." As she picked up Osborne's rod, he opened his tackle box.

"I like a popper," she said as she reached for a lure designed to look like a jumping insect on the surface of the water. Osborne was pleased; he always used a popper himself. "And a longer pole like this gives me more whip."

She stepped over to the edge of the pontoon and cast in the direction of the rock bar. "Hayden, watch this now," said Ray. "See how that popper kind of gurgles on the surface . . . watch the water. . . ." The surface was perfectly still.

Edith cast again. On the third cast—boom! The lake exploded.

Osborne's heart leapt with the fish: a perfect smallmouth moment. These few seconds always made him wonder why he didn't fish smallmouth every time.

"Hey!" shouted Ray, maneuvering the pontoon as the line went taut. Edith stood feet apart as instinct took over.

She set the hook. "Holy cow, Edith," said Ray, "you play that fish like *you* should be in the tournament."

"You got ten-pound mono on this, right?" she called to Osborne. "'Cause this is one nice fish. Y'know, I forgot how much fun this is!" Forget the tournament—from the look on her face, one smallmouth was prize enough.

The water boiled again, then exploded as the bass caught air. Edith's hands started to shake. "He's running, he's running into the rocks." Her hands shook harder. Suddenly the fish was heading toward the boat. Edith played the line, reeling in, letting it run, then in again.

"You got it," said Osborne, sensing the fish had tired. "Easy, easy." He bent over the side of the pontoon, net at the ready. One scoop and he was in.

"Jeez, Edith, you got a beauty. Four pounds easy. Excuse me, Doc." Ray had stepped on Osborne's foot as he leaned back to get a good angle with the disposable camera. "Photo op."

It was a new Edith smiling wide for the camera as she held the bass by its lower lip. Ray slipped the smallmouth back into the water. "See you again, big boy."

But by the time Ray stood up and reached to give Edith a big squeeze around the shoulders, her self-deprecating demeanor had returned. She shrugged off his congratulations. "I shouldn't have taken so long."

"Why did your hands shake so much? That's weird," said Hayden as Ray gunned the pontoon toward shore. She hadn't budged from her seat during all the excitement.

"Hey, babe," said Ray, "we're all like that when we hook a good one. The day your hands stop shaking is the day you put the rod down."

• • •

As they neared the dock, Osborne checked his watch. Ray had kept his word. Plenty of time to make the motorcycle class.

"Hayden," said Ray as he unloaded their gear from the boat, "would you like to take a walk over to Greystone while I do this?"

"No." Her answer was so curt, it put an end to all conversation for a moment. Finally, she offered to help Edith carry some of the video equipment up to their car.

When they were out of earshot, Ray said in a low voice, "I thought it might be interesting to push a few buttons."

"You're likely to end up short a paycheck, bud."

"I don't think so. Parker writes the checks. From where she's had me take her in the last couple days, I think she knows more about this area than she admits to, Doc."

"She went to camp up in Eagle River."

"No, I don't think so. I asked about that and she can't even remember the name of it. Think how many campers come back here for reunions. They don't forget the name of the place where they had the best summers of their childhood. But she sure recognized Greystone. In fact, I never even had to give her directions to my place. When I said Loon Lake Road, she knew right where to go."

Forty minutes later, Osborne walked into the motorcycle class. Each time he practiced on the small bike, he concentrated on keeping his wrist high. By the time the class ended at five-thirty, he was feeling confident enough to tackle the big Harley. He called Lew to see if she would have the time to stand by in case he needed help.

"Of course, Doc. I'll meet you at UPS. Any reaction from your girlfriend on those opened boxes?"

Osborne ignored her teasing. "Didn't you get my message?"

"Doc, I just walked in. I've been dealing with mischief

all day. Had a bar fight over in Tomahawk—two jabones from the St. Croix Loons biker club decided to take on a history professor and a plastic surgeon who rode up from Oshkosh."

"Who won?"

"Before I intervened, the professor and the surgeon had the advantage. One of the Loons had a broken nose. I cited every one of 'em, including the crowd watching. Back to your friend, Doc. I have a stack of messages here. . . ."

"I called in around ten this morning—Cheryl didn't show up for class."

"Ouch."

twenty-two

"Fishing is a world created apart from all others, and inside it are special worlds of their own—one is fishing big fish in small water where there is not enough world and water to accommodate a fish, and the willows on the side of the creek are against the fisherman."

—Norman Maclean

Osborne hurried into the UPS station, where Lucy was busy with one last-minute customer. She looked markedly happier than she had the day before.

"Easy night," she said, glancing up as he walked in. "Not a single delivery for Webber Tackle. Nothing en route for next week either, not even ground. I checked the computer and Chicago double-checked for me. First time in months we haven't had at least one shipment heading in their direction."

"That's pretty odd, isn't it?"

"I think so. But I must say, I'm relieved."

As she was speaking, Osborne heard the soft thunder of a motorcycle. He looked out the window to see Lew pulling into the parking lot on the white police bike. She headed for an open bay, eased the bike in, and parked it next to the big black-and-green Harley. While Osborne lowered the bay doors, she took off her helmet and leather jacket and hung them over the bike. She looked sunburned and tired.

"A little frisky out there, huh?" said Osborne as she walked up.

He had the urge to kiss her but he knew better. The working Lewellyn Ferris was very different from the one in or on water. She had said she was a "sometime" person and she meant it. At this point, he was just hoping that "sometime" came again someday—and he couldn't be sure it would.

Lucy hung around until seven, completing paperwork. "No reason to keep the shop open," she said finally. Osborne and Lew agreed.

Lew made one last call to check in with the switchboard. Things were quiet. "Friday night fish fry—they're filling their faces," she said. "They won't start to party for another couple hours, then watch: All hell will break loose. The good news is Lincoln County sent over six officers to help out this weekend."

"You mean with the motorcycle crowd over in Tomahawk?"

"I mean with everyone, Doc. The bass boys are holding their own, believe me. So let's get you out on the road while it's quiet."

The big Harley was surprisingly stable. Two passes around the block and he felt more comfortable than he had all day on the much smaller Yamaha. Lew motioned to him to follow her out into the traffic along Loon Lake's busiest street. Osborne gulped and followed. But the bike responded nicely, even through slow, short turns.

"You're a natural, Doc," said Lew with a satisfied smile at the gas station where they had stopped for her to fill up. His tank was full.

"Okay, let's head out County C to Hagen Road. I want you to feel familiar with the territory. Then we'll leave the bike at your place and I'll give you a ride back here for your car."

The ride on the highway was just what he needed. Before Osborne knew it, he had shifted up to fifth gear. He felt like he was flying but in control. It helped that Lew kept their speed at a very pleasant 55 mph.

He could do this! As his confidence soared, he relaxed into the ride. Lew's left turn signal went on about a quarter mile before Hagen Road. He slowed and followed her onto a two-lane blacktop road that led back past several small houses. Then the blacktop gave way to gravel. Lew stopped where the gravel started and waved Osborne forward so they could talk. They turned off their ignitions.

"I checked the *Gazetteer*," she said, "and you can get to Willow Creek on foot if you go about a quarter mile down this gravel road and go in off to the right. This is state land up to Patty Boy's property line so you have every right to be here and in the creek bed.

"Thing is, though, I don't want you riding on gravel, Doc. You're doing fine right now but gravel is dangerous—so park here and walk the rest of the way."

"Will they be aware of what I'm doing?"

"I seriously doubt it. That's why you're on a bike. When people come up for the Tomahawk Rally, they come because they love to ride the back roads like these. So you fit right in. Even if Patty Boy's people are patrolling, they'll be looking for cars—and cops."

"Not old fogeys on way too expensive bikes getting lost on back roads."

"You got it. All I want is for you to get a good look at what's happening over there tomorrow morning. Since their cameras are aimed at the road and access to the house from the front and the sides, you'll be out of range and not likely to be seen from inside the house. At least I hope not. And do not use binoculars; that would be a red flag."

"So you want me to check out who's there. Number of cars, motorcycles, that kind of thing."

"Right. Once we have an idea of how many people are involved, the DEA will take it from there. I hope anyway. As of this morning, they were still arguing with Customs over who's in charge."

"When do you want me to start?"

"Midmorning when the place is likely to be humming. If they're expecting as many bikers as I think they are on Sunday, they should be setting up to do a lot of business. The most important thing I can say, Doc, is don't take any chances. Busting these guys is not on the agenda."

"Observe and leave."

"Right."

At Osborne's garage, Lew helped him turn his bike around to face out so he could manage easily in the morning. Before they left the garage, he took her by the elbow and leaned down to brush her lips lightly. She took the kiss with a faint smile but he could see she was preoccupied.

"Rain check—for when this is all over and done?" she said, patting his arm. "I'm just, I'm too wired right now, Doc."

"I know," he said. "What about tomorrow night? Any chance you can make that dinner party at the Steadmans'?"

She shook her head. "Sorry, I can't give you an answer yet. I have to see how things go tomorrow. I promise to let you know as soon as I can."

He finished the leftovers from Brenda's lasagna, then sat out on his deck in the warm darkness, listening to the owl that owned his land. He'd had a phone message from Ray, his voice excited, saying that tomorrow's party had grown to thirty people, including someone Osborne had a personal interest in.

"Bruce Duffy, Doc, old Bert and Harold's boss. He's ranked Number One right now. Maybe that's why the boys picked up those leech traps. I left a message for Lew that she might want to have Roger on the lookout Saturday and Sunday. After that parade Sunday morning, somebody's gonna need to find some big fish fast."

Osborne had forgotten about the parade. Following the qualifying rounds, the parade was the big kickoff for the tournament. Boats, bands, and lots of people. Not like Lew needed more work.

He had one other message, this one from Erin. She was spending the weekend with the kids and Mark out at the hunting shack and would give him a call Sunday morning. She hadn't forgotten he wanted to go along when they picked up Mark's bike.

At least he had no chatty message from Brenda, thank the Lord.

Saturday morning Osborne was up early. He tried to reach Ray but no one answered. He tried Lew at her office, but she had just left for Tomahawk. He asked Marlene to be sure Lew got Ray's message on Bert and Harold. Then he got organized.

He packed his boots, waders, and fly-fishing vest into the roomy Tour-Pak mounted on the back of the bike. The tube with his fly rod fit neatly into the holder that had been rigged up for it between the Tour-Pak and the seat. At the last minute he decided to add a water bottle and a peanut butter sandwich.

Donning his leathers, his helmet, and his courage, he turned the key in the bike's ignition at ten o'clock sharp. It was less than ten minutes to the road near Patty Boy's place. Anxious as he pulled out of his driveway, he felt a visceral sense of relief once he had cruised down Loon

Lake Road and turned left onto a back road that would take him up to the highway. Before he knew it, he had reached the gravel road.

Parking his bike, he pulled off the leathers and stashed everything but his helmet in the Tour-Pak. Then he pulled on his waders and fishing vest, assembled and threaded his fly rod, and set off down the gravel road.

Lew was right—a quarter mile down the road and he could hear the creek. He pushed his way through a dense growth of young aspen, then stepped down the bank and into the water.

Willow Creek was shallow enough that he was able to wade downstream toward Patty Boy's with ease. A couple fallen logs made for detours up on the bank, but within twenty minutes he had the house and barn in sight. The creek widened as it neared the property but the brush along the banks was high enough that Osborne felt hidden as he neared. Someone would have to be right near the water in order to see him.

He sat down on a boulder to thread his fly rod. That's when it occurred to him that anyone who was any good at trout fishing would know he shouldn't be there. The creek was so shallow and the water so warm, no trout would be feeding this far downstream. He had to hope anyone spotting him would know nothing about fly-fishing.

For good luck, he tied on an Adams that Lew had given him. He stood and made a few short roll casts as he waded forward cautiously. The height of the brush and the narrowness of the creek made it impossible to backcast. He rounded a bend and stopped quickly. The brush had been cut back so that the creek was fully exposed from where he stood all the way up to the house and the barn, less than 500 yards away.

Nervous at being in the open without warning, Osborne cast off to his left and cast again without looking in the direction of the house. He did not want to appear curious about anything other than fish. Only when he heard the roar of motorcycles did he look up to see a line of six bikes heading up the long drive to the house.

Now he could see why Lew had wanted him on a bike: The house was situated on a ridge, even with where he was standing, that provided a full view of Highway 45, running north and south, as well as down Hagen Road to the county highway. Even the gravel road where he had parked his bike was visible from where he was standing. No one was going to arrive at Patty Boy's without warning.

As it was, bikers weren't the only visitors. Osborne saw two large semitrailer trucks parked in close to the front of the barn. A silver van like Catherine's was parked near the house, along with two pickup trucks, one black and one red. He counted half a dozen motorcycles parked near the house as well.

Looking back at the semis, he caught glimpses of men loading the trucks, but with the doors open so close to the barn he couldn't see beyond a slight crack between the barn and the doors. As he watched, he became more and more convinced they were not *unloading*. It looked more like moving day—as in moving *out*.

Osborne turned away to make what he hoped were some casual roll casts. As he turned to his right, sunlight flashed off an object in a clearing this side of the house. Casting as he waded, Osborne moved forward about five yards until he could see past the brush. In the clearing was parked a shiny new vehicle much larger than a motorcycle. This was an RV, one he recognized instantly.

Osborne backed up. The last people he wanted to see right now were Bert and Harold, and that was the same RV they had parked up at Birch Lake. Only today, hooked to the back of it, was a trailer carrying a white bass boat that glittered under the sun. Black-and-yellow stripes along the side of the boat matched the stripes on the monster 250-horsepower Mercury outboard—forty thousand bucks' worth of boat and motor. Had to belong to someone very successful, someone like Bruce Duffy.

Funny, for a place that had advertised a "Boats and Bikes" swap meet on the *Help Your Neighbor* radio show, that was the only watercraft in sight.

It was nearly noon when Osborne had safely parked the bike back in his garage. He dashed into the house to call Lew. Marlene said she was still out but had left instructions to patch him through when he called in.

She picked up the radio in her cruiser. Osborne detailed everything he had seen, saving the best for last: "No question, Lew, you're coming to Steadman's with me tonight."

"Doc...."

"Bruce Duffy, who owns that RV, the pro that hired Bert and Harold? The RV is parked front and center at Patty Boy's. And, Lew, Bruce is on Parker's guest list."

twenty-three

*"... not everything about fishing is noble and reason-
able and sane ... Fishing is not an escape from life,
but often a deeper immersion into it, all of it. The good
and the awful, the joyous and the miserable, the comic,
the embarrassing, the tragic and the sorrowful."*

—Harry Middleton, *Rivers of Memory*

The Steadman house was on Lake Consequence, choice
shoreline that Parker's family had owned since the rail-
roads came through in the late 1800s. An old hunting
lodge had once graced the site. For years, when the family
wasn't in residence, native Loon Lakers like Osborne
would drive in to admire the historic structure with its
time-blackened logs and river rock foundation. Now, of
course, it was gone.

The new house was pitched high on the exact same
spot, the point overlooking a deep bay ringed with old
growth balsam, their spires etched black against a hot
apricot-and-lavender sunset sweeping the sky.

"Views don't get much better than that," said Lew,
trudging up the drive beside Osborne.

She wore a sleeveless black dress that circled her neck

and fell to her ankles. A simple medallion of brass and silver nestled between her breasts. Gazing down at her as they walked, Osborne noticed how the setting sun gleamed in her hair and cast a soft glow across her face. Now *that*, in his opinion, was a view.

A wooden fence running along the drive was festooned with tiny sparkling lights, warm and festive even though it was not yet dark. A magnificent spray of the same announced the entrance to the imposing silver-white full-log structure. The lighting extravaganza continued, outlining the wide deck that wrapped the entire house.

"Hell of an electric bill," said Osborne as they entered.

The interior caused them both to stop and stare. Hayden had kept her promise—the furniture was indeed upholstered in camouflage: green and tan accented with black. The walls of the vast living room, two stories high, sported dozens of dead animals. Mounts of species Osborne had never seen before were hung vertically, horizontally, and across the front of the massive stone fireplace anchoring one end of the room.

"A taxidermy outlet?" Lew was amused.

Equally hard to miss as she worked the room was Hayden. As if to match the furniture, she, too, wore camouflage, only she had forsaken her casual versions for a long, flowing chiffon gown with an extremely low neckline. Again the overdone face, the too-white teeth, and a manner as affected as a smiling spider.

"I'll be interested in what you think of Mrs. Steadman," said Osborne in a low voice.

Lew's eyes traveled the room, then settled on their hostess. "First impression . . . she is very attentive to surfaces." That was true and fair. Osborne liked that.

Together they made their way along the perimeter of the room. Twenty-some people had arrived before them. Osborne, looking around, recognized no one. Through French doors running across the front of the house and opening

onto a wide deck, which faced the lake, he could see two
large tables and one smaller one set with camouflage-
patterned tablecloths. He was relieved to see the place set-
tings were a solid color.

Parker Steadman stood just beyond the French doors,
deep in conversation with a tall, thickset man. Looking
up, he spotted Osborne and waved him over.

"Doc," said Parker, "I want you to meet someone.
Bruce Duffy, this is Dr. Paul Osborne, my former dentist
and his friend. . . ." Parker's eyes went up inquisitively.

"Lewellyn Ferris," said Osborne, beckoning Lew forward. "Mrs. Ferris heads up our Loon Lake Police Department—and she's been instructing me in the art of
fly-fishing."

"Bruce here is ranked Number One in the tournament
tomorrow," said Parker. "And if he is one of the five
lucky pros whose names are pulled in our lottery tonight,
not only will he be the proud owner of fifty thousand dollars' worth of the newest models in Ranger boats and
Mercury motors—but he'll have a shot at a first-place
purse of one million dollars. This could be a big night for
Bruce."

With that, Parker raised the drink in his hand in a toast
to the tall, burnished-looking man beside him. Then he
turned his attention to Osborne: "What can I get you to
drink, Doc? Mrs. Ferris?"

"Nothing at the moment for me, thank you," said Osborne. Lew requested a Coke. As Parker signaled a pass-
ing waitress to bring the drink, Osborne put his hand out
to greet the fishing pro, who extended a beefy mitt of his
own. Even though Duffy's face boasted a ruddy tan, his
round cheeks were highlighted with patches of sunburn,
which gave him a clown-like appearance. And he was tall,
all right—a good six foot six or more. He made Lew's
healthy five feet eight inches look midget-size.

A shock of straight, jet black hair fell across his red-

dened forehead. Snappy black eyes looked at Osborne for
an instant then seized on Lew. With a grunt he put his
hand out as if to shake hers, but before she could, he had
plunked it down on top of her head. He held it there, as if
challenging her to squirm away. She didn't move.

"You kiddin' me, Shorty," he said. "You really the sheriff?"

"No, my title is chief of police."

"C'mon. Who you work for? Buncha wimps? You're
too short to be sheriff."

Osborne and Parker stood there, speechless.

"Word around town, Duffy, you're lucky you qualified
for the tournament," said Lew, not moving from under the
man's hand.

"What does that mean?"

"You know what I mean. Why weren't you allowed to
compete on the Bassmaster Tour last year?"

"Who the hell you been talkin' to?"

"I get around," said Lew. With a low curse Duffy removed his hand.

He looked away from Parker, shook the ice cubes in his
drink, then tipped it up, emptied it into his mouth, washed
it through his teeth, and swallowed. He slammed the high-
ball glass down on a table behind him, crossed his arms,
and faced the three of them.

"The goddam competition lied and I was too busy to
deal with it. I'm a professional and I get a lot of respect in
my business. This broad doesn't know what the hell she's
talking about. That's what happens when you put goddam
women in charge."

Duffy's large form weaved forward until he caught
himself and lurched back. Now Osborne understood the
redness in his cheeks: The joker had been drinking for
hours.

Parker took a swallow from his own glass, as if to stall

while he tried to figure a way out of the situation. Lew took charge.

"Say, Doc, take a look at this." She pointed down at the coffee table, where Duffy's empty glass rested. Under the glass top was laid out a collection of wooden fishing lures, each arranged for display alongside the lid of its original box. As Lew dropped to her knees for a closer look, Parker knelt on one knee beside her, either pleased that someone had noticed or intent on directing the conversation away from Bruce Duffy.

"Where did you find these? Some of these are one of a kind!"

"Believe me, she knows her lures," said Osborne, observing from where he stood.

"My former brother-in-law is a dealer, specializes in antique fishing tackle," said Parker. "He dropped these off the other day and Hayden was able to get her decorator to fix up two—there's another table in my den. Come on, since you're interested, let me show you the rest."

Lew and Osborne followed him around the corner and into a small room. It was much quieter. An oak gun cabinet stood in one corner and a large, dark brown leather chair with an ottoman took up most of the room. Beside the chair was a lamp table with glass on top and lures beneath.

"No camo?" said Osborne, looking around.

"I don't let her in here," said Parker. "No camouflage, no decorating, not even a telephone. Peace and quiet. Sounds of the lake," he added, pointing to the open windows. "I miss the old place," he said to no one in particular.

"By the way, Mrs. Ferris, I apologize for Duffy's behavior. Man's under a lot of pressure. If he's one of the five pros whose names are pulled in the lottery tonight, he gets a shot at double the purse—that's a million dollars. I know his results were challenged two years ago, but he's behaved himself since. And he's very well known on the bass-fishing circuit. I need big names to get national exposure for our tour and our cable network. This industry is built on big names and big money."

"And big fish," said Lew with a slight grin. "Don't worry, I'm used to it."

"So you've stayed in touch with the Plyer family?" said Osborne, eager to change the subject.

"No-o-o, not me. Duffy ran into Patty Boy—at the Lake of the Torches Casino. They got to talking and Duff told him I had built this place so he got in touch. He's been big in sporting goods antiquities for a while now. Knowing Patty Boy, I'm sure half are stolen. But hell, Doc—business is business."

"Is that where you got all those mounts? You didn't shoot all those, did you?" said Osborne.

"Those came with the decorator," said Parker. "And they're leaving with the decorator." The three of them laughed. "Hayden is too much the city girl, I'm afraid. I had no idea those were going to be up there until I walked in this afternoon."

"I knew Catherine when she was very young," said Osborne, walking over to take a closer look at a set of framed certificates hanging on the wall next to the gun cabinet. A familiar pattern had caught his eye. "I didn't know you went to Campion," he said, noting the degree from the all-boy Jesuit boarding school.

"My condolences," said Parker. "On knowing Catherine, that is. Yes, I did my time at Campion."

"So did I. My father sent me there after my mother died," said Osborne. "I was six years old when I left home."

"At least you had six years," said Parker. "My mother died in childbirth. The old man remarried but the wicked stepmother never wanted me around. That's why I spent

all my summers up here. My family may be from
Chicago, but I call Loon Lake home."

"Two motherless boys," said Lew smiling over at them
from where she stood examining the treasures in the lamp
table. "Mr. Steadman——"

"Call me, Parker, for heaven's sakes."

"You must have paid a fortune for these lures. They are
some of the finest I've seen."

"Anytime you deal with a Plyer, you pay through the
nose. But they are wonderful to look at, aren't they?"

Osborne assumed he meant the lures.

Looking over the heads of the other guests, clustered in
groups of three or four throughout the living room, Osborne spotted Edith, a camcorder in hand, off to their left.
He motioned to Lew to follow him. They waited patiently
as she completed a scan of the room, then switched off the
camera. She gave Osborne a soft smile.

"Hayden will be very pleased," she said. "I got the Bass
Pro, Ranger Boat, *and* the Mercury people—good stuff.
Candid footage always plays great during sales presenta-
tions."

"Don't you ever take a break, Edith?" said Osborne.

"Of course, I do—like right now." She set the camera
down on a nearby table. "You must be Chief Ferris," said
Edith, pumping Lew's hand without a trace of shyness.
"I've been anxious to meet you." She was so forthcoming
that Osborne was surprised. This was not the timid young
woman he had seen in Ray's kitchen.

"I must talk to you about my father. Ray told me that
you and Dr. Osborne are reviewing the case? I hope you
are because I know he did not kill that girl. I want his
name cleared."

Lew, caught off guard, stammered, "Well, I thought . . .
Doc said you. . . . Edith, would you have time to sit down
with us on Monday or Tuesday before you leave? I would

do it sooner but we're overloaded this weekend. I shouldn't even be here tonight but Dr. Osborne insisted—"

"Of course. And there's someone else you should know about—"

At that moment a loud bong rang through the house. Ray appeared in the doorway. Resplendent in his trout hat and a crisp white butcher's apron, he carried a heaping platter of fish fillets high and in front as he marched into the living room. Positioning himself in front of the fireplace as the ringing faded, he announced, "Fresh-caught walleye, folks. Follow me . . . to the buffet."

"Excuse me," said Edith, reaching for her camera. "Parker plans to sign Ray for the show and I need footage of that tray of walleye before it's served. Can we talk later?" She rushed off to the dining room.

Shaking his head as they followed her, Osborne wondered how it was that Ray always managed to take over the party. Jeez Louise.

When everyone had heaped their plates with sauteed fresh walleye fillets, French fries, potato pancakes, applesauce, and cole slaw, they took their places at one of the three tables, now lit with candles. Osborne and Lew chose the smallest table, which was situated off to the right of the others and closer to the house. A couple from Minneapolis, Parker's stockbroker and his wife, joined them.

Ray remained standing until everyone was seated, then raising his hands as if he were the Pope, he said, "A blessing . . ." A few nervous looks were passed around but everyone politely bowed their heads as he prayed, "Bread feeds the body . . . flowers the soul . . . Amen."

"Hear, hear," said Parker from the first table, raising a glass of white wine.

"A toast—to the star of our newest feature on The Fishing Channel, 'Ray's Fish 'n' Fry,'" said Hayden, saluting from where she sat at the second table.

As Ray sat down, a figure stepped through the French doors from the living room. The girl was very tall, her height exaggerated by a cap of wild white-blond curls. Wearing faded green shorts, a wrinkled black T-shirt, and a face identical to her father's, there was no doubt who she was. She dropped a scruffy backpack onto the deck. It hit with a loud thud just as Parker and Hayden leaped to their feet.

"Jen!" Parker crossed the deck quickly to his daughter. "I had no idea you were coming—how are you, sweetheart?"

"Dead broke, Dad. Nice of you to ask." Her voice quivered. Her body was thin but wide-shouldered, and even through the dusk, Osborne could see she was trembling. Lew gripped Osborne's forearm. The entire dinner party was silent, forks in the air.

"What? Why didn't you call?"

"I did. I've been trying to reach you for three weeks. *She*"—the girl pointed at Hayden—"wouldn't put my calls through."

"That's nonsense." Parker looked over at Hayden.

"I told you he would call you next week. We have been very, very busy," said Hayden through gritted teeth as she sat down.

No one moved; no one even coughed.

"Jen, come with me," said Parker. Reaching down for her backpack, he beckoned for her to follow him into the house, closing the French doors behind them.

"Okay, folks, don't you dare let that fish get cold," said Ray, his words sparking a polite buzz of conversation as everyone worked hard to pretend nothing unusual had happened.

Parker, apparently forgetting the windows were open so that everything he said could be heard clearly by the four people seated at the small table, pulled his daughter into his den. "Jennifer, what the hell happened? That ranch of yours is worth over a million dollars."

"Mother came to visit three months ago. You know her name is on the property until I turn thirty. . . ."

"Yes, but—"

"She refinanced it, took the cash, and left town. Never told me either. Then the weather turned on us. The rains were very bad this year, Dad. We had flooding and mud-slides and all the livestock were washed down into the ocean. . . ."

"Jennifer, this doesn't make any sense. I made sure you had a good manager—"

"Mother was so horrible to him, he quit. I've been try-ing to call you for weeks, Dad, but all your personal calls are routed through that monster—"

"Okay, okay, we'll deal with that later." The soft sound of a girl's sobs came through the window. "Come on now . . . everything will be all right. This is your old dad, here. Let's go find you a bedroom. . . ."

"Where is this ranch?" whispered Osborne to the stock-broker.

"Maui. This isn't the first time Catherine has done something like this. Poor kid."

"Is it true what she said about Hayden and the phone calls?"

"Oh, yes indeed. That woman is a guardian lion if you know what I mean."

"She's awful," the broker's wife confided, "but it's his fault, he lets it happen."

"Hey, you, Ray Pradt!" Parker was still in the house when Bruce Duffy's voice rang out from the first table to where Ray was holding court at Hayden's.

"Yes-s-s?" said Ray. He rocked back in his chair and gave Duffy his full attention. Osborne recognized the ex-pression on Ray's face: It was the look he had when he changed lures, angling for the big one, setting his drag the way a musician tunes his instrument.

"I hear you're so successful a fishing guide that you have to dig graves to make a living."

"Now Duff, old man, if that's a job application— you've got to change your attitude." Ray's chair rocked. People shifted uncomfortably. Hayden opened her mouth, then closed it.

"Yeah, right. How is that bishness, the grave bishness?" Duffy winked heavily at the wife of the Mercury Marine marketing director seated to his right.

Ray let his chair fall forward. His face brightened and he waved a fork in the air. "Since you asked, the truth is we're getting hammered with cremation. Just hammered. But I have to tell ya, even though it's a no-growth business—it is steady. As reliable a customer base as you'll ever find."

Duffy grunted. He wasn't sure if he was being put on or not.

Hayden finally found her voice. She jumped to her feet. "Okay, everyone, I have an announcement. Parker surprised me today with my very own pontoon boat. I've already christened her: *Serenity.* And every evening at the stroke of six, if you're in Loon Lake when we're in Loon Lake, you are invited to join Parker and myself on a cocktail cruise of Steadman Bay. Our maiden launch departs in five minutes—so everyone on board for dessert and after-dinner drinks!"

Just then the French doors opened and Parker stepped onto the deck.

"Parker," Hayden said, her voice unnaturally gay, "I've just invited everyone down for a maiden voyage on our new boat."

"You can only get ten people on at a time," said Parker. He sounded very tired. "Go without me."

Hayden paused for an instant, then looked around at the

tables. "Tally ho, then." Somewhat reluctantly a number of the guests agreed to join her. They did not include Bruce Duffy.

The pontoon had been gone for about ten minutes when Edith, who was sitting at Parker's table, pushed back her chair and gazed around the deck. The remaining guests were having coffee, chatting quietly in the candlelight. Jen had joined the group, taking an empty chair between her father and Edith, where she was hungrily attacking a full plate of food.

"Chief Ferris?" Edith called softly over to the small table. "Ray said you're quite the fly-fisherman. I've been thinking about giving it a try. Tell us, how did you start?"

"Girl shit," muttered Duffy. The woman beside him poured more coffee in his cup and shoved it in front of him.

"Well . . ." Lew hesitated.

"Go ahead, I'd like to hear, too," said Osborne. Now that he thought of it, he had never asked about that himself.

"I have an uncle that I worked for as a kid," said Lew. "He managed a sports shop over in Minocqua. He loved to fly-fish but I was never interested. I wanted muskies— big fish.

"Anyway, about fifteen years ago, my son, my oldest, was killed in a bar fight. I had a call from my uncle the day after the funeral and he told me to come by his place. He had a little cabin on the Bearskin River, which was full of brookies in those days. He knew I was in bad shape.

"When I got there, he had a fly rod all set up for me . . . and a few trout flies . . . some waders, which didn't quite fit," she chuckled.

Lew paused. The deck was very quiet. "He gave me a few pointers, a couch where I could sleep when I needed

to, and told me I couldn't come out of that river until . . ."
She stopped.

Everyone waited. Finally Edith said, "How long were
you in the river?"

"Twenty-two days."

No one said a word, not even Duffy.

"When I was ready to go home, not only did I know
how to fly-fish, I had made up my mind to try to get a job
in law enforcement."

"I don't get the connection," said Edith.

"There isn't any," said Lew. "It just so happened that
both my son and the boy who killed him were high on
speed that night. I made up my mind that if I could catch a
brook trout, maybe I could nail a drug dealer—I have my
own opinion as to which of those two is smarter."

Just then the door from the kitchen opened and a young
woman called out, "Chief Ferris, phone call."

twenty-four

"(Angling) is tightly woven in a fabric of moral, so-cial, and philosophical threads which are not easily rent by the violent climate of our times."

—A. J. McClane, *Song of the Angler*

While Lew was gone, Osborne made small talk with the stockbroker and his wife. He hoped that phone call was from the DEA agent who was in charge of the team from Chicago. It was getting late and Lew still had no details as to their plans for the raid on Patty Boy's place.

Lew poked her head out the French doors, her face serious. She motioned to Parker. The two disappeared into the living room.

Osborne looked around for Ray. No sign of the guy. He was sure he hadn't gone out on the pontoon.

"Look this way, Doc." Ray's voice came from over his left shoulder. He was standing behind Osborne's chair with Edith's camcorder in his hands. A pinpoint of red signaled the camera was running. "Getting some home movies here. . . ."

"Ray—" Before Osborne could protest, a blaze of light illuminated the entire deck as Parker and Lew stepped out. Parker's face was flushed purple under his white hair.

"Duffy!" he thundered.

"What?" Bruce Duffy roused himself slightly.

"You're out of the tournament. I'm pressing charges."

"What the hell—" The fishing pro moved clumsily to his feet.

"Chief Ferris just had a call from our headquarters— your name showed up in the ballot box for the lottery twenty-five times. It should have been in there *once*."

"Wha—? I have nothing to do with that. For Chrissake, I've been here all night."

"The Loon Lake police arrested two men who were seen coming out of the tournament booth after they locked up late this afternoon. Bert Kriesel and Harold Jack-somebody."

"Jackobowski," volunteered Ray, moving the camera from Parker to Duffy and back again.

"Never heard of 'em."

"Mr. Duffy," said Lew, stepping forward, her eyes dark under the bright lights, "I have a witness who was told by those two men that they have been working for you."

"Yep, that's what they told me all right," said Ray, camera on Duffy.

"You have compromised this entire tournament circuit," Parker's voice thundered. He was so apoplectic, Osborne worried he might have a stroke. "You have compromised my entire investment in this enterprise. I want you arrested."

At that moment, Hayden came running up the stairs to the deck. "What on earth? Parker, what's happening?"

"And you. I want you out of my face tonight. You hear me." Parker was shaking. "*Out of my face.*"

While Lew waited for Roger to drive out from town and pick up both herself and Bruce Duffy, she and Osborne stepped into the foyer, out of earshot.

"Doc, for once, Roger did his job. After Ray called in about the leech traps, he found those two just where Ray thought he might. He stayed on 'em all day. He watched them go in the booth after the guys working it took a dinner break. They were behind a curtain so he wasn't able to see what they were up to but he suspected no good. So when they held the big drawing tonight, it was Roger who suggested that they check the ballot box."

"What a stupid thing to do."

"Stupid is one thing, but why risk your career? That man," Lew observed, looking through the doorway to where Bruce Duffy sat slumped on a camouflage-upholstered loveseat, "must be desperate."

Back in the big house, Osborne hunted for Ray. He found him in a rear room, an office area packed with video monitors and equipment. Ray was alone, lounging in a chair with one leg crossed over the other.

He winked at Osborne. "Told you it'd be a good party. I'm making myself a copy of tonight's tape for the family archives," he said. "Edith got some terrific shots of me in the kitchen."

"Ray, I don't think Bruce Duffy likes you."

Ray laughed. "Did you see how fast people cleared out of here?"

"Lew asked me to thank you for tipping Roger off to those two razzbonyas."

"Put one foot in front of the other, you can't lose. You in the parade tomorrow, Doc?"

"I forgot about that. No, what time is it?"

"Seven A.M. I'll be on guard duty, I guess. Haven't heard otherwise yet, though after tonight, who knows."

When Osborne got home, he had a message from Ralph's Sporting Goods. Ralph was nicer than usual, saying that he hoped Osborne could ride on their float in the morning. They had been counting on having a dozen

members of the local Trout Unlimited chapter to dress up
in their fly-fishing vests and waders and throw candies to
the kids along the parade route. Four people had had to
cancel for various reasons. Ralph promised to up his do-
nation to TU if Osborne would substitute.

Osborne called him at home and said he'd do it. Then
he tried Erin's number but no answer. Assuming she and
the kids must still be out at the hunting shack, he decided
to stop by the house after the parade. He knew Mark and
Erin wouldn't let the kids miss the big parade.

Just as he was about to fall asleep, the phone rang. It
was Lew.

"Still no word from the DEA, Doc. And no one answers
my calls, not even their cell phones. I don't know what to
do about this—I can't stand by and let Patty Boy sell
drugs and stolen goods out there tomorrow."

"Lew, I am sure you will hear something in the morning. What else can you do? How did it end with Duffy
tonight?"

"I didn't have enough to hold him. Those sidekicks of
his had made bail by the time I got there. Once I have a
chance to interrogate those two, I'm sure we'll have
Duffy on fraud. That's on my plate for Monday. Right
now, I'm worried sick about this other situation."

"Nothing you can do tonight, Lew; try to get some
sleep. Will you be at the parade?"

"Yes, I will be at the parade." She sounded beat.

twenty-five

"God never did make a more calm, quiet, innocent recreation than fishing."

—Isaak Walton

The parade was to launch from the parking lot of the Lutheran school at the top of Main Street. It was just shortly after six when Osborne parked on a side street, but the place was already buzzing with activity. Looking down toward the center of Loon Lake, he could see families already setting up their chairs along the parade route.

Looking for Ralph's float, Osborne strolled past band members tuning instruments, a couple dressed like a hooked bluegill with a bobber putting last-minute touches on their float, and members of Kiwanis handing out steaming cups of coffee.

Parker Steadman's car was at the very front of the line. His crew had decorated a vintage white Cadillac convertible with streamers of gold and silver. As Osborne headed toward the back of the line, where he knew he would find Ralph's float, he saw Parker leaning against the convertible, a cup of coffee in his hand as he talked to a group of men crowding around him.

Jen was sitting in the car, watching her father with an admiring smile on her face. They both looked happier this morning. The simple tableau of father and daughter reminded Osborne of Erin and Mallory and how they had filled that hole in his heart after Mary Lee's death. No wonder Hayden didn't like the girl.

A vintage Thunderbird convertible was parked immediately behind Parker's Cadillac. Hayden, her eyes covered with dark sunglasses, sat slumped in one corner of the back seat. Edith, sitting beside her, was intent on a clipboard resting on her lap. She glanced up as Osborne walked by and gave a cheery wave. A banner rigged over their heads featured their names and titles under large black letters announcing THE FISHING CHANNEL. Their car did not flash gold and silver. Parker had definitely separated family from employee.

Prepared to walk alongside both cars with a video cam in a shoulder harness and a large battery pack with an attached microphone hanging off his hip was Rob, the young cameraman that Osborne had met at the airport. At the moment, he was deep in conversation with Ray. Osborne strolled over.

"Employed?"

"One more hour. I'm driving the T-bird in the parade and then, as far as I know, I'm done for the day. That's fine with me; those two aren't speaking this morning and I'd just as soon be out of the line of fire."

"You sure got Parker's attention for that 'Fish 'n' Fry' idea," said Rob. "I heard him on the phone to New York yesterday afternoon before it all hit the fan. Sounds to me like you might have a deal." He dropped his voice to say out of the corner of his mouth, "With or without Hayden."

Ray beamed.

"What's the story with Edith?" said Osborne to the cameraman. "She seems so much happier than when you folks arrived earlier this week."

"Yeah, I noticed that, too. I dunno, maybe it was when she found out Jennifer was coming."

"Oh, so she knew ahead of time."

"I think so. I know I heard her on the phone with Jen. But hell, who knows what makes women happy." Osborne laughed with him.

A pistol shot at seven started the parade pouring down Main Street. Osborne searched the crowd from his seat on board Ralph's float. He had been handed a bucket full of hard candies and given a metal folding chair to sit on. Midway through the parade, he caught sight of Erin, Mark, and the kids under the time and temperature sign at the corner of the First National Bank.

He waved and shouted. They waved back but he knew they couldn't hear him. Oh well, he'd catch up with them at the house shortly. Several times, as the float moved past intersections, he saw some of the deputies Lew had corralled from neighboring towns and counties, but no sign of her.

The parade ended at Loon Lake Beach, a large public swimming area and boat launch. In front of the boat launch was a baseball field. Today it was filled with tents and booths draped with banners announcing THE STEADMAN PRO-AM BASS TOURNEY and BUDWEISER. To no one's surprise, the beer was already flowing.

As his float rounded the corner, Osborne could see two blocks down past the tents to where the lead cars had pulled up next to the boat launch. Striped awnings decorated a nearby stage where the opening ceremony for the tournament was scheduled to take place as soon as the entire parade had wound its way down.

Osborne's float came to a standstill while the Loon Lake High School Band high-stepped their way through a rousing march. The smell of brats on the grill wafted up from the tents as he watched the kids in the band. His bucket was empty and the morning sun felt good. It was one of those small moments in life that he loved.

Looking down toward the water, he saw movement in both the lead cars. Parker sat alone in the Caddy, its metallic streamers framing him with flashes of sunlight as Jen walked off toward the concrete block building housing the ladies' rest rooms. The Thunderbird behind the Cadillac was empty.

He heard the BOOM right through the music. Seconds passed, maybe two, and the Cadillac levitated, flames bursting with enough force that two men standing twenty feet away were knocked to their knees. Later the fire chief would estimate that the fire was so intense it had burned at a temperature over 2,000 degrees Farenheit.

Flying down the baseball outfield, Osborne saw the three women come running out of the rest rooms. Jen's arms reached for the sky and he could see the howl on her face. Edith was close behind. A second explosion and the women fell back, covering their heads. Sirens were screaming. People ran down the field from every direction.

A hundred feet from the burning car, Osborne saw Ray.

"Doc, you stay back!" he shouted. "That other car might go."

Osborne did as he was told. "Where's Lew?"

"I have no idea—you stay here. I'll be right back."

"Ray—where are you going!"

"I'm damn sure that was fired from across the lake. I want to see what's there before it's too late."

Ray ran toward a police cruiser that had just pulled in. It was Lew. Ray jumped into the front seat with her and they took off across the baseball field.

Jen was hysterical. It was all Osborne and Edith could do to restrain her from going too close to the flaming wreckage. Hayden stayed back, her face drained of color and her mouth slack. Two firemen were brave enough to put the Thunderbird's standard shift into neutral and push it back out of danger.

Osborne, arm firmly around Jen's shoulders, watched the fire. He couldn't help but think of the irony of Parker Steadman's death: No amount of money could save his life. Sure his daughter would be wealthy but all she would have of her father now would be a handful of gold fillings, several slumped porcelain crowns, and maybe some dental posts.

twenty-six

". . . until a man is redeemed he will always take a fly rod too far back. . . ."

—Norman Maclean

Twenty minutes later, Lew and Ray were back, Lew threading the cruiser down the baseball field through people, bicycles, and baby strollers. It seemed like all of Loon Lake was descending on the beachfront, anxious to view the smoldering remains of the man who had just led the biggest parade in the history of their little town. Leaving Jen in Edith's care, Osborne hurried over to where Lew had parked.

Ray was right: The salvo had been fired from across the lake, off Walkowski's Landing. A ten-year-old kid walking down to see where the music was coming from had stumbled onto a man setting up what sounded to the two adults like a shooting bench, a bipod and a spotting scope.

"He said the gun was much bigger than his dad's deer rifle," said Ray. "And he thought it was pretty heavy because the guy had to carry it upright and he grunted when he was moving it around."

"We caught the boy running down the road to his house

as we drove up," said Lew. "Scared to death, poor little guy. He said at first he thought the man was out for target practice aiming at the old warehouse down by the bridge. Then he saw the explosion."

"Had to be a .50 caliber sniper rifle to take out a car from that distance," said Ray, shaking his head in disbelief. "I know some nuts around here that own those. You know, Doc, the same ones who own AK-47s and Uzis. One guy used his on a deer last year. The bullet entered the chest, traveled the whole body, and blew off the entire right hind leg. All he had left was two pounds of hamburger."

"I know those guns are out there," said Lew. "They make the damn things right over in Waunakee and you can buy one just as easy as you can a .22 for shooting squirrels."

"But the explosion?" said Osborne. "How the hell do you hit a fuel tank from that distance?"

"Doc, it's a military gun. It uses bullets tipped with phosphorus that explode on impact," said Lew. "With a scope, sighting his target from that distance was a piece of cake. All he had to do was hit the car."

"Did the boy say what the shooter looked like?"

"He was too impressed with the gun—and the guy's vehicle." She gave a grim smile. "Fortunately the kid was smart enough to stay hidden behind an RV that was parked there. A *big* RV. Bruce Duffy's from the sound of it. I've got an APB out for what it's worth—too much traffic. The few cars I've got available are crawling.

Hayden, making a remarkable recovery, insisted on taking charge. The tournament goes on, she demanded, giving directions every which way.

"Edith, call NBC! Network news should be covering this. This is a national story."

Edith ignored her. She remained right where she was on

a bench near one of the tournament tents, her arms around Jen, who had collapsed into her shoulder. An ambulance pulled up beside the tent, and Osborne watched as two EMTs dashed over to the women. He recognized the one who knelt beside Jen—Jessie Lundberg. Jessie reached over to give Edith a quick hug; apparently the two knew each other.

"Lew, is Marlene on the switchboard?" said Ray. "Why don't you have her give Father Vodicka a call. I don't know if Steadman was Catholic or not but the good priest will know how to help these women get things under control."

"Tell you what, Ray. Go ahead and use the radio in my car and *you* call Vodicka—okay? You know him, I don't," said Lew.

She turned to Osborne. "I haven't had a chance to tell you the bad news. The DEA is still having a turf war with Customs over the situation out at Webber Tackle. They put a hold on everything until Wednesday.

"But you saw Duffy's RV parked out there yesterday, right? So this isn't 'interstate,' 'international' anything anymore, Doc. This is murder—and Loon Lake is responsible. *I* am responsible and I want Bruce Duffy in custody. As far as Patty Boy and his operation, I'll just have to play it as I see it."

"You can't go in there alone," said Osborne.

"Of course not. I'm going to ask Roger to take over here. I'll have him reassign all deputies and officers on duty to traffic control only. Of those, we'll put two teams on roadblocks up on Highways 45 and C. That way at least I can keep people out of the area. Then you and Ray come with me. But I want you armed."

"My gun's in the back of my truck, Chief," said Ray, "parked back at the Lutheran school."

"Doc?"

He threw his hands up. "Lew, I want to help but I have

got to get over to Erin's. She and Mark think they're picking up that motorcycle out there. I have got to tell her
what's going on. I can't let them—"

"No, you're right, you're right. C'mon, I'll drop you
two by your vehicles, then meet up with me at my office.
Ray, you got more than one gun? Anything Doc can use?"

"Twenty gauge okay?"

"Fine with me," said Osborne, jumping into the back
seat of the cruiser. Never good with a pistol, he was comfortable with a shotgun. Not only that, at close range a
shotgun is deadlier than a revolver, which anyone who
knows guns knows. And if anyone knows guns, it would
be the Plyer boys.

Shotgun in hand, he would feel competent. Safe was
another question. But if Lew had to take the risk, he sure
as hell did not want her out there alone.

"So we're going by your office first," said Ray, confirming the plan.

"I need to get the Wausau lab boys up here right away."
She looked over at the smoke pouring from the wreckage.
"They'll have to handle this."

The front door to Erin's house was wide open when Osborne pulled up in front. Before bounding up her front
steps, Osborne realized he was still in his fly-fishing vest
and waders. He'd forgotten he was wearing the damn
things.

"Erin! Mark!" he called through the front door. He
could hear kids squealing and laughing in the back. A
young girl he recognized as one of Erin's baby sitters
came running through the living room.

"Hi, Dr. Osborne. If you're looking for Mr. and Mrs.
Amundson, they left already," she said. "Someone called
a little while ago and told them they had to pick up their
motorcycle early, that the afternoon party was canceled."

twenty-seven

On bass: "This is one of the American freshwater fishes; it is surpassed by none in boldness of biting, in fierce and violent resistance when hooked."

—W. H. Herbert (Frank Forester), *Fishes and Fishing,* 1850

"**You're** right, we go in from the back," said Ray after Lew had laid out a plan. They were standing over her desk with a well-worn *Wisconsin Gazetteer* open in front of them. "You'll have the roadblocks out here, right?" He pointed.

"Right."

"But have them hold back until we have a chance to go in. Otherwise Patty Boy and his people will be warned and outta there before we even arrive."

"You think he knows another way out?"

"I know he does. That's why he picked this location in the first place. Doc, you remember old man Plyer had a cottage up on Shepard Lake?"

"Vaguely."

"Well, he did. Those kids grew up out there. Something not many people know about because it's not on any map is there's a tributary from Shepard Lake into Willow Creek. Right here." Ray stabbed a finger on the map.

"It runs through a four-foot-wide culvert under the old railroad trestle and empties into Shepard Lake. You can't walk the wetlands to get there, but you can wade in easy or use a canoe. I know it well because every spring I seine minnows downstream from a big beaver dam that's back in there."

"So why isn't it on the map?" said Lew.

"Same reason you got roads with no fire numbers, Chief," said Ray. "Lazy humans make those things. And I don't have to tell you the rest," he said. "Once you hit that lake, you're home free. If you have a boat waiting, it's a straight shot across to the landing and the highway. Even if you don't have a boat, Shepard Lake is shallow enough; you can wade along the shoreline to a point where someone can pick you up. Then you can just hustle on up those back roads. Not likely anyone can find you once you're north of Eagle River."

"Can the three of us fit in your truck?" Lew headed for the door. "Doc said they have a partial view of that road into Willow Creek—so we sure as hell don't need to arrive in a cop car."

In less than half an hour, they had pulled off the gravel road at the point where Osborne had walked in the morning before. A distinct rumble of motorcycles could be heard off in the distance. They checked their watches. It was almost nine and Lew had given directions for the roadblocks to be held off until nine forty-five.

"Is this the section of the road you could see when you were upstream yesterday?" said Lew as she yanked on her waders. Like Osborne's, her waders came up to her chest with wide straps over the shoulders. They made carrying a gun in a holster impossible.

"No. They can see the stretch of blacktop but that pine

plantation hides this area," said Osborne. "We're well hidden wading, too, until we reach that bend in the creek where they've cut back the brush."

"Good." Lew threw her belt with the holster for her .40 caliber SIG Sauer onto the seat of Ray's truck. She would wade in gun-ready.

Ray was messing around in the bed of his pickup, which was always a disaster area. First he found his hip waders and pulled them on. Then, stepping between a stack of plastic buckets and several long-handled fishnets, he picked up a tangled mess of seining equipment. Under that was a locked metal cabinet. Watching Ray, Osborne kept a lid on his impatience. He knew better than to let his worry over Mark and Erin bungle everything. Determined to make fear work for him, Osborne inhaled and relaxed, letting a fierce calm override the panic.

Leaning over the side of the truck, Ray handed Osborne the .20 gauge side-by-side and a box of shotshells. He kept the deer rifle for himself. Osborne crammed eight shells into the inside top pocket of his waders. Two more went into the gun. He checked the safety.

They waded into Willow Creek, keeping to the right as much as possible. Osborne looked back. A Great Blue heron stood watching, grave and skeletal. Grasshoppers popped up and down along the bank. The rumble of motorcycles rose and fell. No one spoke as they moved forward. The creek had a nice burble, enough to cover the sound of their wading.

Just as they neared the final curve in the creek, Osborne, who was in the lead, felt a tug on his sleeve. It was Ray, pointing off to their left.

A swath of grass and brush along the creek bank was trampled and muddy, the mud marked with footprints. Osborne, eyes intent on seeing Patty Boy's house before the house saw them, hadn't even noticed. Ray touched one of the prints—"Wet, maybe less than an hour ago given how warm and sunny it is." He stepped up and over the boulders lining the creek to take a look.

Walking in about six feet, he stopped to peer over a healthy stand of tag alder. He waved at them to follow. Grabbing a branch, Osborne hoisted himself up onto the bank, then held out a hand to Lew.

"I'm afraid you're down a couple witnesses," said Ray, his voice low.

Osborne stared at the two bodies. He felt like he always did around death: numb. Numb and inept.

When he had got the news that Mary Lee had died on the operating table, all he could think in those first few moments was who to call to cancel the bridge party she had planned for the next day. Right now all that came to mind was the fact that Bert Kriesel would never have to worry about having those black pants laundered.

Osborne inhaled, then exhaled slowly, feeling the weight of the shotgun in his arms. This was not going to be easy.

Lew moved closer to the bodies. Harold lay across Bert. No movement. A cicada shrilled. An edge of paper stuck out of one rear pocket of Harold's jeans. Lew tugged at it. Out popped a fishing lure still in its clear plastic wrapper. She glanced at it quickly then held it out for Osborne and Ray to see.

A new Frenzy Diver, Medium. Looked like the Crawdad pattern but Osborne couldn't be sure. Lew tucked the lure back into the dead man's pocket.

"Poor guy," she said.

"Bert wasn't all bad," said Ray as if he were giving a eulogy over the grave. "He had a good sense of humor."

Osborne's eyes raked the ground around the bodies, looking for signs of blood or tissue. "Hard to tell if these two took it from the front or the back—"

"I can answer that for you," said a familiar voice. "After you set those guns down. Ver-r-y slowly."

They spun around.

Bruce Duffy stood in the water, lips tightened into a grim smile. He was wearing Neoprene chest waders, which may or may not have been why he was sweating so profusely. A blood vessel running up his left temple throbbed—but his right hand was steady. And in that hand was a .357 Magnum revolver. It was pointed at them and there was no question: The gun was loaded.

"Do exactly as he says," said Lew, her voice even. Osborne had no plans to do otherwise.

"Now empty your pockets, and I better see knives."

They obeyed. Osborne and Lew worked the tops of their waders down slowly, carefully, until they could reach their pockets. Ray didn't have to. When they were finished, three utilitarian pocketknives rested in the grass by the guns.

As Duffy waved them into the water, Osborne could see deep circles under his eyes, which were flat and hard. The face so ruddy the night before was ashen gray this morning. He looked like a man teetering on the brink of the DTs or coming off a drug high. Whichever it was, he looked dangerous.

twenty-eight

"Fish die belly-up and rise to the surface, it is their way of falling."

——Andre Gide

Rounding the bend, they had a full view of the barn and the house. A U.S. Mail truck was parked in front of the barn. People, maybe twenty or more, were milling between the barn and the house. Several cars were parked in the circle drive that fronted the barn and beyond the cars stood a number of bikes, maybe ten or more, chrome glinting in the late morning sun.

As they got closer, two more motorcycles pulled into the drive. Obviously the roadblocks were not yet in place. No sign of Mark's black pickup. Osborne's heart lifted. But he couldn't see around to the front of the house so he couldn't be sure.

"Walk up on shore right there," said Duffy, directing the three of them to the far right edge of the property. No one would be able to see them from the front of the house. "Then up to the clearing, then over to the back door."

It was the same clearing where the RV and the shiny

white boat with its black-and-yellow stripes had been parked.

"Patty Boy, here we come," said Ray.

"Patty Boy and Dickie are long gone, wise ass."

"How's that? We're buddies from way back. Same grade school. I've been looking forward to this." Ray made it sound like Patty Boy would be equally thrilled.

They were crossing the clearing toward the house now.

"The boys got a phone call the other day, had to rush off on a business trip."

"Is that why they're shutting down shop here?" said Lew. "And you stayed behind because you thought you had a guaranteed win of the top purse in the bass tournament?"

Duffy's silence answered her question.

"Just how deep are you in to Patty Boy?" Lew kept her voice soft and low, soothing. "Look, I know the man's a loan shark and I know you've got gambling debts. He has to be strangling you, Bruce."

Duffy's eyes remained grim and unflinching as they approached the stairs leading up to the back door. He paused to wipe the sweat from his forehead with one hand. "He's got me for two point three mil—not counting today's interest. And I'm not his biggest customer." He gave a hoarse laugh. "You better believe I wanted that million-dollar purse—if I could've picked my own guys, I'd have had it, too."

"Bruce, the Feds are in on this—we could work a deal."

"Open that door, old man, real slow." Osborne did as he was told.

"A deal? Yeah, right. You know damn well I'd die in prison. And Patty Boy's pals would make it real unpleasant. Don't talk to me about deals. I got deals up the wazoo."

"Witness protection," said Lew. "Works for some people."

"Not me, woman. The only thing I know how to do is fish. You think it'd take Patty Boy long to find me? I don't."

Duffy had started up the stairs behind Lew when he stumbled but quickly caught himself. Osborne had thought it was the weight of the water when they were wading that caused the man to move so slowly, so out of sync. Now he wasn't so sure.

The back door led directly into a big kitchen. The house had to be at least sixty years old. The kitchen sure looked it. The walls were a dingy institution green with matching grease-stained linoleum on the floor. A rusty porcelain sink off to the left was piled high with dirty dishes. A window over the sink was shoved open to expose a ripped screen where dozens of flies banged off the screen and the smudged windowpane.

Between the sink and an ancient, formerly white refrigerator was a plastic trash can heaped with crushed beer cans, pizza crusts, and watermelon rinds. It dawned on Osborne that that was why the RV had been parked in the clearing. He bet anything Patty Boy had been living in splendor, leaving his minions to make do with the crud.

Duffy motioned for them to stand back against a cupboard off to the right of a small square table, painted white, that took up the center of the room. On the table was a paper plate full of crumbs, a banana peel, and a rectangular metal box with its lid down. Before Osborne could take his place beside Lew and Ray, the door to an outer room swung open.

"Paulie, you made it. Why'd you come in the back way? Wha—?"

Cheryl stood in the doorway. Her smile disappeared at the sight of the gun in Duffy's hand. "Put that damn thing down, you. This is my friend. I've got something for him out in the barn." She held the door open behind her.

"D-a-a-d?" an uncertain voice came from the other

room. Through the open door, Osborne could see people, most of them in leathers, lined up in front of a card table. They included Erin and Mark, who were now walking toward the kitchen.

"Who the hell is that?" Duffy did not take his eyes off his hostages as he barked at Cheryl.

"Just somebody picking up one of my bikes. Why? Are you gonna tell me what's going on here, shithead?"

Without letting his hand or eyes waver, Bruce Duffy kicked back hard with the heel of his right boot. He got her on the shin just below the kneecap. Cheryl crouched in pain. "Jee-zus, man, what the hell?"

"Get that girl in here."

"What girl?"

"The one buying the goddam bike, the one that just talked to you."

"No. That's my bike and my money and this here's my friend from my motorcycle class. And don't you kick me again, you—"

Too late. Erin stood in the doorway behind Cheryl, Mark beside her.

"Dad, you found us okay. . . ." Erin's eyes traveled around the room. She saw Ray and Lew . . . then Bruce Duffy and his gun.

"Oh," was all she could muster.

"Get in here and shut up," said Duffy. He waved the gun toward the cupboard. "Over there, both of you. Cheryl, we'll talk about it later. Wind up your business right now, we're outta here in ten minutes."

"Ten minutes! I got half a dozen bikes getting picked up, man. That's fifty thousand bucks. Jimmy's got a couple more boats he needs to get paid for, too. *You* leave in ten minutes, you dumbshit."

"Okay, I will. You take your goddam time, but I'm taking that truck."

"No, you don't. You go without us, man, and Patty

Boy'll hear. Your ass'll be grass and you know it. Shit, I got people waiting." She left, slamming the door.

"Cheryl!" Duffy called after her.

"Erin, Mark, do what the man says," said Osborne. He stepped sideways to stand next to Lew, leaving room for Erin and Mark. Ray caught his eye for an instant as he edged up to make room, almost out of Duffy's range of vision.

Lew gave Osborne a subtle nudge with her elbow. He followed her gaze. Cheryl's head appeared at the kitchen window. She held up a finger as if telling Osborne to wait, then she ducked and was gone.

The five of them stood silently against the cupboard. Duffy, his gun pointed and his eyes on them, flipped open the top of the rectangular box. He gave a quick glance down. It was full of cash. He flipped the lid shut. Picking up the box, he tucked it under his left arm, then waved the gun toward the door they had just come through.

"Out. Over to the barn."

At the barn, Duffy instructed Ray to open a side door near the rear of the building. Inside was a darkened office. Another door was set into the far wall. It was made of steel and featured a deadbolt. Duffy opened the door, flipped on a light, and stepped back for them to enter.

It was a storeroom with a twelve-foot ceiling, empty except for tall racks of heavy steel shelving lining three of the four walls. The shelving units, about five feet wide each, were not attached to the walls. In sharp contrast to the kitchen, this room was pristine.

It was also, in spite of the eighty-degree temperatures outdoors, quite cool. If Osborne had to guess, this was where Patty Boy stored drugs, away from sun and heat and locked up tight.

"Whoa," said Ray, "is this where you keep the heavy artillery?"

"Shut up," said Duffy.

"Just thought it'd be fun to see that .50 caliber behemoth of yours up close and personal. A dying man's last wish, doncha know." Erin looked at Osborne with dread in her eyes: Wasn't Ray pushing all the wrong buttons?

Lew saw the expression on Erin's face. She caught Osborne's eye. They both knew Ray was trying to buy time. If they could stall until the roadblocks, they might have a chance.

"What the hell are you talking about?"

"The gun you used to incinerate Steadman this morning," said Lew. "That was an amazing shot, Bruce."

"Steadman's dead?"

The man looked at them, his jaw on his chest. The look in his eyes was sheer terror. His entire body started vibrating. "What makes you think I did that?"

"Your RV was parked right there," said Lew. "We've got witnesses."

Duffy shook his head like he was fighting dizziness.

"Well, if it wasn't you, who was it?" said Lew.

Duffy opened his mouth but nothing came out. A door opened somewhere.

"All right, all right," hollered Cheryl from the outer office. "Duffy, I got Jimmy packing up. He got rid of the boats okay—but you gotta tell me what's going on."

At the sound of her footsteps coming their way, something happened to Duffy's face—like maybe he was no longer taking orders.

"None of your goddam business, Cheryl. I said we'd talk later. Now butt out."

Cheryl stepped into the room behind Duffy.

"*You* butt out. This is my friend here. I left him a message this morning to come early 'cause I got him a set of custom chrome wheels for his new bike. These two people owe me money. Now why the hell are you doing this?"

"Because he's married to the goddam sheriff, that's why. That one, the broad with the black hair. How much more do I have to tell you?"

"Is that true?" Cheryl's eyes searched Osborne's. He was very aware that she was keeping her hands behind her and staying back behind Duffy. Knowing that something about him appealed to her, he gambled.

"Not exactly. We're not married. But I am a deputy with the Loon Lake Police," said Osborne. "I'm not going to lie to you, Cheryl. I've been working undercover with Chief Ferris here." He nodded toward Lew.

Duffy's eyes widened as he spoke. Ray edged off to the left, slowly, slowly. He backed closer to one of the steel racks.

Osborne talked louder. "We know Patty Boy has been running Ecstasy and stolen bikes through here. We know Mr. Duffy shot and killed two men that were working for him. Then, this morning—"

"They weren't working for *him*, they took orders from Patty Boy." The derision in her voice made it clear what she thought of Duffy. "The only people giving orders around here are Patty Boy and Catherine. You ever meet Catherine? She's married to my brother."

Cheryl gave a slight smile of pride as if that put her higher in the organization. At that moment the cash box slid out from under Duffy's arm. It hit the floor with a loud crash.

"Duffy, what are you doing with that?" As Cheryl stepped forward, Ray moved back another step. "You weasel—first you don't tell me you got cops here. Now you got our money? What the hell? You planning to leave me and Jimmy holding the bag?"

"Jesus, Cheryl, I'm trying to tell you—"

At that moment the rack behind Ray began to tip. It teetered, then plunged forward. Duffy saw it coming. He twisted, stumbling back and firing as he hit the floor.

A geyser of blood shot up from below Mark's waist. Erin screamed.

"Stop! Everyone stay right where they are." Cheryl was on her hands and knees behind Duffy. She had her own .357 and the revolver's barrel was angled deep into the side of Duffy's neck.

Mark writhed. "My leg, my leg!"

"Ohmygod, he hit an artery," said Ray, scrambling onto the floor with Mark and Erin. "Please," Ray pleaded with Cheryl, "let me tie off the leg, please, he'll bleed to death." He was already ripping the belt from his pants.

"Go ahead," said Cheryl. "Just no one get in my way or you'll get hurt."

Osborne dropped to his knees. Blood was everywhere. This was wrong. Mark couldn't die. Osborne was the oldest—why couldn't that wild bullet have hit him?

"Cheryl, stop——" Osborne heard the strangled sound of Duffy's voice far, far away.

"Doc, here." Lew was ripping off her waders. "Use these for pressure."

Erin had her leather jacket folded and ready.

"Payback time," Osborne heard Cheryl's voice as he and Lew pushed the jacket hard against Mark's leg, then twisted the waders tight. Only then did he look over at Cheryl. She had her head down close to Duffy's. "What were you thinking when you busted into my room the other night?"

"Oh, for Chrissake. I had too much to drink."

"You never asked permission, Brucie."

"Permission? Woman, you are one well-traveled highway——"

She raised the muzzle a little higher and tipped it ever so slightly.

Blam. It wasn't so much what the bullet did to Duffy, it was what it did to the floor behind his head.

•   •   •

"We've got to get Mark to a hospital," said Osborne, kneeling next to his son-in-law. His vision blurred with worry: he was determined not to let the father of his grandchildren die. "He can't lose much more blood. . . ."

"Please, let these two young people out, let them get help," said Lew, looking up at Cheryl from where she was helping Osborne keep the pressure on the wound. Their hands were slippery with blood but the spurting had stopped.

Erin had her arms around her husband's head and shoulders. Ray was holding the belt in place. "The rest of us—"

But Cheryl was backing out of the room, the .357 pointed at them. She had scooped up Duffy's gun and the cash box. "Paulie's your old man?" she said to Erin.

Erin nodded.

"You're lucky. He's a nice man. I coulda used a father like him."

"Cheryl, please "

"I'm sorry, Paulie, I don't want to hurt anyone, but I can't let you people go. My brother works for Patty Boy, too. If we don't get the job done, we'll all be dead." Then she was gone, the door slammed shut behind her. They heard the deadbolt turn.

"Don't move, Mark. We've got to keep pressure on that," said Ray, holding the belt tight. "You're gonna be okay. We just gotta get us out of here. Doc, any ideas?"

"Look around, Doc," said Lew. "I can manage this fine."

Osborne stood up and looked around the room. No windows, no opening. The gunshot had splattered blood and tissue and penetrated the wood floor but there was solid dirt beneath. The locked door was the only way out.

Lew checked her watch. "The roadblocks go up in ten minutes—"

"We can't wait for someone to get all the way out here," said Osborne. "Who knows how long that might take. If one of us can just get out. . . ."

"Listen, everybody." Mark's voice was tight.

"Shh, Mark, don't talk," said Erin.

"No, I know about this stuff and they don't," he managed, tipping his head toward Ray and Osborne. "It's just Sheetrock on those walls, like maybe an inch thick. If you got something sharp, you can cut a hole easy, push back the old siding behind it. That siding's rotten."

"Sharp? Duffy took our pocketknives, dammit," said Osborne.

Lew's eyes lit on Osborne. "Erin, you take over here." Erin moved quickly and Lew jumped to her feet.

"Doc—your fishing vest. What've you got in there?"

Before he could answer, she had yanked down the straps on his waders and was reaching in for the long, narrow pocket running down the front of his vest. She pulled out the silver forceps he used to remove hooks.

Pulling it apart, she ran over to the wall and tried stabbing it into the Sheetrock. It penetrated easily. She tried slicing down, but the point kept sticking.

"Try the clippers, Lew." Again, she broke the tool in half.

The cutting edge of the clippers was sharp like a knife—it worked. She handed the other half to Osborne.

"Don't worry about cutting all the way through," said Ray. "Mark thinks all you have to do is etch in deep enough, you can push it the rest of the way."

They worked swiftly, slicing at the Sheetrock until they had an irregular rectangle about seventeen by twelve inches. It couldn't have taken more than three or four minutes. Meanwhile, Ray and Erin kept the tourniquet and the pressure on Mark's leg. Outside, they could hear motorcycles leaving, one after the other. Then a brief silence followed by the sound of an engine turning over.

"That must be the mail truck," said Ray. "Think they'll let 'em through the roadblock, Lew? It's either stolen or a good fake."

"I don't really care," said Lew. "I just want to get Mark here to the emergency room."

With one pound of Osborne's fist, the Sheetrock caved in. Behind it was a vertical panel of siding as old as the barn. He hammered at a knothole with the blunt end of the forceps until he was able to get a good grip on the panel itself. He pushed. The damn thing buckled out but it wouldn't come loose.

"Let me try," said Lew. Osborne stepped back. Maybe she was stronger or maybe it was because she pushed up at an angle, but the board gave. Through the opening, they could see the drive running up to the house. Except for two bikes, it was empty.

Erin looked up from where she was holding Mark.

"Dad, I know I can make it through there easy," she said.

Osborne changed places with her.

"Erin," said Lew, "run down that driveway—the road-block will be right where it meets Highway C."

Mark's face was dead white. Ray inched the belt tighter. Lew pressed.

Osborne held him in his arms.

"You're not alone, son," he whispered. "Please . . . hold on. You're not alone. . . ."

twenty-nine

"The fish are either in the shallows, or the deep water,
or someplace in between."

—Anonymous

The emergency room was hot, humid, and packed with
summertime disasters: fishhooks attached to body parts,
motorcycle road rash, jet ski collision concussions, a
chain-saw gash, and spider bites.

Osborne sat next to Erin, his arm across the back of her
chair, as they waited for news of Mark's room assignment. The surgery had gone smoothly. Mark would be
fine.

Right now, even though Osborne felt both exhausted
and relieved, a dark hole had opened in his heart. A hole
filled with dread over what could have happened. He
knew it would be a long, long time before he would ever
forget one moment of these hours. He knew he had made
a grievous error for which he could never forgive himself.

"I feel so responsible for this," said Osborne. "I should
have said something when Lew told me there was a connection between that bike you two were buying and her
investigation of Patty Boy Plyer. We just couldn't risk red

flags too early, but jeez Louise, Erin—what was I thinking!"

"Dad, don't beat yourself up. How could you have known we would go out there early? Remember now, I had promised to wait for you." She patted his knee reassuringly. "Look at it my way—it brought us closer together."

"Erin, that's dumb. Your husband could have died."

"But he didn't. This whole week—planning for the bike, talking about our lives—it's been good. We know now what really matters to us. And maybe"—Erin punched him lightly in the shoulder—"we got ourselves a free motorcycle. That woman never did take our money."

Osborne gave her a grudging smile. "If the police can't trace it back to the original owners, you just may. What about school—you still thinking about a law degree?"

"Absolutely. I'm working on my applications this week. But we're being practical. Mark's going to continue with the Kasmarek law firm and hope something opens up with the city. He'd love to be back in the D.A.'s office— less money but better people."

"That's wise," said Osborne. "If he hadn't been working for Chuck, he'd never have heard of Patty Boy and he wouldn't be here almost losing his leg."

A group of EMTs strolled by, on break, from the relaxed expressions on their faces. Jessie Lundberg was one; she held a cup of coffee. She stopped when she saw Osborne and Erin and waved her colleagues on.

"Hey, Dr. Osborne. I hear Mark's doing fine."

"Yes, thank goodness. Erin, you know Jessie, don't you?" Erin nodded. "Jessie, I saw you with Jennifer Steadman this morning. Do you know how she's doing?"

"Yeah, that poor girl. Losing her father like that. You know, I was so surprised to see Edith Schultz. We were best friends in grade school. Hadn't seen her in a long time."

Jessie took a sip of her coffee. She had an easy, gentle way about her. As she stood, she looked around the waiting room, then back at Osborne. No one was sitting too close. She dropped her voice and leaned forward, like someone looking over a bridge at a dangerous current.

"What do you know about that woman?" From her tone, Osborne knew exactly whom she meant.

"Hayden?"

"Dr. Osborne, that woman is so horrible. I can't believe she showed up here."

"How do you know *her*?"

"I know her from when her name was Harriet Carlson. She's the reason I got out of television."

Just then one of the nurses beckoned to Erin.

"I'll wait here," Osborne told his daughter. But when he turned back to Jessie, her eyes were dark and worried. "You have time for another cup of coffee?" She nodded. "Erin, I'll be in the cafeteria when you're ready."

"I hope you don't think I'm a gossip," said Jessie as they walked down the hall. "But there are some things you and Chief Ferris should know, and someone needs to warn Jennifer Steadman."

"We knew all about her before she got to *Outdoor America*," said Jessie. "I was a senior producer and weekend anchor at the time and that little cable network was really taking off. It was a neat job." She stirred her coffee. They were sitting at a table far enough away that no one could hear them.

"Television is a small universe. Everybody knows everybody—what jobs are open and why. So we knew Harriet got her first reporting gig at a small affiliate outside Portland, Maine, because she was sleeping with the station manager. When she moved up to the owner of the station, she got promoted to anchor.

"Now," she smiled slightly, "to a certain extent, that is a

tradition in the business, but Harriet was different. Creepy, really, which became obvious when Parker Steadman bought that station. She would find out when he was in town and hang out in the restaurant and the bar at his hotel. One day she grabbed the dry cleaning from the maid and delivered it to his room. And waited there.

"Here's where it gets creepy, Dr. Osborne. She had not even met the man but she had already decided what she was going to do. Harriet didn't sleep her way up so much as she *stalked* her way to the top."

"She was waiting in his room and she had never even met the man?"

"She had a plan and she made it work. Harriet Carter was glued to Parker Steadman after that." Jessie gave him a look, half-smiling, half-serious. "I'm sure you wouldn't understand, Dr. Osborne, but Harriet, I mean Hayden, has special talents."

"You're right, Jessie. I haven't a clue. Go on, this is very interesting." said Osborne.

"It was shortly after they got together that he bought part ownership of *Outdoor America* and guess who arrived as part of his entourage. That's when I met her.

"The day she arrived, she demanded an anchor position but she didn't have the experience. Her audition was awful. The next thing that happened, everyone on staff had to deal with lies she told about us. Bald-faced, outrageous lies. She alleged that one of the news reporters molested children, that our executive producer was stealing money. Total lies. But management was so intimidated by Parker, they never really looked into the allegations, they just fired people.

"Anyone who crossed her ended up without a job. The more control Parker Steadman had, the more she had.

"It all came to a head for me one weekend when I was covering NASCAR. It was a big story: six cars crashed, two people killed. This was a story that would air nationally. She and Parker were at the track because he owned a NASCAR team that was racing that day.

"I was all miked and one minute from going on-air when she came running up, yanked me out of the chair, ripped off my mike, and said, 'Move, I'm doing this.'"

"No one stopped her?"

"Nope. No one ever said a word. Two weeks later, she was promoted to anchor. That was it for me. I came home. Now I've got a nice little business of my own and I like being an EMT. A lot less pressure, no evil people. But I stay in touch with several friends who are still in television. That's how I heard she was telling people they were married."

"Isn't her name Hayden Steadman? That's how she introduced herself when we met."

"No—he's refused to marry her. I'm not sure why; he certainly hasn't ended their relationship. But she's such a snake, who knows what she's got on him." Jessie talked as if Parker were still alive.

Maybe it was just too much trouble, thought Osborne. He could see that.

"If her name isn't Hayden Steadman, what is it?"

"Hayden *Sterling*—close enough that you might think you heard it wrong. You'll notice she never corrects anyone either. She changed it about, oh . . . three years ago. Just before she got the anchor job.

"Dr. Osborne, you can see I hate her guts. But that aside, I sincerely believe that Jennifer needs to be careful. That woman is entirely capable of forging papers, telling lies. She'll steal the business right out from under Jennifer. She cheated to get where she is; she'll cheat to stay there."

"Does Edith know all this?"

"She must. I've known about Edith's work over the years, but we were never in the same place at the same time. She's really made a name for herself in outdoor television. I'm sure she's the reason the Fishing Channel is off to such a good start. It isn't easy, you know. You think it's tough to make golf interesting on TV? Try fishing, for God's sake."

Jessie stood up. "I better get back to work. If you see Edith, would you ask her to give me a call? I haven't seen her since we all went off to college. I went to Marquette and she went to Northwestern. Oh, right—and that's where Harriet says she went—Northwestern. I mean Hayden. I'll bet she lies about that, too."

Osborne got home at five-thirty, exactly twelve hours after he'd left. Poor Mike, the dog was beside himself. He let Mike into the house, fed him, then walked out onto the deck. Osborne leaned over the railing and let his eyes rest on the water. The western sun streaked across the lake, leaving paths of diamonds in its wake. Up on the deck, a light breeze dismissed the heavy heat of the afternoon.

What a day. He needed a nap, a long nap. He didn't even check phone messages, just collapsed onto the redwood chaise longue and fell sound asleep.

"Doc?" A gentle hand shook his right shoulder. He knew that voice, dammit.

"Doc, sweetie, did you forget?"

Sweetie? His heart froze. He had a horrible feeling he was the victim of amnesia and was about to wake and find himself married to Brenda Anderle. Oh, dear God. Mike nudged from the other side, his nose wet on Osborne's limp hand.

"Did I forget what?" Osborne forced his eyes open. The faces of three women hung over him. Two were miniatures of Brenda. Osborne blinked. "Brenda, what on earth?" He sat up.

The women were nicely dressed and made up, ready for an event of some kind. Each one held a round foil tray, filled with food and covered with Saran Wrap. He saw raw vegetables, a ring of shrimp, and bowls of what he imagined were dips of some kind.

"I left you a message the other day that my daughters were visiting this weekend and I thought we could have cocktails at your place and dinner at mine. I said to call if you had a problem with that. You didn't get my message?" The poor woman was so stricken, Osborne felt like a heel.

"Brenda, I've been at the hospital—a family emergency." Hastily, he dramatized Mark's brush with death. By the time he had finished, all three women had tears in their eyes and everyone was off the hook.

"I understand completely," said Brenda. "Your poor man."

"Golly, Dr. Osborne." The two younger women shook their heads in sympathy.

"Let me get everyone a cold drink. Brenda, what will you have?"

A quick dash into the bathroom to splash cold water on his face and Osborne was in full operating condition. He opened some soft drinks, grabbed the bottle of wine he had forgotten to return to Brenda earlier in the week, and hurried back to the deck. He wracked his brain for the names of the two daughters.

As he slid back the screen door to the deck, Brenda said, "Holly and Marsha are wondering if you've seen Harriet Carlson since she's been in town. I hear Ray Pradt's been working as her security manager. You know, the girls were all such friends that summer."

"What summer was that?" Osborne poured Brenda a glass of wine, then set the bottle on the table near her elbow. He would make sure she took it home.

"That summer she was staying at Greystone Lodge. And now she calls herself Hayden. Hayden Steadman. An improvement over Harriet, most definitely. Harriet is so old-fashioned."

"Sterling is her last name. She's not married." Osborne poured Coke over ice for each of the two younger women.

"Oh? Marsha thought she was. They're the same age, you know. Marsha, weren't you two pen pals for a while?" Brenda basked in her little bit of fame by association.

"Yes, Mom. Now you're happy about that but you were so upset back then."

"Of course I was. What mother wouldn't be? That girl was something else."

"What are you talking about?" said Osborne. He settled back with a glass of ginger ale.

"Oh, Doc. Come on," said Brenda. "It was such a scandal. Harriet was fourteen that summer and she had an affair with the father of the family she was staying with. You know, that was the family whose baby-sitter was murdered. The Thorntons. The wife was an heir to the Kendall Boat fortune. I'll never forget that day when your little Erin found the body—"

"I never knew about a girl named Harriet."

"Well, you spent all your time fishing, that's why. Mary Lee and the rest of us knew. We felt so sorry for his wife. Of course, we never talked about it in front of our children, but we knew what was going on. What those two did on the swimming raft—Millie still talks about what she saw."

Brenda looked at her daughters and gave a dismissive wave of her hand. "Men—they never pay attention."

thirty

"I know several hundred men. I prefer to angle with only four of them."

——Frederic F. Van de Water, author

"Harriet Carlson," said Osborne. "Sound familiar?" It was after eight when he was finally able to reach Lew at home. She sounded tired as she picked up, then relieved to hear his voice.

"I know the name, Doc. It's on one of those samples we sent down to Wausau. If I remember right, that's the name of the young girl who was staying with the family. One of their kids' friends that they brought along for the vacation."

"Lew, that's Hayden's real name. She changed it several years ago." Quickly, he related everything Jessie Lundberg had told him.

"Nothing surprises me anymore, Doc." Lew sighed. "By the way, your friend Cheryl? She and her brother blew right by my roadblock in that mail truck. I should've known better than to expect Roger to score more than once a decade."

"Don't be too hard on the guy, Lew. Anyone would

have let them through. The DEA would have let that truck
by."

"Actually, Doc, you're right. I'm not being fair. Speaking of the DEA, boy, did I let them have it. 'Course now
they're blaming everything on Customs."

"Are they coming up Wednesday?"

"No. They're going straight up to Canada; they think
they've got a chance at intercepting Patty Boy and Dickie
up there."

"What are you doing in the morning?"

"Paperwork and more paperwork. Why?"

"I thought I'd take you out to breakfast."

"Thanks, but I don't have that kind of time——but how
about coffee in my office at eight? One of the lab guys
who came up from Wausau today said the results on the
tests they ran on the Schultz samples should be ready
early tomorrow. They're e-mailing them up."

At seven-fifteen the next morning, Osborne found himself
held hostage in his own living room, forced to view the
high points of his neighbor's brief career in cable television.

"How much longer, Ray? I'm due in Lew's office in
thirty minutes. Could we finish this later?"

"Just this next part, Doc. This is cool."

Osborne wanted to be kind. Chances were good that
Parker's death had put an abrupt end to Ray's dream. He
kept that in mind as he watched minute by long minute of
Ray catching walleye, cleaning walleye, frying walleye.
At the moment, the tape showed Ray holding his tray of
walleye fillets high in front of the big fireplace in Parker
Steadman's log home.

"Edith did great, didn't she?" Ray sat forward on the
ottoman, his eyes fixed on the screen. "And with just a
camcorder. Think how excellent this would be with the
right lighting and professional cameras. . . ."

"Okay, okay, I know you gotta go, Doc." As Ray stood to click off the VCR, the lighting changed on the screen. It darkened, the lens shooting with only the glow of candles to light the faces of the guests. Osborne's profile came into view, then Lew stepped through the French doors and motioned to Parker, who followed her back into the house. The lens panned past faces, jerky and shifting—Ray's was not the sure hand of Edith.

Suddenly the screen lit up. Parker had returned to the deck where lights were blazing. "Oh boy," said Osborne, eyes riveted. Ray had captured the scene with Parker confronting Bruce Duffy. Now Hayden entered the frame from the side and Parker shook his finger at her. The camera panned the tables and the dinner guests, shocked faces all around.

Osborne picked out Jennifer Steadman sitting at Parker's table, Edith next to her. Jennifer held her fork in the air, stunned.

The camera pulled back as people stood up but the focus remained on Parker's table. It held steady as Jennifer leaned toward Edith, who put her arm around the girl's shoulders and brushed her brow with a kiss. The video was now a blur of people moving around on the deck.

"Stop, go back, Ray."

Ray hit the rewind button. Again they watched the moment of tenderness between the two women.

"What do you think?" said Osborne.

"I think they know each other . . . pretty darn well."

thirty-one

"Fishermen are born honest, but they get over it."

—Ed Zern, *To Hell with Fishing,* 1945

By the time Osborne got to Lew's office, the morning had turned muggy. She didn't seem to mind.

"I can use some rain, Doc. It'll keep the fishermen in their boats and the motorcycles off the road. Give me a chance to get out to the Steadman house. I need to sit down with all three of those women."

"What's your theory, Lew? A family grudge? Like maybe way back when Parker did something and Catherine's been biding her time?"

"That could very well be. I'm hoping a search of Parker's office out at the house and his personal effects might help. The fact that Hayden can't be trusted doesn't make things any easier. Pretty strange she kept insisting *she* was being stalked, isn't it?"

"Ray's convinced it was her way of getting attention from Parker. Attention and sympathy, a good way to keep him on her side."

Marlene stuck her head in the door. "Chief, your e-mail came in from Wausau—I printed out two copies."

She handed one each to Lew and Osborne. Osborne studied the first page, then the second. He looked out the window.

"What?" said Lew.

He walked over to her desk. "May I use the phone? Phone book?"

Brenda answered on the first ring. Pleased to hear his voice, she was less happy when he asked for Marsha. But Marsha had the answer to his question.

Osborne set the phone down gently. "Bud Thornton died of prostate cancer two years ago."

"Damn," said Lew. "He never had to answer for it, did he." She hit a button on the telephone console. "Marlene, would you get Hayden Steadman for me, please?"

Osborne refilled his coffee cup. Neither spoke while they waited.

"Hayden? This is Chief Ferris. Sorry to intrude during this difficult time but we need to discuss a number of things today. How soon can you be available?" Lew waited. "No, no, I'll come out there . . . no earlier than that?" Again, a long pause.

"Well, all right then. But if anything changes, please call in. If I'm out, dispatch will know where I can be reached. Otherwise, I'll see you at four this afternoon. Please, will you remind Jennifer not to disturb any of her father's effects until I've had the opportunity to look everything over? Thank you."

Lew looked over at Osborne. "She's tied up with funeral arrangements until late this afternoon."

Marlene stuck her head in the door again. "Chief, you have a visitor—Edith Schultz." Before Lew could respond, Edith walked in behind Marlene.

"I'll leave," said Osborne, standing up.

"No, you stay," said Lew.

Edith looked at them both. "It's my fault he's dead."

She was trembling. Her face was a mess. She looked like she'd been up all night.

"Okay, Edith," said Lew, walking around from behind her desk to take Edith by the elbow, "why don't you sit down here and we'll talk."

She pulled an armchair over from the wall, then closed the door to the office. Edith sat on the edge of the seat, arms folded tight across her chest. Osborne nudged his chair in closer. Edith looked like she might pass out.

"Coffee or water?" asked Lew, walking over to the table with the coffeepot.

"A little water please," said Edith in a tiny voice. She gulped the water, then took a deep breath as Lew sat down behind her desk.

"Did you pull the trigger?" Lew's question was so abrupt, Edith was startled.

"Of course not, but—"

"Did you hire the person who pulled the trigger?"

"No!"

"Does this have anything to do with your father?"

"Kind of, but—"

Lew raised a hand. "Before you go any further, Edith, I want to share some news with you. Something I learned just this morning."

"But—" Edith looked like she was going to burst into tears. She raised a faltering hand to her lips, which were shaking.

"Edith," Lew said, leaning forward over her desk. "I have no idea what you feel you have to say, but *how* I hear it is going to be greatly affected by something that I now know. Does that make sense?" Lew waited until she had a nod from Edith.

"The other night at the dinner party, I told you that Dr. Osborne and myself have been reviewing the file on your father and the murder of that young woman. We sent all the evidence, which has been in storage over the years, down for testing at the crime lab in Wausau. The results of those tests came in this morning and confirm the simple, awful truth that shoddy police work all those years ago led to your father being falsely accused. The man who held my position at the time took the easy way out; he did not question the opinion of an alleged eyewitness."

"Why would he do that?" Edith's voice was a whisper.

"Chief Raske was lazy, he was mean, and he wasn't very bright," said Lew.

She glanced down at the report on her desk, then looked back at Edith. "We're fortunate that a young police officer on the force at the time had the foresight to take significant physical evidence, blood samples and nail clippings, from anyone who might have seen the victim in the forty-eight hours before her death. In addition, he had very good quality photos taken of the crime scene and other physical evidence. And he carefully preserved the burlap sack in which the body was found.

"His efforts are a good example of how ignorance can work to advantage in interesting ways. The fact is DNA testing, like we know it today, did not exist at the time of the girl's death. But the investigating officer wasn't thinking DNA when he took those nail clippings.

"Instead, not knowing the limits of the forensic microscope, he had hoped that something in the physical characteristics of a good-sized shard of fingernail that he found stuck to the bag holding the body might be a clue. He hoped it would match similar patterns or characteristics on the nail of the individual he suspected to have murdered the girl—much like fingerprints match or, in those days, markings on bones could provide clues to cause of death. Enough to keep the case open. So he didn't really know exactly what he had when he found the nail shards stuck in the burlap but he felt it could be good, tangible evidence.

"That plus this." Lew held up a copy of the close-up of

the bite wound on Bud Thornton's neck. "The crime lab has confirmed that the teeth that made these marks belonged to the victim.

"But even better—they tested the DNA of the nail clippings against the shards found on the burlap bag. Edith, your father's nail clippings do not match. His blood test clears him as well. The blood smears and the nail shards found on the burlap bag link two other people to the victim."

"I've always known that my dad was innocent," said Edith. "I couldn't prove it but I've always known it. That's why I did what I did."

She pressed both hands hard over her eyes. Lew reached for a box of Kleenex and set it on the desk near Edith.

"Listen to the rest, Edith. Of the two samples that match the nail shards, one person is dead. That is Bud Thornton. He was the father of the family whose baby-sitter was murdered. The other belongs to a friend of the family's who is very much alive today: Harriet Carlson. The woman you know as Hayden Sterling.

"Now you keep this confidential, Edith. I'll be taking Hayden into custody later today, but Wausau does need to run one more blood test before she can be formally charged. Nevertheless, I feel confident she will be charged as an accessory to the murder of Gloria Bertrand."

Edith's shoulders relaxed as if a heavy weight had been lifted. "Chief Ferris, all these years I've known this. My father told me that the girl—that Hayden lied. She told the police she saw him in the woods with the girl who was killed. She said she saw him leave the woods afterwards. But he swore to me that he was never there."

Lew leaned back in her chair. "And he was not. Based on these reports from Wausau and the officer's notes from years ago, my theory is that Gloria, the baby-sitter, stumbled onto Bud Thornton in a compromising position with the young Hayden. She may have confronted him. Who knows?

"One interesting fact that the investigating officer noted was the family was quite well to do but the money came from the wife's family. Bud couldn't risk divorce. Did he think that the baby-sitter was going to tell his wife?

"One thing we do know for sure: Hayden was there when that girl's body was forced into the burlap sack. Only Hayden knows what really happened. Whether she'll tell the truth, who can say? But we have DNA proof that she was a party to a crime for which the statute of limitations never runs out."

"Then why?" Edith looked at her. "Why did my father kill himself?"

Lew gazed down at her desk for a long moment, then up at Edith. "The man who was the police chief in those days was a bully. He was vicious and he was powerful. When he got the eyewitness report, he decided your father was guilty and told him he would see that he got a life sentence. Your father had no witnesses to prove his side of the story, no DNA testing like we have now that might have challenged that witness. He had been out fishing alone that day. He probably fished a special, secret spot like so many of us do—and no one saw him."

"May I say something, Chief Ferris?" said Osborne. Lew nodded.

"I knew your father, Edith. And I remember the circumstances at the time. As a father myself, I think he was desperately afraid of what the whole scenario would do to you and your sisters. Sometimes when we're accused of things, even though we didn't do it, we feel guilty. Just the accusation smears you. That on top of your mother's leaving—it was too much. He wanted it over."

A lengthy silence filled the room. Finally, Lew said, "Edith, can I trust you not to say anything about this to Hayden? I know you're staying at the Steadman place and you're bound to see her before I do later today, but anything you might say could jeopardize the case against her."

"Please, I understand," said Edith.

"We have another witness, too," said Osborne gently. "An elderly woman here in Loon Lake. She can document the love affair between Hayden and Bud Thornton. She saw them together. Hayden is about to find herself boxed into a very tough spot."

"I'm not sure I feel too much better," said Edith. "I still feel damned responsible for Parker's death."

"You'll have to tell me why," said Lew, "because I don't see it."

Edith stared at the floor before answering.

"You have no idea how obsessed I have been over avenging my father's death. I was able to keep track of Hayden through high school. I knew she lived in Evanston. We both went to Northwestern, too, though our paths didn't cross often enough for her to be aware of me. She was in a sorority, I wasn't. She was a communications major, I was in theater.

"I lost track of her after graduation. Then, by some twist of fate, we both ended up working in television. I couldn't believe it at first. I was working on one of ESPN's fishing shows when I heard about Parker Steadman and his plans to expand his cable channels. Then I heard about Hayden and that's when I decided . . ." Her voice trailed off.

Then Edith stuck her chin out. "I'm not proud of this but the fact is that I've known for a long time that if I did it right, if I took my time, I would find the moment when I could destroy her. Not hurt her physically, but destroy her career. That's what I've been working for.

"It's no accident I landed this job with the Steadman group two years ago. I went in knowing that most women who do what I do are very attractive, very stylish, very competitive. My production skills are excellent and I have solid experience shooting outdoors but most important"— Edith looked from Lew to Osborne—"I know how to be a good mouse.

"They had over thirty candidates for the job and Hayden picked me. She needed a grunt and a purse carrier— so she picked the homely one. Enough years had gone by, she didn't recognize my name. She barely read the résumé. She didn't know until last week that I grew up here in Loon Lake.

"Once I was on board, I bided my time. I knew I'd have the opportunity and I wanted it to be perfect."

Edith dropped her face into her hands again. "This is all so pathetic."

"It's understandable, Edith," said Lew. Edith lifted her head and relaxed back into the chair.

"The first thing I noticed when I started working there was how protective Hayden was of Parker. No one gets to that man without going through her. I was so surprised when I found out he had a daughter. Jen came to visit once, for a very short time, but I could see the affection between them. And Hayden was so jealous.

"That's where she was vulnerable. That plus the fact that when Parker isn't around, she's a raving maniac. A total bitch. Without her knowing it, I befriended Jen. I would call her on weekends to see how things were going. I encouraged her, all the way from Maui, to send her father notes and little gifts. She would mail them to me and I would sneak them into his office. Bugged the hell out of Hayden.

"About three months ago, things got tense between Hayden and Parker. Even though her ratings are lousy, she has been demanding a bigger role on the new cable channels. He wanted someone the audience would like better. Meanwhile, I learned that Jen had this financial disaster and was trying to reach Parker by phone, but Hayden wouldn't put the calls through. She was just a bitch.

"That's when Jen and I cooked up a little trap. Jen would call, get Hayden on the phone, and tape the nastiness. That's all, just let Hayden rave on, then hang up. Eventually Hayden refused to take the calls."

"Is that when she alleged someone was stalking her by phone?"

"Yes—and all the time it was poor Jen trying to reach her father. When Jen stopped calling, Hayden pretended to get calls—always when she could milk the attention.

"Jen had stopped calling because I was helping her arrange to come here to Loon Lake. Things were dicey enough between her father and Hayden that I thought she could push that relationship over the edge. I was right. Jen played those tapes for him Saturday night after everyone left the dinner party. He couldn't believe it.

"Before he went to bed that night, he told Hayden he wanted her off the property the next day, after the parade—and he would personally see that she would never work in television again."

"Edith, none of this explains how you could be remotely responsible for some jabone taking him out with a .50 caliber sniper rifle," said Lew.

Edith's eyes brimmed. "I'm the one who added Loon Lake to the tournament circuit. We weren't coming here originally. You know, this area is really too small for the kind of bass fishing you need for a million dollar purse.

"I talked Parker into coming here. He always told me how much he loved Loon Lake. I had this crazy plan. I thought if they were a family—he and Jen—on the lake with all the memories. I never realized. . . ."

"How could you know he had former family members who are hardened criminals? Parker himself was nicknamed 'the Predator.' He was no innocent, Edith. You are not to blame for that man's death," said Lew.

Edith pushed at her eyes with a Kleenex.

Lew tapped her pen on her desk. "Edith, who do you think fired that gun?"

"You know those guys they caught cheating on the drawing for the boat? Because of that, Bruce Duffy will never be allowed in another professional tournament. He's furious. He did it or he hired someone to do it."

"Good theory," said Lew. "Except Bruce Duffy is dead. And I happen to know he didn't fire the gun that killed Parker."

"Oh," Edith said in surprise. "I didn't see that on the news."

"No, and you won't until I decide to make it public."

Lew thought hard for a minute. "Edith, how would you feel about doing something for me? Have you and Hayden already discussed the fact you think Duffy is behind Parker's death?"

"No. She never talks to me—she barely *sees* me. She's all over Jen, trying to make up."

"Good. When you go back to the house, see if you can find the right opportunity to let Hayden know that you're convinced that Duffy killed Parker and you don't understand why we haven't made an arrest."

"And see how she reacts?"

"Right. If she doesn't agree, that's a good indication she knows Duffy is dead. That tells me she's in touch with the people who killed him."

"You think Hayden—"

"She met Patty Boy when he delivered all those antique lures, didn't she?"

"Yes, they had quite a conversation now that I think of it."

"All it takes is money and a phone call. Money and a phone call and the arrogance to think she can control the daughter like she did the father."

As Edith stood up to leave, Osborne stood, too.

"Edith," he said, "Hayden told us you've been under the care of a psychiatrist relative to your father's suicide. She instructed us not to discuss it with you—that it would cause a severe emotional reaction."

Edith laughed. "So she finally figured out who I am. Even after Parker told everyone that I grew up in Loon Lake, I wasn't sure she put it all together. That's a lie, by the way. I haven't been seeing a shrink—which isn't to say I don't need one."

"What Dr. Osborne is trying to say is—be careful, Edith."

After Edith had left, Osborne said, "You're comfortable letting her go out there?"

"Edith is smart, Doc. The kind of work she does requires attention to detail. Visual detail. She knows what I'm looking for. And she knows Hayden's face. Be interesting to hear what she has to say when we get there this afternoon."

"Oh, so I'm included," said Osborne.

"I thought you might enjoy landing a big one for a change."

thirty-two

"Only dead fish swim with the stream."

—Anonymous

A light rain christened the windshield of Lew's cruiser as they pulled up the drive to the big log house. Stepping out, Osborne inhaled. Nothing smells so good as summer mist in the pines.

Hayden's Mini Rover and the Chevy Suburban were parked in the drive. They walked past the cars and through the portico leading up to the front doors with their etched glass panels. Lew knocked. No answer. She peered through the windows. No movement indoors either. She knocked again.

Lew started around to the lakeside of the house and Osborne followed. Edith was standing on the dock, looking out at the lake through a pair of binoculars. They walked on down. It was still misting.

"Hayden took Jen out on the pontoon boat an hour ago. She said they would be back by four," said Edith, pushing her hair out of her eyes. The sun was trying to break through the clouds and a stiff breeze was blowing out of the north.

"She insisted on taking Jen out alone. Wanted her away from me, I guess." Letting the binoculars drop against her chest, Edith thrust her hands deep into the pockets of her jeans. She was wearing a T-shirt and Osborne could see goose bumps on her arms.

"Not like either one of them has a clue how to handle that boat. It took them half an hour to get started after Hayden flooded the engine. I was checking to be sure they aren't stranded out there somewhere."

"What would we do if they were?" said Lew. She looked around. The only other boat in the vicinity was an aluminum canoe tipped over on the grassy bank next to the dock. "That canoe will be difficult to maneuver against this wind," she said.

"May I see those?" said Osborne. Edith handed him the binoculars. Lake Consequence was one of the region's bigger, deeper lakes. The bay in front of Parker's home was just one finger of a long, winding body of water reached through a narrow channel at the far end of the bay. Peering through the lenses, Osborne swept the bay, then focused in on the channel. "No sign of them."

Dropping the binoculars, he looked up and down the nearby shoreline. Several summer cottages could be glimpsed through the dense growth of birch and white pine that crowded the lake in both directions. Nothing was as grand as the Steadman home.

"What's going to happen to this place?" Lew turned to look back up the hill at the massive log structure. "And"—her eyes twinkled—"all that camouflage?"

"We can make fun of it," said Edith, "but the public relations director for the cable channels has *Instyle* magazine shooting a spread here next month. That's if Jen agrees—all this is hers now. I hope Parker's death doesn't change everything with the TV group. A photo spread like that is great for our sponsors."

"Are those two getting along?"

"Can't tell. Jen was in her room when I got back. Hayden was on the phone all morning. Then the two of them went in to see the funeral director. They got back about an hour and a half ago."

"So Hayden could have met with me earlier," said Lew.

"Oh, yes. And I brought up Bruce Duffy just like you said."

"And?"

"No reaction. Nothing. As much as I hate to say it, Chief Ferris, I don't think Hayden had anything to do with Parker's death. If you really think about it, it's hardly to her advantage with Jen in the picture."

"Hey, you two, here they come."

The pontoon's green-and-white-striped awning was vivid against the soft gray of lake and sky. It came at them rhythmically, bouncing over the waves. As the pontoon reached the middle of the bay, Osborne heard the purr of an outboard motor.

From a dock down the lake, a fishing boat nosed out. Osborne watched it idly. It was a big bass boat. Again the grayness of the day exaggerated the boat's color: glitter white edged with stripes of black and yellow. The driver kicked the engine into a higher gear, the stripes morphing into streaks.

As the boat sped off to the right of the dock, Osborne raised the binoculars. He could make out two people: one wearing dark green, the other something patterned in black and white like the plumage of a loon. The boat hydroplaned, making it easy for Osborne to focus.

He dropped the binoculars. He knew that boat—and he knew the loon.

"Tattoos," he said. "Lew, that's Catherine Plyer's husband in Duffy's boat—the one I saw at Patty Boy's."

"You sure?" Lew had her gun out.

The pontoon continued toward them, on a diagonal

from the channel. They could see the women sitting side by side in the bucket seats at the front.

The bass boat swerved toward the pontoon, closing the distance between them at high speed. The women on the pontoon jumped to their feet, waving and shouting. They must have thought the driver of the bass boat couldn't see them.

"Shoot," urged Osborne.

"I can't. The boat is in line with the pontoon—I'll hit the women." Lew crouched, left hand supporting the SIG Sauer in her right, waiting.

A figure stood up in the bass boat. The line of a rifle barrel etched the sky.

"He's got a gun, Lew!"

Two shots. One of the figures on the pontoon fell forward, hanging over the rail. The other dove for the deck. The pontoon chugged forward, up and down over the waves. The bass boat curved away and up toward the channel. Lew fired. Again and again.

"Too far away, Doc."

"Go for the outboard."

"I did." She got off two more shots. Edith stood silent beside Lew, her fist to her mouth.

The pontoon kept coming, closer and closer, aimed straight at the dock. The figure on the deck lifted its head as the body hanging over the railing fell back to one side.

"How do I stop?" screamed the woman, now on her knees. She had light-colored hair.

"Jen," cried Edith. "Grab the wheel."

Jen lunged for the wheel. Holding it with both hands, she swung down onto her knees. The boat went into a sudden spin, barely missing the dock.

"Turn the key! Turn off the ignition," Osborne shouted, hoping she could hear over the noise of the engine.

The boat stopped with a lurch. Edith, who had pulled off her sandals, dove into the water.

"Get that boat over here," said Lew. "Hurry!"

Osborne and Lew helped Edith and Jen up onto the dock. It was too late to do anything for Hayden. Together they swung her limp form off the boat. Then, jumping onto the pontoon, they took off.

Winding their way through the channel, they saw the boat. The driver, unfamiliar with the shallow channel, had run it up on a sandbar. She was in the water pushing away at the big boat.

"My brother!" cried Cheryl as they pulled near. Osborne crouched behind one of the bucket seats. Lew knelt behind the console of the pontoon, gun out. "My brother's bleeding to death! Help us, please help us!"

Time was not on Jimmy's side. One of Lew's bullets had ripped through his upper back, and blood was all over the place.

Two hours later, Osborne and Lew sat with Cheryl in Lew's office. A matron on duty in the jail had found her some dry clothes. She sat sobbing quietly in the same chair Edith had occupied that morning. She had waived her rights to a lawyer. She wanted to talk. She seemed relieved to talk.

"Jimmy was just following orders," she said. "It was Catherine's idea. She and Patty Boy made him do it. He needed me to help," she sobbed harder. "He was my brother, my big brother."

"Made you do what?" said Lew, her voice kind but firm. "Cheryl, be specific. The more you tell us, the easier it'll be for you."

Before the drive into town, Cheryl had taken them to the RV, which was parked at a cottage, farther down the bay, where she and Jimmy had put in the boat. It was a summer place that had not been opened that year. The shuttered cabin was located at the end of a long overgrown drive. They could have hidden in there for as long as they wanted if their provisions had held out.

"Catherine and Jimmy scouted the place earlier this summer, while all the work was being done on Parker's house," said Cheryl. "Catherine knows this lake real well from when she and Parker lived out here years ago.

"At first, she planned for Jimmy to take Parker out from somewhere around here—you know, just get him through those big windows some night. Then Patty Boy got wind we were gonna get busted, so they had to hurry it up."

"How'd he hear that?" said Lew.

"He's got friends in Customs up in Canada. Very good friends."

"That .50 caliber sniper rifle—is that around here?" said Lew.

She showed them the gun, cased up and stored in the bedroom that Bert had been using. A box of ammunition held cartridges six inches long.

"Jeez Louise," said Osborne.

In the kitchen, they found two boats of Ecstasy. "Jimmy was kind of upset he couldn't deliver those— that's forty thousand dollars' worth, y'know," said Cheryl.

Before they left the RV, Osborne checked the livewells: the smallmouth bass were gone, the water drained, and the pumps had been turned off. He hoped the fish were okay.

"When Catherine heard that Parker was building a place up here, she set it up. She wanted him dead—before he married that girlfriend of his, the one on TV."

"Jealous after all these years," said Lew.

"Oh no. She wanted the money. If Parker got married, then their daughter would only get half, see."

Cheryl wiped tears off her cheeks. She was calming down as she spoke.

"Catherine didn't want that to happen. Her plan at first was to kill just Parker. But when she found out their daughter was coming—that's why we had to finish up today."

"So your brother was trying to kill Jennifer, not Hayden," said Lew.

"Catherine figured if Parker was dead—and Jennifer— she was next of kin. Being Jennifer's mother, she would inherit everything. But Jimmy shot the wrong person."

Cheryl looked from Osborne to Lew. "That's Catherine's fault. She told him he would know which one was Jennifer because she's so tall. She never said they would both be tall."

"She should have watched more television," said Lew.

"Not Catherine. She hated Parker. She wouldn't watch his stuff for nothin'."

thirty-three

"Believe me, my young friend, there is nothing—ab-solutely nothing—half so much worth doing as simply messing about in boats. Simply messing."

—Water Rat, *The Wind in the Willows*

It was Friday night and Osborne's deck was a busy place.

"A beer, Lew?"

Lewellyn Ferris shook her head. "No, thank you, I'm just fine, Doc."

She was lying on the chaise longue, eyes closed, the setting sun caressing her face. Osborne liked how it looked as if she belonged there. She was dressed for fishing, though he was hoping they might just take it easy that evening. Maybe he could persuade her it was one of those "sometime" times.

Meanwhile, he had other guests. They did not include Brenda Anderle. He had managed to cancel their fish fry date by saying he had paperwork to complete on the Schultz murder case. She was disappointed but impressed. He would deal with that another day.

• • •

The week had rushed by. On Wednesday, the fishing tournament had hobbled to a finish. Even the million-dollar purse seemed anticlimactic after the tournament's explosive opening. Following Ray's advice, Jennifer turned the awards ceremony into a wake for her father. He attended—in a birchbark container that Edith found at Ralph's Sporting Goods.

The motorcycle rally ended the next day. The year's count was better than in the past: only three fatalities, eleven accidents, and one serious bar fight. Osborne found himself reluctant to part with the big Harley and his borrowed leathers. He was mulling over a possible purchase, particularly if Erin and Mark were able to keep their bike, most particularly if he could ride with Lew.

Only Hayden remained unresolved, her body awaiting burial plans. The Carlsons, her adoptive parents, were deceased and a search was under way for her next of kin. Mark was helping with that.

And so the mood on the deck that evening was lighthearted. Ray had dropped by with Edith and Jen in tow. They wanted to celebrate a decision made by Jen earlier that day: She and Edith would do their best to maintain and expand the Steadman television dynasty. Plans were still in place for the "Fish 'n' Fry"—to be hosted by a certain Loon Laker. Ray was beaming.

"But, Ray, if that happens, you'll have to give up your grave digging," said Edith. "Hey, given you spend so much time around headstones, any thoughts on your own epitaph?"

"You betcha," said Ray. "Got it in my will: 'High Risk, High Reward.'"

The women thought that was hilarious. Osborne and Lew had heard it many times before.

"All right, all right, enough of that baloney," said Osborne, raising his bottle of Coke. "A toast—to three happy fishermen. Here's wishing you good ratings and tight lines."

Edith sat down in a deck chair next to Lew. "I want to thank you, Chief Ferris, for seeing that justice was done on behalf of my father. If Hayden were alive, I know that——"

"Dr. Osborne is the one to thank, Edith," said Lew. "Because justice is not punishment; justice is never forgetting. Doc, like yourself, never forgot."

The deck was quiet. An owl hooted. Ray cleared his throat. "Okay, girls, down to my place. Fresh bluegill is the entrée this evening, seasoned with a spicy beet salad on the side."

"Beets?" Edith had a funny look on her face.

"Jen," said Lew, standing up as the three prepared to leave, "I'm sorry I wasn't able to do much about your mother and those brothers of hers. The Canadian authorities are convinced they made it to Tokyo on false passports."

"Do you think she would ever try . . ." Jen stopped. She couldn't say it. No one could say it.

"All I know is they will be back," said Lew. "You be vigilant, I'll be waiting." Lew paused, then she said, "Jen, we never know why people do things. Whatever it is that motivates Catherine happened to her long before you were born. You've done nothing to deserve a mother like that."

"I know," said Jen. "That's something my dad told me, too."

Lew and Osborne leaned over the deck railing, side by side, watching the three young people as they walked the lake path over to Ray's.

"How could Parker Steadman have fallen in love with two such cruel women?"

"He told you, Doc. He never knew his mother."

"But I never really knew mine."

"Maybe you did, just enough."

It was nearly midnight when Osborne reached up for the small box he had hidden behind the clock. Shopping had been good that morning at the Loon Lake Market. He found wrapping paper with a white-on-blue fish pattern that was perfect. For ribbon, he used a strand of Orvis's braided white Dacron twelve-pound test line.

He held the box out to Lew. She hesitated, a grave look on her face. She pulled at the bow, then undid the paper, taking care not to tear it. She lifted the lid from the box. The original box.

"Oh . . ." She was speechless. The wooden lure glowed pale yellow in the light from the candle.

"Night Radiant Moonlight Bait #1000, four treble hooks . . . very rare," said Osborne. He knew better than to add, ". . . like you."

"Doc, this cost thousands of dollars. I can't accept this."

"I made a deal with Jen. She gave it to me on the condition that you and I warn all predatory females away from Ray until she has an opportunity to get to know him better."

"Isn't Edith closer to his age?"

"I made a deal with Edith—"

"Oh, you!"

Enjoyed *Dead Frenzy*? Be sure to pick up *Dead Hot Mama*, the next book in the Loon Lake mystery series!

It's ice-fishing season in Loon Lake and Doc Osborne is trying to convince Police Chief and fishing pal Lew Ferris to give it a chance. But fish aren't the only things lurking below the surface. The bodies of two snowmobilers have just been pulled out of nearby Two Sisters Lake. And a beautiful woman's corpse turns up in a snowdrift. Is it payback for a drug deal gone bad? Or is it something more sinister? Osborne and Ferris once again team up to get to the bottom of a very murky mystery.

Please enjoy the following brief selection.

A sudden flutter to his right, and Osborne's shotgun was up and firing. Yes! He got it on the wing. Osborne watched the bird fall. Oh, he was a happy man.

Trudging forward, eyes focused on where he was sure the bird had landed, he felt his right foot give way too far and too fast. Down he went, down and back, bouncing along on his rump as he struggled to keep his shotgun up and out of the snow. To his surprise, he landed in a very comfortable position, cushioned from behind by a snowy hillock and snuggled up against a decaying tree stump.

Leaning to his left, against the stump, he fished around in the pocket of his hunting vest, hoping to hell he had something he could use to wipe the snow off the butt of his gun. He found a packet of Kleenex. After wiping the wood dry, he was reaching back with the Kleenex when his eye caught a flash of white inside a hollow in the stump. Mushrooms? At this time of year? He bent forward to take a closer look.

Thirty-two teeth greeted him: a full set of dentures.

Osborne stared at the disembodied grin. Now that was damn strange. And they were set so carefully, too—not like the wind had blown them into place or an animal had stashed them. No, some human had set these dentures down quite carefully.

Osborne looked overhead and all around. Had there been a deer stand here? Flat-line winds two years ago had reconfigured the forest, and he knew many hunters who had lost their stands in the blowdown. Losing a deer stand was one thing, losing your teeth was another. He hadn't heard of any locals with *that* kind of bad luck. But then, he was three years into retirement and out of touch. The more he thought about it, he decided maybe he shouldn't be so surprised.

More people over age fifty misplace their teeth than lose their eyeglasses. One of those little-known facts that allow dentists to retire early.

Osborne reached into the hollow. Even without his reading glasses he could see the teeth were finely made. He'd bet anything they were imported.

Osborne turned the dentures over, tipping them this way and that, but the light was too dim for him to make out either the owner's name or the Social Security number, which he knew he would find somewhere inside each.

Oh well. He took out the Kleenex packet again and wrapped each section with care, then tucked the dentures into the upper left pocket of his vest. He could check for the identification at home, then get in touch with the owner or their dentist. Someone would be very pleased.

Grabbing the branch of a nearby balsam, he pulled himself to his feet. The sun was dropping fast, and he'd better hurry if he wanted to find that bird and get out before dark. He scoured the shallow ravine in front of him but no sign of the grouse. Maybe he could see better from the rise behind him.

Osborne turned to start back up the hill. Looking up, he was startled to find he wasn't alone.

"Of the pike: It is a fish of ambush."
—J.H. Keene, *The Practical Fisherman*

"Make voyages. Attempt them. There's nothing else."
—Tennessee Williams

Within you there is a fire
Within the fire
An expanse of water.
—DoDo Jin Ming, contemporary artist

A few words from the author:

I was born and raised in Rhinelander, Wisconsin, in the heart of the fishing culture that backgrounds my mysteries. I grew up fishing for walleye and bluegills and muskie—and when I turned fifty, I learned to fly fish!

I've always had an aptitude for writing (not singing, for sure, as the nuns at St. Mary's told me to "just move your lips") and won a full scholarship to Bennington College in Vermont. Went on to have three children, marry and divorce twice. My second husband was 9 years younger, hence my non-fiction book, *Loving A Younger Man*, which I wrote 25 years ago. We broke up for reasons that had nothing to do with the age difference.

After a decade of magazine and newspaper feature writing—the source of my non-fiction books—I directed promotion and publicity for Andrews & McMeel/Universal Press Syndicate, during which time I had the privilege of working with outstanding writers and cartoonists such as Abigail Van Buren, Gary Larson, Erma Bombeck, and Garry Trudeau. Later I joined Jane Mobley Associates, a public relations firm based in Kansas City.

I moved back to Rhinelander in 1996 (having been gone for more than 30 years) where I now hunt, fish, and write mysteries. Over the years, I have published 23 books—a fact that surprises the hell out of me as I never finished college. I am just starting my fourteenth Loon Lake Mystery.

My influences are the happenings in the world around me and I continue to be a fanatic newspaper reader, devouring *The New York Times* and *Wall Street Journal* daily. My favorite authors are Willa Cather, Edith Wharton (Rhinelander is named after her uncle who brought the railroad through in late 1800s), early Hemingway and early John Updike, Raymond Chandler, and Ross Thomas. Growing up I was an avid Nancy Drew/Agatha Christie fan. Oh, and G.K. Chesterton's Father Brown series, too. I'm not a card-carrying member of Oprah's Book Club. However, I do enjoy biographies such as the one about Steve Jobs. And poetry! I don't think I could get through the day without some Mary Oliver and Billy Collins to name a few.

I love movies—*Argo*, *Zero Dark Thirty*, *Silver Linings Playbook*, *The Descendants*, *Pulp Fiction*, and *Gone With the Wind*—and music. I'm currently listening to Calexico, Avett Brothers, and Sea Wolf. Other favorites range from Elvis, The Beach Boys, Roy Orbison, Bob Dylan, and The Beatles to Adele, Emmy Lou Harris, and Aimee Mann. Classical music and jazz round out my listening.

When it comes to the books, I have always worked on a Mac and just treated myself to an iPad. When not writing, I run, play tennis, and do Pilates. Oh, and I fish!

A Guide for Book Club Readers of the Loon Lake Mystery Series

Q. *How does the author use fishing as a device within the mystery?*
- What happens while characters are fishing?
- Are there differences in personality types between the people who fly fish and those who bait fish (as in fishing for muskie, walleyes, bass, and bluegills)?
- What is the role of the female characters who fish?

Q. *What role does water play in the mystery?*
- Are there differences between lakes and rivers and streams? Do they attract different types of people?
- Is the water always safe and lovely?

Q. *What role does dentistry play in the mystery?*
- Is that valid in contemporary investigations?
- What other characteristic of Dr. Paul Osborne helps to solve the mystery?

Q. *Are you familiar with the regional vernaculars used; i.e. "razzbonya," "goombah" and "jabone?"*
- What do they mean?
- How are they pronounced? (Hint: two of the words are pronounced with a long "o" sound.)

Q. *What role does the northwoods landscape, which has the second-highest ratio of water to land in the world, play in the stories?*
- Would you want to visit the region?
- If you did visit, would you want to go fishing?
- And would you prefer to fish *on* water in a boat—or *in* water with flyfishing gear?

Q. *How does Point of View (POV) figure in the mystery?*
- Is it clear and satisfying?
- Do you agree with the author's approach?

Printed in the United States
By Bookmasters